# SISTER HOLLYWOOD

By the same author

*The New Poetic: Yeats to Eliot*
*Pound, Yeats, Eliot and the Modernist Movement*
*In the Glass Case: Essays on New Zealand Literature*

POETRY

*Between*

# SISTER HOLLYWOOD

## C. K. Stead

St. Martin's Press
New York

Library of Congress Cataloging-in-Publication Data

Stead, C. K. (Christian Karlson).
    Sister Hollywood / C.K. Stead.
        p.    cm.
    ISBN 0-312-04423-2
    I. Title.
    PR9639.3.S7S57    1990                                          89-77946
    823—dc20                                                        CIP

First published in Great Britain by William Collins Sons & Co. Ltd.

First U.S. Edition
10  9  8  7  6  5  4  3  2  1

This one especially for Kay

Also for Los Angeles friends Cal Bedient, Joe Beaton, Jim Generoso, Blake Nevius, and Marion Weinstock

Los Angeles had been coming at me all my life, but this was the first time I had come to it. Prejudices are useless. Call Los Angeles any dirty name you like – but the fact remains that you are already living in it before you get there.

CLIVE JAMES

# SISTER HOLLYWOOD

# 1

It's a Lincoln Trader. The name seems odd, so I look twice to make sure there's no mistake. It has two doors, long enough to let a passenger into the back seat, so they swing inconveniently wide. It has a long broad flat snout, sloping slightly towards the front – a very satisfactory rumble of suppressed power comes from under it. She switches off the engine and gets out.

We're parked just off a steep winding road that goes up into the hills, at the entrance to a narrow paved path marked 'Private Drive'. On one side there's a big clump of cactus I knew in my childhood as Prickly Pear. Around it are various waxy flowering shrubs. Some are green and healthy-looking, others brown and dry. On the other side, by the Private Drive sign, there's something tall and stalky waving in the light breeze – 'bambooiform', as one of the American poets calls such plants, but not bamboo. And there's a young eucalypt, its leaves healthy and green.

But now I'm looking beyond the eucalypt, across the green-brown gully to the hills beyond. There it is, almost at the hilltop, in big white letters: HOLLYWOOD. Just right of the D there's some kind of radio or television mast – battleship grey with banks of small dishes.

She calls. She's across the road now under a clump of huge gum trees. She has picked up two of the seeds that fall under them – gum-nuts we used to call them. She's squeezing one and breathing the eucalypt smell. She holds the other out to me. There are tears in her eyes. She puts her hand on my arm and points back across the street to the hills. I see now the big white sign reads SISTER HOLLYWOOD.

She says, 'I want you to kiss me.'

I do, but she says, 'Not like that. Kiss me properly.'

I begin to kiss her 'properly'. Something tells me this is not right and I struggle to wake. I open my eyes. I know this room but I don't know it. I've been in such a heavy, jet-lag sleep I can't remember who or where I am. I know this is one end of the earth or the other, north or south, but I can't remember which. The uncertainty is painful. I fight it. It seems after a moment I do know where I am, and the sense of relief sends me right back to sleep.

We're sitting beside her pool. Her dog, Kapai, is chewing on something under her deckchair. I stare, trying to see what it is. It appears to be a doll. 'Don't worry,' she says. 'There are plenty more.'

Kapai growls and shakes the doll this way and that.

She tells me Bogart came to work every day with two sandwiches and a bottle of beer in a lunch box. 'He reminded me of the Hippo,' she says. 'He wore the same kind of hats.'

Now we're dancing. 'Kiss me,' she says. 'Go on. Kiss me.'

We're in the Lincoln Trader, racing across an empty desert landscape. I'm struggling to wake up.

# 2

It's not possible for me to be exact about dates, but towards the end of the war – the big one that went on during my childhood – my grandmother must have been in her late sixties. She seemed to me a very old woman. She had one obsession and it was Hollywood. Every week three or four women's magazines were put aside for her at a paper shop in Dominion Road, Auckland. She called them her 'books'. I don't know whether any of them were exclusively about Hollywood – probably not – but I know they all contained Hollywood news and gossip which was what she read first, and re-read. She knew all about the stars, and she 'went to the pictures' (as we said then) more often than anyone else known to us. So often that it was embarrassing. Her other pastime was walking. Or as my sisters and I, her brutal grandchildren, used to say, her hobby was hobbling. There was something wrong with one or both of her knees; and she used to cut holes in the tops of her shoes to make room for her bunions. She lived with us, but in public we children did our best to disown her. Our grandmother was an embarrassment.

I suppose one or another or several of her 'books' ran the syndicated Hollywood columns of Hedda Hopper and Louella Parsons – I'm sure I remember those names from that time; and maybe also one of the columnists from the rank just below those two – Sheilah Graham, for example. So knowing what I know now – and what I know now is what is to follow – I like to invent a paragraph of a kind my grandmother might well have read (and in fact I will chance my arm and say it's certain she did read such a paragraph) but the significance of which, and I mean the significance to her, she wouldn't have been able to guess.

Paragraphs of that kind, the Hedda Hopper/Louella Parsons kind, were not truthful or accurate in detail. They weren't meant to be. But they were true to their purpose, and I suppose their purpose was the dissemination of myths. They were true to Hollywood. So for example a 'starlet' (and someone has said that in those days every young woman in Hollywood not actively engaged in a brothel could be called a 'starlet') might call Hedda, or Louella, and tell her (to the consternation and wrath of the one *not* called) that she, the 'starlet', and one of the male stars were secretly dating, hopelessly in love, and about to be married. It was a secret. No one was to know. The chosen columnist would then explain through fifty, or a hundred, or however many, newspapers and magazines throughout the world, that these two were in love, and that no one but their few closest friends knew that they would soon be secretly married. That it was a secret was true. That the world had to know was also true. The world simply had to be trusted to keep the secret. Trust in their readers was implied in every sentence those women wrote.

So we have to imagine my grandmother reading the Hedda or Louella paragraph with interest, but without *special* interest – without any recognition that it might contain a clue to help solve a mystery with which our household at that time was preoccupied. And because she lacked that recognition, we have to imagine her reading and forgetting. It was just another single brush-stroke in the enormous and always growing mural that lined the wall of her consciousness; a picture which, if it had a name, would have to be called something like Stellar Paradise, or Life in Celluloid City, or the Star-Gazer's Guide.

What the Hedda or Louella paragraph explained was that the new young Australian star, Rocky Tamworth, who would soon be signed up for seven years by Warner Brothers, had been seen with his pretty young starlet wife Arlene, also Australian, at a party at Constance Bennett's on Carolwood Drive, in the company of Humphrey Bogart and Lauren Bacall.

The young actor, Hedda or Louella added, must have been celebrating his seven-year contract. He'd got somewhat the worse for wear as the evening went on, and at a late hour had fallen into Miss Bennett's pool from which he was dragged by a surprisingly good-humoured and patient Bogart.

A lot of the details of the paragraph were wrong. Hedda and Louella couldn't be everywhere in Hollywood and they relied a good deal on hearsay. For example if Rocky Tamworth, as the young Australian had decided he was to be called, got drunk that night it was out of anxiety about his proposed contract with Warners, not in celebration of a signing. Nor was his wife a 'starlet'. Nor was she 'also Australian'. Finally, the party was not at Constance Bennett's; and there was, as far as Arlene is now able to recall, no pool – or if there was, Rocky didn't fall into it. Her recollection is that he complained that there was no pool and, late in the evening and boisterously drunk, rolled about in a fountain that decorated the drive at the front of the house. But even that she's not sure of. Rocky was to get drunk so often in those years, the recollections get run together.

Nevertheless the paragraph is based on something that happened. Arlene (and let's stick to the name Rocky had persuaded her to take in Hollywood) remembers that the party was at the home of Charles Laughton in Pacific Palisades. It was true that she and Rocky arrived with Bogart and Bacall, and that Bogart looked after them. That was because Rocky was a keen yachtsman. His agent had introduced him to Bogart one Friday when the star was a man short for weekend sailing out of Newport on his yacht *Santana*. Rocky was taken on. He proved himself a good sailor, and a thirsty one, and since then had sailed most weekends with Bogart.

In Arlene's recollection they arrived before the sun had quite gone down. Someone took them through the house showing them the paintings, and then out into the large back garden to look at the ocean. They stood among olive trees, with the scent of orange blossom coming from some other part of the garden, and with a fresh, just faintly damp flow of air coming up from the sea. She was surprised they were so high above the water, that the cliffs dropped so steeply and so far – and in fact a part of the garden was fenced off where the cliff-top had crumbled and fallen to the Roosevelt Highway (as it was then called) which ran between the cliff base and the wide beaches. The sun was out of sight, but away to the right it still seemed to be laying a sheen down over the water. There were strange sculptures in the garden, and someone said they were 'Pre-Columbian' but she didn't know what that meant. She was also told not to mention to Mr Laughton the collapse of the cliff, which had happened after heavy rains, because it was an event that had upset the actor. Sometimes when it was spoken of, Laughton sweated and his hands shook.

More and more people arrived. There was food as well as drink. For a time the party seemed to break into two groups, men and women, and that surprised Arlene – she thought it was one of those things peculiar to New Zealand which she'd left six thousand (and emotionally a million) miles behind. So she lost sight of Rocky, and when she next saw him he was drunk. The night was mild and beautiful, as nights in Southern California mostly seemed to be, and at some time in the middle watches of the party she found herself in the kitchen, and then out in the garden among the statues, with a strange little man with short-cropped hair who smelled of fresh sweat and old cigars, and who talked to her in a German accent as if they'd been friends for years. He talked about the architecture, the guests, the garden, the soil, the statues, Los Angeles (which he said was 'Tahiti in Metropolitan form') – never about himself; and he asked her no personal questions. When she asked him was he a film director (there were a lot of German directors in Hollywood then) or an actor he said he was neither; he was Mr Laughton's tailor.

Much later she was out in the garden again side by side with Humphrey Bogart in a hammock chair above some concrete steps. She told him she'd been talking to Mr Laughton's tailor – and she described him.

'That's not Laughton's tailor,' Bogart told her. 'That's Bert Brecht. He writes plays.'

Across the garden, over the heads of the people who had

spilled out from the house, she could hear Rocky singing 'Waltzing Matilda'. She said she wished he wouldn't.

'Let him have his head,' Bogart said. 'Don't crowd him. At least he sings in tune.'

She explained that Rocky was anxious about getting a contract. His agent kept saying 'Soon. Be patient. It's on the way,' – but nothing happened.

Bogart said agents were like that. And Hollywood was all about waiting.

They sat silent, looking out at the moon that was over the ocean. There were lights in the garden. Gradually the party was shifting out of doors. It was then the exchange occurred which Arlene remembers so clearly. In that conversational gap she was worrying about Rocky. She knew what Bogart had said was true – so many people had said it to them. In Hollywood you have to be prepared to wait. She would wait as long as it took, but already she knew her nerve was stronger and her head cooler than Rocky's. She needed work – and that was what she said to Bogart.

'Sure you do,' he said. 'But like I told you, you've just got to sweat it out. Wait for your chances. Breaking into movies is everybody's headache in this town.'

But she didn't want to break into movies – and that was what she explained to Bogart. 'Rocky's the actor,' she said. 'I'm a typist.'

He didn't laugh but his eyes were smiling. He shook his head and drew on his cigarette and went on staring at her. Finally he said, 'Shorthand?'

She nodded. 'Shorthand typist.'

And then he laughed out loud. 'Come here,' he said. He took her by the arm and pulled her to her feet. In a group not far away there was a tall man in his late thirties or early forties, with slicked-down hair and horn-rim glasses.

'Jesse,' Bogart said. 'I want you to meet my young friend here. Mrs Arlene Tamworth. Arlene, this is Jesse Fischer.'

So she met the director-producer whose name was well known to her, and at that moment she felt nothing at all except a kind of embarrassment, which she thought he felt too. But

Bogart didn't notice; or if he did, he didn't care. 'Isn't she lovely,' he said. 'And she's looking for work.'

On Mr Fischer's face came a look of surprise and irritation. Hollywood producers didn't go to parties at the home of stars expecting to have 'starlets' thrust at them. Bogart was breaking the unwritten rules.

Jesse Fischer managed to be polite, but only just. He mumbled something about it being a tough world when you're getting started, but added that with her looks and figure she would surely make it. He wished her luck. Then he looked down at his glass, which wasn't empty, and said he needed to freshen his drink.

She was thinking her looks and her figure were pretty run-of-the-mill in Hollywood – and in any case, she hadn't been offering them for appraisal. But Bogart hadn't finished. He had that truculent look he was famous for, and you couldn't tell whether or not it was an act. His hand restrained the producer who was turning away. 'Hang on Jesse. I told you – this kid needs work. Tell him what you can do Arlene.'

Arlene said something like 'Oh please Mr Bogart . . .' She must have looked as distressed as she felt, because for the first time Jesse Fischer looked straight at her. He stared a moment, then turned to Bogart. 'What is all this Bogie? You're making the poor girl uncomfortable.'

'Well look sweetheart . . .' Bogart put his arm around Jesse Fischer's shoulder and spoke like a character in one of his movies. 'Here I am at an Industry party, see? – and a good-looking dame tells me she wants work. Haven't I heard that before? And then she tells me she's a – typist.'

This time they both laughed.

'Shorthand,' Bogart added, and they laughed again, louder. Then they looked at Arlene, and apologized, and explained, although the explanation wasn't necessary. Everyone who looked like Arlene was a 'starlet'. To meet a typist – a shorthand typist – it was unheard of. It was wonderful.

She wasn't really the butt of their joke. If there was a butt it was the 'starlets'; or maybe it was themselves for thinking every young woman in Los Angeles had the same ambition.

But it was embarrassing too. She was glad when she got away from them.

But before the party ended Jesse Fischer had come up to her again. He had a little tear-off sheet of notepaper, folded once. 'Put this in your pocket-book,' he told her, and she did, without looking at it. By then Rocky was in the fountain and he had to be got out and dried so the Bogarts could drive them back to their hotel.

In those days Rocky was always hopeful in the mornings, depressed towards evening. If he drank, that delayed the depression. If he drank a lot, it was delayed a long time. But sooner or later it arrived. That night it arrived in the Bogarts' car. Rocky wept, and got them to stop while he was sick in the gutter, after which he sighed and groaned all the way to North Hollywood. The Bogarts were patient with him, and kind to Arlene. They'd seen it all before.

Arlene loved him, and decades later she would still remember those terrible days with nostalgia. Rocky was a kind of phoenix. Every night he burned himself to the ground. Every morning he rose fresh from the ashes, full of hope, and with a kind of enthusiasm that could sweep her along. The self-destruction was painful to watch, but the hope was worse. During the hours of daylight he never went far, or for long, from their hotel room, in case he missed the call from his agent that would open the big door. Meanwhile he practised – fencing, shadow-boxing, reading aloud, making faces in the mirror, above all working on his accent. He knew he had to do something about those Australian vowels, and although he worked hard at it, and always believed, until the evening gloom settled over him, that he was doing well, to Arlene's ear it never sounded convincing. Rocky's model in those early days before he turned to Method acting was Errol Flynn, also Australian, but whom the studios passed off as Irish, and who affected a kind of stage British full of 'old boy' and 'old sport'.

A day or so after the party Arlene looked at the little folded sheet Jesse Fischer had given her. She needed work. And although she could probably have found it easily enough anywhere in Los Angeles, working inside one of the studios might be useful to Rocky. She could keep her ear to the ground for him.

Jesse Fischer's note told her what to say at the studio gate, which building to go to, what person to ask for. She supposed that once through the cordon she would see him, but she didn't. She saw a senior secretary. But she was expected – he hadn't forgotten – and after an interview and a test of her skills she was given a job in a rather poky office with two other girls who told her Mr Fischer was a nice boss.

A few days later he looked in to say hullo and to ask if she was OK. He appeared to be in a hurry, but she thanked him and he smiled distractedly, waved a hand at the others, and left.

# 3

I have now, by way of explanation, to track back a little in time and a lot in distance. The excuse is Hollywood. It was ubiquitous. It knew no bounds. Distance was no obstacle and neither, it seemed, was language. Before the war, when Edward G. Robinson went to Paris to buy paintings, little children ran away from him in the streets and men on building sites made rat–tat–tat noises with imaginary machine guns. After the war it was the same when Bogart went to film on location in Rome.

In Auckland, New Zealand, my grandmother with her obsession wasn't different from the rest of us; she was just an extremist. We lived in Mt Eden in a big wooden bungalow which my grandfather had built in the style of an old colonial farmhouse. It belonged to our grandmother but she'd signed it over to her only child, our mother. As you went down the wide hallway that ran from the front verandah right through to the kitchen at the back you passed on either side my parents' bedroom, the bedroom of my two older sisters Edie and Ellie, my grandmother's room, and finally my younger sister Cassie's – a room I'd shared with her until I grew old enough to be shunted off to a glassed–in verandah at the side.

I couldn't be bothered with all that gossip stuff my grandmother read, but I was mad about the movies. I think in those days, before television, everyone was. There were four picture theatres in easy walking distance – the Capitol, the Princess, the Astor and the Crystal Palace – and if, like my hobbling grandmother, you were willing to cover an extra mile or two, there were more. In the middle of the week the Astor had something called Guest Night when you could get in for half price. I think half price was ninepence for adults and threepence for children. And then there were the Saturday afternoon matinées, which ran pictures for kids preceded by one or two adventure serials. I remember in the evenings hearing my parents talking about whether or not to go to the pictures. Sometimes they would think of it, look at the evening paper to see what was offering, and then decide against it. That always seemed to me crazy. To be able to go and to choose not to – I couldn't understand how anyone could do it.

I and my sisters grew up in Hollywood's greatest years. It was the dream city. From our place on the globe where the Pacific began its curve down under towards the southern pole, the world of the European war and the great European cities was unreal. But Hollywood was a degree of unreality beyond that again. You could no more believe it possible to go there and put your feet on the ground and touch real people than you could go to the land of Oz and shake real hands with its wizard. We thought of Hollywood as the place of ultimate success, a bit like Heaven only a lot better. We didn't know – nobody did, nor wanted to – that to be the place of success it had to be even more a place of failure.

I remember reading once – not then, of course, but as an adult – about an actress called Peg Entwistle who'd had some success on the stage in New York in the late 1920s and who came to Hollywood to be a star. After I'm not sure how long – a year, or maybe longer – she knew she hadn't made it and wouldn't. She must have been a strong young woman because she climbed forty feet up the letter H in the huge HOLLY-WOOD sign (in those days it read HOLLYWOODLAND) in the hills above the town and jumped off, to her death. That happened in the year that I was born. The date is neither here nor there except that it signifies the era I and my sisters belonged to. Hollywood was in reality a matter of life and death. Peg Entwistle has no star set in the pavement of the Walk of Fame. Her absence stands now for a million absences. One of them was to go by the name of Rocky Tamworth.

I was very young, not much more than five years old, when I first saw a piece of movie film. A boy down the street was given a toy projector. It was made of red metal, it had a lens, and a light inside, and you wound the film through by turning a handle, projecting images on to the wall of a darkened room. A few small reels of cartoon went with it. I used to hold the film up to the light and see the tiny changes from one frame to the next. It seemed magic stuff to me and I wanted a projector more than anything I could imagine. They were very rare. I saw one just once in a toy shop and it was thirty shillings – too much, I was told.

Some years later a reel of movie film was stolen from outside the Capitol theatre. A few weeks before, I'd found a couple of feet of film lying among fennel in an empty section at the bottom of our street. Someone told the local policeman that I had it, and he called on us. I knew it couldn't be from the stolen reel but he took it away just in case. He said the stolen reel was from a Bob Hope movie, and he held my piece, which was of an elderly actress called Dame May Whitty, upside down, stared at it, and said it might be Bob Hope. I couldn't argue with him, but I remember how I hated handing it over.

My primary school years were the war years and the celluloid years. My sisters while they were young enough played with celluloid dolls; and movie films were printed on celluloid. The celluloid dolls were named after the celluloid stars. The sisters dressed up, or dressed their dolls, like Shirley Temple, then like Deanna Durbin. They skated like Sonja Henie, and sang like Judy Garland with a terrible vibrato. I wanted to play the piano like Jose Iturbi; and I remember once riding my cousin's horse into the purple west (I was staying on a farm north of Auckland) and in a confusion of movie influences trying to sing, like Nelson Eddie, songs from *The Chocolate Soldier*.

Our father ran a small business as an accountant. I liked to visit his office in town. It was all brown and rather dingy, with a lot of pencils and wire baskets and stationery and old typewriters, and it wasn't too difficult to think of it as the office of a private eye. He was also a big wheel in the local Labour Party. When he became Auckland President we referred to him around the house as the President, or President Harper. Then because names in our household had a tendency to shift from one thing to something near to it, and from that to something else again, our father became President Harpo, and finally Resident Hippo.

Resident Hippo was a great believer in the family. He was proud of his offspring. And because he had political aspirations I think he thought the family added to his public prestige, or to what would be called these days his image. Every Saturday night five or six seats in the front row upstairs at the Capitol were reserved for the Harper family. I'm a little hazy now about whether this was really the permanent and unvarying booking it seemed, or whether it was just something that happened often; but certainly we thought of that front row as ours, in the same way that a family in an earlier century might have a pew reserved for them in the local church.

My life in those years consisted of degrees of boredom. Primary school was a form of slow torture from which I escaped into fantasy, and it's bizarre to reflect that probably more often than not the forms the fantasy took had been manufactured in the brains of Louis B. Mayer, or Jack Cohn, or Walt Disney, or Sam Goldwyn, or Darryl Zanuck. Or rather, it had probably been manufactured in the brains of their army of cohorts, but it had had to satisfy one or another of those all-powerful studio bosses before it began to be made and again before release. My earliest fantasies were pretty straightforward, though they involved a few pieces of basic equipment, like a bow and arrows (easily made from bamboo which grew on an empty section close to the school) and a rope for swinging from tree to tree. Any old stick made a rifle. So there was no problem about being Errol Flynn as Robin Hood, Johnny Weissmuller as Tarzan, or any number of stars being any number of cowboys.

Then the real war started getting into the movies. At first it must have been by way of British movies; or anyway they had British subjects – *Brief Encounter*, *Mrs Miniver*, *This Above All*. Soon the Americans came into the war too, and the war got into Hollywood, but as Hollywood presented it it never seemed to me quite real. I suppose that was because the New Zealand army had gone away to fight in Greece and Crete, and in the Middle East; but after Pearl Harbor and the start of the Pacific war, Auckland filled with American soldiers. So there were two wars, one near, one far; and I could never feel that the Pacific war was as real or as important as the one we – I mean *our* army – was fighting further away. Yet at the same time I was frightened by the one in the Pacific, because I thought that to be overrun by the Japanese would be terrible, whereas to be overrun by the Germans might be some kind of adventure.

I couldn't sort all that out, and there's no need to try and make sense of it now. I suppose my point is only that the great world out there existed in images, and for everyone, not just for children, one of the big image-forming forces, perhaps the biggest, was Hollywood. Sometimes we let the Hollywood cameras decide how we saw the world; at other times we resisted. But always as a force it was there.

Recently, in the course of the quest which will have to become part of this story, I was having lunch in Hollywood just across the street from Grauman's Chinese Theatre at a place called Hollywood on Location. All the time I was there the sound system was relaying songs and theme tunes from movies of the 1940s and I was amused, and fascinated, and finally appalled, that although I couldn't have deliberately called to mind more than three or four of them, as soon as each one started I remembered it – not only the tune but the words as well. It was as if someone had put a long ladder down into the lowest levels of my memory and taken me down with a powerful torch and revealed the heaps of rubbish that had been thrown there and never cleaned out.

So the influence was powerful, and at the same time it was resisted. Even children, or some children (or maybe especially children) knew that Hollywood manufactured treacle. Louis B. Mayer was the sugar-daddy to beat them all. He liked to weep, and he wanted the world to weep with him. There's a story – one Mayer liked to tell – about the filming of an Andy

Hardy movie. Mickey Rooney as Andy Hardy was standing weeping outside the door of the room in which his mother is dying. Mayer came on the set and made them do it again. Andy shouldn't be standing. He should be on his knees. Tears, yes; but prayers as well – and that's how it was done. When Mayer told this story he always acted it out. He went down on his knees, he prayed for his old mother, and the tears ran down his cheeks. Those were the movies that made us think Americans were sponge-hearted and weak-brained.

I suppose everyone knew Hollywood wasn't a balanced intellectual diet. Like any dietary issue, some people cared more than others, but everyone agreed children were inclined to excess and had to be restrained. I don't think my father gave it a lot of thought; my grandmother was herself childishly addicted; my mother was our intellectual conscience. If a famous novel was made into a movie she called it a travesty. If a great stage actor like Laurence Olivier appeared in Hollywood she said he was prostituting his art. If she heard Richard Tauber, or later Mario Lanza, singing opera in a movie she said he was doing it because he wasn't good enough for the real thing. And Jose Iturbi, whose style at the piano I once thought I might emulate, she declared to be an inferior performer. I remember on one of those Saturday evenings at the Capitol we saw a movie about a young violinist. Joan Crawford played an older rich woman who promotes his talent. She falls in love with him and in the end drowns herself. I found it pretty boring but I quite liked the music. After it was over I saw that my mother was in a rage. She kept saying to my father, 'How could they do that to Wagner?' – and my father shook his head as if it was terrible, but I don't think he knew what she meant. I didn't either. I didn't think there was anyone called Wagner in the picture. Years later I saw it late at night on television, and of course my mother had been right. The movie ended with music from *Tristan and Isolde* done as a soupy violin concerto. Just so they could get the hero's best friend, a pianist, into the final sequence, they added a piano to the orchestra. It turned great music into sludge, and the recording sold in millions.

In those days I used to wonder whether my mother was right

when she told us one thing was better than another, and if she was, how she knew. Once I set a trap for her. A record of Jose Iturbi playing Chopin was coming from the radio but there was a conversation going on around the table and no one was listening. I interrupted to tell my mother it was Paderewski, her favourite pianist, whom she'd once heard play in Auckland. She stopped talking and listened. 'Wonderful,' she said.

'Better than Iturbi?' I asked.

'Much better.'

'But it *is* Iturbi,' I said.

I wasn't triumphant. I think I was disappointed. And in any case I didn't think the test was conclusive. If she'd listened longer she might have begun to doubt. But all that was second-ary to the immediate effect of what I'd done. My father was aiming a side-swipe at my ear. My sisters were declaring sisterly outrage. And my mother was weeping. This wasn't the family according to Louis B. Mayer – but ours seldom was.

The years from age five to age twelve were the forever years. I suppose that's so for most people. There was the boredom and there were the escapes from boredom. There must have been much more but it's not my purpose to dig deep into that particular midden. No period since, not even all of it run together, has seemed so long. It may be that in some sense time didn't begin until . . . And then I have to ask myself at what point do I draw the dividing line, because there is truly some sense of a radical division, a before and an after. I could draw it outside myself and my family and say it was marked by the end of the war. The war was timeless. I grew to consciousness during something that was called 'the duration'. The clocks started when it was over. Or I could draw the line inside the bounds of the family and say that time began when my sister Edie disappeared.

When the war ended – that's to say when the Japanese surrendered – the headmaster of my school came beaming into the classroom. He picked me out and told me to go and ring the school bell and just keep on ringing it. Everyone in the whole world knew that war was bad and peace would be good, so together with the whole world I was pleased. More immediately I was pleased to be chosen to ring the bell. But along with that there was a curious anxiety. I couldn't remember a time when there hadn't been, not just *a* war, but *the* war. It had gone on in continuous session like the movement of clouds and the rising and setting of the sun, a public international drama with a cast of millions. Now the curtains were closing, the dead were being counted, the curtain-calls taken and the reviews written. There was something too new about it for me to feel quite easy.

As for the other event – the disappearance of Edie – I'm not able to date it more exactly than to say it happened around that time. It might have been between the German and the Japanese surrenders. Or maybe a little later. It didn't happen like an explosion; or if it did, it was kept from me. Gradually I became aware that Edie wasn't there, then that nobody knew where she was, and finally that this was causing my parents and my grandmother anxiety and distress.

Edie was the oldest of us – she must have been nineteen when she vanished, so she might have been expected to leave home quite soon. But she would have gone, as everyone did in those days, to get married, to live in a nearby suburb perhaps and raise a family. Or at worst she might have gone to another town to take a new job – in which case she would have written letters and come on visits. But it wasn't like that. Edie was gone, silent, vanished into an implacable and (it came to be realized) deliberate non-communication. She was AWOL, as the war had taught us to say – absent without leave. She was probably not even in New Zealand (and sometimes I heard them talking about Sydney) – but even that wasn't certain.

It must have been clear right from the start that she hadn't been abducted or murdered, or fallen down a well. Again I don't remember the details. She must have packed suitcases, gathered up the things she specially valued, drawn her money and closed her bank account. But if she did all that it can't have been while anyone was standing around arguing about it. Somehow she managed to get away unnoticed, without expla-

26

nation and without dispute. It was brutal in its effects but I have to admit it was practical. If it had come to an argument I can imagine how violent our father would have become and how hysterical our mother. But having got away, why did she not then make contact? In the answer to that question, if there was an answer, I've always supposed a story must lie waiting to be told.

I missed Edie. Ellie, who was three years older than I, and Cassie, two years younger, were of an age for me to quarrel and compete with. The parents were just that – parents – and in those days parents were bosses. My grandmother wasn't entirely with us. She was a loving old soul, but she missed her dead husband so much she'd made herself into a receptacle for the worst treacle Hollywood could manufacture.

Edie had always listened to me, entertained me. Some time after she left I had a dream about her. It's still vivid when I recall it, even after all these years and decades. Our bungalow was built on uneven ground and at the back, where the land sloped away, there was a kind of basement where firewood and garden tools were kept. In the dream I was standing there and a beautiful blonde young woman came towards me in the half light and kissed me. That's all, except of course the atmosphere, and the fact that the moment was very long and slow and passionate and beautiful. When I woke and recalled the face it was Edie's, and that seemed to cast me – although she was no longer living with us – into a different kind of relationship with her. She became a kind of talisman, a love object. Her absence made it easier for me to think of her in that way, and I kept a photograph of her in a drawer under handkerchiefs and socks.

So although she was seven years older and probably thought of herself as insignificant in my life, her disappearance was something I felt keenly when I came to realize it was permanent, and that even if, as everyone anticipated, she would soon make known where she'd gone, she certainly wouldn't return. I was in love with her in a strange, unreal and dreamy way; and that feeling for her got mixed up with my reading of the poetry of John Keats.

It must have been at least two, more likely three, years after she left. Already I'd discovered literature. From John Buchan and R. L. Stevenson to Scott and Dickens and the Brontës – I was well along that path. But I was discovering poetry too. Sooner or later it had to be Keats and sooner or later it was. I remember sitting in one of those Grammar School desks reading the 'Ode to a Nightingale' again after the class had left. I was due at a soccer practice. I wasn't hanging back for lack of keenness on soccer. It was more serious than that. I had entered another world. It was the fifth stanza that took me away – the one in which the poet, following the sound of the nightingale, enters a garden he can't see in darkness. Because he can't see, he invents the garden as he goes.

> The grass, the thicket, and the fruit-tree wild;
>   White hawthorn, and the pastoral eglantine;
>     Fast-fading violets cover'd up in leaves;
>       And mid-May's eldest child,
>   The coming musk-rose, full of dewy wine,
>     The murmurous haunt of flies on summer eves.

The words seemed to point to beautiful things, and at the same time they were beautiful in themselves. I had no idea what 'pastoral eglantine' might be, but the phrase, and the stanza, and in fact the whole poem, effortlessly took up residence in my mind and haven't ever left.

But after the garden stanza came one that stirred me even more profoundly, and it's this one that got strangely intertwined with my thoughts about Edie.

> Darkling I listen; and, for many a time
>   I have been half in love with easeful Death,
> Call'd him soft names in many a musèd rhyme,
>   To take into the air my quiet breath;
> Now more than ever seems it rich to die,
>   To cease upon the midnight with no pain,
>     While thou art pouring forth thy soul abroad
>       In such an ecstasy.

The poet stops imagining the garden. He simply listens to the nightingale until he's all ears – nothing but hearing. Gradually he's extinguished by the song.

> Still wouldst thou sing, and I have ears in vain –
> To thy high requiem become a sod.

What on earth did that mean? I didn't know – I didn't need to know. It meant exactly what it said. It was a kind of magic I hadn't encountered before, and would probably never feel so keenly again.

So I went off to soccer practice and probably by outward appearances I wasn't in any way changed. But inside my head those stanzas were repeating themselves. I kept coming back to the line 'I have been half in love with easeful Death.' I thought of Easeful as well as Death as having a capital letter. Then it shortened to initials. 'I have been half in love with E.D.' And then it became 'I have been half in love with Edie.' It was as if the poem had signalled to me secretly. My mind was playing tricks – even, if you like, silly tricks; but they were in keeping with the spirit of Keats. Or it seemed so to me. That night I looked at my photograph of Edie, and the dream of kissing her under the house returned.

But there's something else about her I haven't yet recounted which explains, or helps to explain, why she was so much on my mind. I think it happened some time late in my first year at Grammar; or perhaps it was early in the second. Edie had been gone more than two years, nothing had been heard from her, and she was mentioned less and less often in the family. A sullen silence was gathering around her name, broken only by occasional maternal outbursts. It was a subject we were learning to avoid because whenever it did come up the talk ended in recriminations between my parents, each blaming the other for having driven her away. It would have been easier if they'd been able to join forces in blaming her, but it never happened.

I had a sense of the family breaking apart and of my father trying to hold it together. My grandmother was more and more disengaged from us all. She'd taken up smoking, though she wouldn't admit it, and she sat in her room with the windows open and the door shut, reading about Hollywood and throwing the butts out into the garden. Then, late in the afternoon, she would set off hobbling towards town for a five o'clock session at the pictures. If she liked a movie she would go to it every night of the week.

My father's business seemed stable but his political ambitions weren't prospering. I could tell he wasn't happy but I didn't want to know about it. Ellie had boyfriends and was leading her own life, more or less undisturbed by the parents who had probably lost confidence in their authority since Edie had run away.

Those Saturday nights at the Capitol were pretty well over. Ellie and I were too old to enjoy family outings; but just occasionally, when there was something to celebrate, or a particularly good movie, my father would book seats in that front row upstairs. Cassie enjoyed it. Ellie and I went, I think, out of a feeling of sympathy for the Hippo.

So there we were one Saturday evening back in our usual places eating chocolate-coated ice-creams and watching a picture called *Out on a Limb*, one of those slightly seedy tough-guy detective movies of the period. In it one of the suspects is a businessman. He's not a serious suspect, or not for long – just one of those possibly guilty parties detective story writers add to make it a bit harder to pick the real killer. There's a scene in which he goes out of his office into the next room and asks his secretary for a file. She's sitting behind her desk, typing. She looks up, says 'Certainly Mr Fronsett. It's right here.' And she gets up, takes something from an open drawer in the filing cabinet, and hands it to him.

It's difficult to describe the effect that scene had on us. My mother let out a shriek and then clapped her hands over her mouth. Cassie yelped. Ellie beside me made a kind of choking sound. The Hippo let slip a packet of chocolate peanuts and they rattled out on to the floor. In a moment the scene was over and we were saying to one another 'That was . . .' 'Was it . . . ?' 'Wasn't it . . . ?' until people in the rows behind began making shushing noises. We sat in a state of nervous apprehension through the rest of picture. At its end no one had a clear idea of what had happened, what the story was all about. We'd just sat there waiting for the secretary to reappear. She never did. Had the actress been Edie, or hadn't it?

# 4

Jesse Fischer put his head into the office where the three secretaries worked. Two were seated typing, one was standing at a filing cabinet near the door. She could see he was tense, in a hurry, but still when he pointed at her, clicked his fingers and said 'You . . .', trying to remember her name, she was offended. But it was an enquiry and she answered it.

'Arlene,' she said. 'Arlene Tamworth.'

'Mrs Tamworth,' he said, looking at the ring on her finger. 'Grab a notebook and pencil and come with me.'

He walked out and down the stairs into the courtyard. She clattered after him in her high heels and tight dress. He stopped outside the door and now he was feeling in the pockets of his jacket. She stood beside him. He didn't look at her. She knew he'd picked her because she was nearest the door. It could just as easily have been one of the others. She wasn't sure whether he remembered their meeting at the Laughton party.

'There's supposed to be a car,' he said; and at that moment it arrived – not a real car but a little open vehicle for getting around the lot.

He sat beside Arlene behind the driver and the car trundled them past the administration building and the commissary, between rows of sound stages that looked like warehouses or aircraft hangars, and down towards the back lot. The car turned in at a big door and drove through a building filled with unimaginable junk from every part of the world and every period of its recorded history.

Jesse Fischer talked to two men, checking items that had been chosen for setting up an interior scene. One of the men had a shooting script which they consulted from time to time.

Each item had a storage number, and as the choices were confirmed Arlene took note of them so Mr Fischer would have his own list.

An hour later and long past the usual time for lunch they were upstairs in a yellow-plastered Spanish-looking building where the studio's writers were housed, going through problems Mr Fischer had found in his latest check over a script. The writers, a man and a woman, suggested ways the problems might be overcome. When there was agreement Mr Fischer dictated to Arlene the scene number and a sentence or two summarizing what was to be done.

From there they went to one of the sound stages. A scene was set up and the cameras were ready but the female lead was still in her dressing-room, not answering the call. An explanation was whispered to Jesse Fischer. He let himself drop into a chair beside Arlene.

'Stomach cramps,' he told her.

'Hunger,' Arlene suggested, and he smiled, and then squinted at her in the dazzling artificial light.

It was hot and oppressive. The huge interior space was crowded with technicians and equipment. The star emerged from her dressing-room, smiling and apologizing. The director patted her, called her sweetheart, and told her she looked great. She was dressed in khaki jodhpurs, boots, a bush shirt tight on her very full chest, and a pith helmet. The scene was a heap of yellow sand, some palm trees, the façade of a bungalow that seemed to be made of bamboo and seagrass, and a big blue painted backdrop of sea and sky. The lights, representing a tropical sun, blazed down on it all. The camera was slightly elevated on a boom. The star had to come through the door of the bungalow, look into the far distance, see something, and then turn excitedly and call back behind her to someone indoors. They did it three or four times.

'Looks alright,' Mr Fischer said to the director between takes. The director nodded and tipped back the peaked cap he wore to keep the lights out of his eyes. 'So-so,' he said. 'We're getting better. Have you had time for yesterday's clips?'

'I'm on my way there now,' Mr Fischer said.

When they got outside the little car was gone. Arlene watched Mr Fischer. There was a wave of irritation, and then what looked like a successful effort to suppress it. He turned back indoors, but didn't go up the stairs. In a moment he was back, wheeling two of the studio bicycles that were left about the lot. He held each cycle by the centre of its handlebars. As he came towards her he was smiling. 'Can you ride?'

In a moment it was obvious she was much more practised on two wheels than he was. He led the way back through the maze of studio streets and she followed, watching him wobble as they went around corners.

Back at the administration building they went straight to the projection room. While the rushes were being set up he ordered coffee. Arlene, who took hers black, ordered it with cream (she'd learned to call milk cream) and sugar. She hoped some biscuits might come too, but none did.

The clips were of a scene, apparently inside the thatched bungalow, between the lady packed into the khaki shirt and a male star so astonishingly handsome it hardly mattered that he acted like a block of wood. The two grew impatient with one another, then angry, arguing about whether it was safe for her to go on with him (wherever it was he was going). Then in a moment of fierce passion he took hold of her, and turned on her the full beauty of his blazing brown eyes. The first time it happened Arlene didn't quite manage to suppress a laugh. As the takes repeated she heard Mr Fischer sigh now and then, and once he wiped his hands over his eyes.

When the lights went on he turned to her. 'What did you think?'

She hesitated. She was going to say 'Don't ask me,' but he had asked her. She was no expert, but he knew that. She said, 'It seemed pretty awful.'

He absorbed that. 'What made you laugh?'

'Oh that.' She thought for a moment. 'I think it was surprise.'

'What surprised you?'

'It was – well, it almost comes off. I mean, he can't – he's not much of an actor.' She hesitated. 'Is he?'

'Go on.'

34

'But he's so beautiful.' And then she realized what it was she had at the back of her mind. 'It's like one of those old silent movies – Rudolph Valentino. If you had the whole scene without dialogue you'd get away with it.'

'Can't have no dialogue.'

'Well, less.'

He stared at her for a moment, then nodded and turned away. He sat staring at the blank screen. 'When we get back to the office I want you to call O'Donoghue's office. Leave a message for him to call me as soon as he gets away from the sound stage.'

She made a note of it.

By now she'd given up hope of lunch. It was mid-afternoon and Mr Fischer hadn't finished with her. She found a moment to call Rocky. She didn't like doing it because she knew when the phone rang his hopes rose. But she told him what was going on and that she wasn't sure when she would get away. She asked him would he cook something. He was a good cook – better than she was – but he said he hadn't been out and there wasn't much in the kitchen. She said she would bring hamburgers – or they would go to the local Mexican.

Since she'd been working as a secretary they'd rented a little house on Pacifica Street, Santa Monica, and with the last of the money Rocky had brought from Australia they'd bought a used car, a big old four-door Chev.

When she got back that evening it was almost dark but there were no lights in the house. She found Rocky asleep on a couch in the sitting-room. He smelt strongly of wine and she couldn't wake him. He groaned and rolled away from her, saying 'Go away. Leave me alone.' She made herself strong tea and ate two crackers and some dry cheese. She tried again to wake Rocky but he was determined to sleep. She turned on the lights and the radio and sat in a comfortable chair, trying to read. It was no good – she couldn't.

Half an hour later she was eating a hamburger and walking along the sand of Santa Monica beach. The waves rolled in, there were a few dismal lights along the pier, and she felt homesick.

She woke in the middle of the night hearing Rocky making tea in the kitchen. She called to him and he brought her a cup and sat with his on the edge of their double bed. He said he was sorry. He'd done it again.

She sat up and sipped her tea. 'You've got to be able to get out,' she said. 'You'll go mad in here. Everyone says you've got to know how to wait in Hollywood. But waiting's got to be possible.'

He nodded. 'Give me the word, Captain. How's it done?'

'You phone Charlie Beltane in the morning.'

'He won't be there. It's the "Don't-call-us-we'll-call-you" treatment.'

'Phone his secretary. Tell her you're here between – whatever you like. Say nine and twelve in the morning. Or nine and twelve-thirty. If they have anything for you that's when they should call. If you haven't heard by twelve-thirty you forget about Charlie for that day. Get out of the house for a while.'

He smiled and patted her cheek. 'Oh mistress mine why art thou so fucking smart?'

'Will you do it?'

'I'll do it, Captain.'

'And don't say fucking,' she said. 'Not unless you meant it.'

He climbed into bed with her.

Next morning she was typing in the office she shared with the two other secretaries when a call came through. Mr Fischer wanted her in his office. It was almost eleven.

'I'm sorry,' he said. 'I meant to say to you last evening – I want you in there.' He pointed through to the little adjoining office that belonged to the woman who was known as senior secretary. Arlene looked where he pointed, then back at him for an explanation.

'Just in the meantime,' he said. 'Until things shake down – you know.'

She didn't know. Had the senior secretary left? Was she on holiday, or ill? Had he sacked her?

She moved the things that were hers out of the top drawer of her desk into the senior secretary's, and waited. Nothing happened. Mr Fischer worked in his office, made a few phone calls, went out. There was a receptionist to take calls and keep unwanted visitors from the inner office. Arlene read a newspaper, went to the commissary for lunch, phoned home and was pleased when Rocky didn't answer. Late in the afternoon Mr Fischer came in and dictated two letters. That was all.

She got used to changes of pace, not knowing from day to day whether she would be busy or have little to do. Mostly Mr Fischer didn't appear in the office until around eleven. When he worked late he sometimes asked her to stay on, sometimes not. Usually he went home in time for a meal with his wife and children. He had a projection room at home and he often watched the rushes of current movies there in the evenings.

One afternoon when they were running late he phoned home and said he wouldn't be in for a meal. He suggested Arlene do the same, and they settled to a long session of dictation.

When they were finished they drove to a little place called the Formosa Cafe. It was small and narrow, painted barn red, with banana palms growing front and back. It reminded her of an old tram or railway carriage.

'It looks like a diner,' Mr Fischer said. 'But it's good food. Everyone comes here.'

Across the street she could see the gates of the Sam Goldwyn Studio. Somewhere not far away were Paramount Pictures and RKO.

They chose a combination of rice, vegetable and fish dishes, and drank Chinese tea while they waited for a bottle of wine.

Mr Fischer asked how Rocky was doing.

She shook her head. 'It's terrible for him. When you have that kind of talent, and that kind of energy – waiting's very hard.'

'No contract?'

'No contract.'

'A screen test?'

'He's had two. Everyone sounded so enthusiastic he was sure the contract would come through. I don't like to tell him but

37

I think I'm learning the language. Everyone in Hollywood says, "Sweetheart that was beautiful, a great scene, a great movie, you were stunning" – but then you have to work out whether they mean it.'

Mr Fischer nodded. He refilled her tea cup. Their dishes had arrived and she was sharing them out. 'It looks lovely,' she said. 'I'm hungry. I'm always hungry.'

'But you don't put on weight.'

'I have skinny genes.'

'You have very nice genes.'

'I think it's Rocky's accent that's the problem. Nobody wants to hear our kind of English in movies. But when he changes it it doesn't sound quite right – unless he's doing something big like Shakespeare. For modern roles it seems to take the sting out of his acting.'

She asked Mr Fischer about his family. He told her his wife was a painter – those were her abstracts in his office. His three kids were at junior school – two boys and a girl, called Danny, Delores and Doug.

Arlene thought she hid her surprise successfully. 'Alliterative names. That's unusual.'

'Judith chose them. She wanted something . . . decorative, I guess.'

'So you two are alliterative as well. Judith and Jesse.'

'Yeah well . . .' It was the first time she'd seen him show a faint shade of embarrassment. 'This is Hollywood.' And then, taking command again, 'Wouldn't you like some wine?'

She asked about his role as a producer. He shrugged. 'What's there to say? I'm a man with talent in the process of becoming a hack.'

That surprised her. She said she believed in the talent, not in the hack.

He hesitated a moment. 'Well . . . It's like this. I want to make pictures. I started as a scriptwriter. Then I became a director. Now I'm an executive producer – but I've had it written into my contract that I can direct one picture a year if I find something I want to do. Marvin Major doesn't like that. He wants me in there making sure the studio meets its annual schedule. Twenty, thirty pictures – whatever we've decided on. You've seen what I do. I buy a property. I get some writers to work on it. I find a director. I maybe look over the casting director's shoulder. I keep an eye on progress. I might take a hand at the cutting – or anyway I look at the final cut. I'm everything and nothing. But I do have some power, whereas a director has none – unless he's a very big shot with an Oscar or two. He gets told what to make. He's given a script and a cast. He's overruled in the cutting room by anyone from Mrs Nightingale to me to Marvin Major to someone in New York he's never met. When he's finished, the studio might decide to bring in someone else to shoot a different ending, or to cut his favourite scene – anything. But that's the Hollywood system. It's a team effort. We all know it, and we all hate the guys who protest and say they're being made to prostitute their art. The answer's always the same. If you don't like the brothel, stop cashing the cheques.'

He was so relaxed she thought it might be a good moment to mention the job she seemed to be filling. Was it vacant? Was he looking for someone to fill it?

At once he looked wary and she regretted having begun, but she rushed on, if only to get to the end. 'I mean – if it's vacant I'd like to apply for it – to be considered along with whoever else is after it.'

He was silent for a few seconds. 'You're in the chair aren't you?'

'Yes, but . . . OK. I'm sorry. I can see I shouldn't have mentioned it.'

'No. You can mention it. Say whatever's on your mind.'

She shrugged. 'I've said it.'

Again there was silence. Then he said, 'You must know you've done a good job.'

'Have I? That's good. You've never said so.'

'I haven't complained.'

'That's true.' She smiled. 'Thank you for not complaining.'

He returned the smile. 'OK. I apologize. You've done a good job.'

'Now you've made me feel I was fishing for compliments.'

'Whereas really you were fishing for the job.'

She put her head down and thought about that. 'I think I was asking where's the proper place to go fishing. You keep talking about the system. I'm trying to learn it.'

He nodded. 'Let's put it like this. You keep doing the job. If we still like one another after a month or so, it's yours. How's that?'

'It's wonderful. It's much more than I expected. Thank you.'

She asked what happened to the previous secretary.

'Miss Pickett? She was called to the great white office in the sky.'

'She died?'

He laughed. 'No. Just called to higher things. You haven't seen Marvin Major's suite. We must sneak you in there one day when he's out of town. It's all white. White desk, white cocktail bar, white chairs and couch, white walls, white phones. His wife's photograph's on the wall. They say it's mounted on a hinge with the wall safe behind. It's a good story anyway.'

Some time later when he'd called for the bill he said, 'There's one thing I should say to you.' They'd finished the wine and he chose his words carefully. 'You mustn't see this job as a way to help your husband. I don't mean the studio's closed to him. But if he comes in as an actor it has to be by the same door as everyone else.'

She felt embarrassed – and there was disappointment too. To help Rocky was what she wanted more than anything. She didn't reply.

'You're not offended, are you?'

She managed a smile. 'No. Or maybe yes. It doesn't matter. I've got the message.'

'I suppose the warning wasn't necessary.'

'Not really,' she lied. And it wouldn't be heeded, either.

Their cars were parked some way apart. He walked with her to hers. 'Drive carefully,' he said, holding the door while she got in. 'And thank you for your company.'

She thanked him in return. There was a little coldness between them now. Or there was on her part, and she didn't conceal it.

Driving back through the empty streets she turned on the car radio. The Inkspots were singing, 'Into each life some rain must fall, But too much is fallin' in mine.' Then came a favourite of hers – Ella Fitzgerald and Louis Armstrong singing 'Stars fell on Alabama.'

Lights were on in the little house at 1011 Pacifica Street. She could hear the radio as she approached the back door. It was tuned to a broadcast of classical music. On the kitchen table were some empty wine bottles. In the bedroom Rocky was more or less unconscious on the bed, still in his clothes.

# 5

From the opposite side of Pacifica Street the bungalow looked like a child's drawing, a door in the middle for a nose, a large window on either side for a pair of eyes. In front was a small patch of grass and a path to three front steps that went up to the door. A narrow drive along one side went to a single garage at the back. The front door opened straight into the living-room. Beyond that, through a curve-topped doorless opening, was a small space for the dining table, and beyond again, the kitchen. There were two small bedrooms and a bathroom. That was all, except for a laundry space beyond the kitchen, opening on to a back porch. The back garden was enclosed by a wall. A gate in the back wall opened on to an alley where the rubbish bins were kept.

They rented the place furnished. It had a décor that was very common in those days in the houses of Californians who wanted to be up-to-the-minute but whose resources were limited. The rugs on the bare polished floors were Mexican style, though Rocky, inspecting the label, found they'd been woven in a factory in California. The curtains were a heavy dark velvet and hung on wooden rods with knobs like big arrow-heads. The furniture in the living room had fabrics woven in what must have been Spanish-Indian motifs. Arlene remembers squat birds with dark grey bodies, pink beaks, and white outstretched wings and tail; also pink flowers with black centres, and grey flowers with pink centres.

She liked the house and so did Rocky. But he wanted to change it, especially to lighten the effect of all that dark velvet and heavy weave. It wasn't a plan. It began one day when he bought a Japanese screen. He tried it in the living-room but it didn't match what was already there, so he put it in their bedroom. Then he began to look for things that would go with it. Gradually the bedroom lost its Mexican look and became Japanese. The birds now had long wings, long necks and long legs, and stalked or flew among fine wavering grasses. The lampshades and blinds were of paper and thin wire, so the Southern Californian light that had been checked by the velvet came pouring through. There were two beautiful blue vases, inlaid with flowers; and on the wall, three Japanese prints, one of a Samurai, one of women with umbrellas in a rainstorm, and one of geishas, their heavy black hair skewered with what looked like chop-sticks.

All this happened gradually. When the bedroom was done Rocky turned his attention to the dining space. He found a table of stainless steel with a glass top; then chairs that matched the steel, and a small, steely-looking art-deco sideboard with mirrors.

One day Arlene came home to find a piano in the second bedroom. It was a small-size grand which he'd bought second-hand. Soon after he bought a silver metronome and a collection of six silver-framed photographs of Hollywood stars of the 1920s and '30s. He kept the top of the piano down and arranged them on it. He liked to set the metronome waving and tocking among the stars. Sometimes, half-ironic, half-serious, he let the metronome pace him while he intoned lines from Shakespeare.

> Tomorrow, and tomorrow, and tomorrow,
> Creeps in this petty pace from day to day,
> To the last syllable of recorded time;
> And all our yesterdays have lighted fools
> The way to dusty death. Out, out, brief candle!
> Life's but a walking shadow, a poor player
> That struts and frets his hour upon the stage
> And then is heard no more.

They were starting to like Santa Monica. On the weekends Arlene liked to walk down to the beach where the little white wooden houses with the rust of salty nails coming through flaking paint reminded her of houses on beachfronts where she'd gone swimming as a child.

Rents were low, houses cheap to buy. Los Angeles was spilling over the hills and out into the San Fernando Valley. A popular song went

> I'm gonna settle down and never more roam
> And make the San Fernando Valley my home.

Young couples settling down in those post-war years were more interested in a new house in the Valley than in older ones in Santa Monica. So when the agent told Arlene the house was for sale, and that when a buyer was found they would have to move out, she asked about raising a loan. That was before her evening with Jesse Fischer at the Formosa Cafe. After it, when she collected her next pay-cheque, she found she was officially called senior secretary and her pay had almost doubled. That afternoon she left the studio early, called on the house-agent, and arranged to buy the house. Instead of paying rent, they would pay off a mortgage. It was to be a surprise for Rocky. But as the weeks went by she kept putting off telling him.

It was April and the daytime temperatures began to go up into the eighties. The air was full of the scent of lemon-flowers mixed not unpleasantly with gasoline. It bore grass-pollens too, blown down by the warm dry wind, the Santa Ana, from the hills. You didn't know the pollen was there until suddenly you were seized with a sneezing fit.

They had a little iron table and chairs out in the back garden under a bottlebrush tree, and Arlene liked to get home from the studio in the late afternoon and drink chilled fruit-juice mixed with soda-water, sitting on the cool iron chair and smoking a single cigarette, her first of the day. Often Rocky would be cooking. Sometimes they went out and ate Mexican food. There were also times when she got home and found he'd been drinking and there was nothing to be done with him.

In the weekends she worked hard to keep him occupied; and he could still, when the mood took him, sweep her along on

44

the crest of a wave of enthusiasm and almost insane cheerfulness that might last hours, or a whole day, before it broke. They went often to movies, and sometimes to plays, or to a concert at the Hollywood Bowl. They even went once to a football match at the Los Angeles Coliseum. Lunch on Saturdays was at the Brown Derby in Hollywood, or the one in Beverly Hills. There was always the beach – they were both strong swimmers. And Bogart was still glad to have Rocky on board *Santana* to make up his crew. It would have been a good life – it was a good life. But still there was no contract.

The little garden seemed minimal compared to the gardens she was used to in Auckland, but still she loved hers and watered it every day to keep alive and flourishing its grass, its flowers and shrubs and its few small trees. The soil seemed like brown powder – it had no body, no dark accumulation of humus, and if you watered without a sprinkler you saw it washing away down the drive into the street. She remembered the little German who had said he was Mr Laughton's tailor telling her, as they looked over the Laughtons' garden and the cliff-top that had been washed away in a rainstorm, 'Scratch the surface and you find the desert.'

Arlene lay flat on her back on the thick springy grass in the shade of bamboos that ran down one fence-line, watching a pair of mocking-birds watching her from their perch on the electric wires. They had a nest in the bougainvillaea that sprawled over the back wall. They seemed to think she might steal their eggs, but even if she'd wanted to she couldn't have got her hand through the spines that guarded it.

Often when the heat seemed too much to be tolerated, a cooler breath would come up from the sea. It was palpable. It was something Santa Monica and Pacific Palisades were famous for – a wonderful, faintly chill, faintly damp wash of air up from the ocean and over the burning sandy suburbs.

As the sun went out across the Pacific towards (as she always thought) New Zealand, the coastal suburbs seemed to fill with a peculiar magenta light. The temperature dropped and her energy came back. She liked to walk at night. The streets were poorly lit – away from main thoroughfares the only lights were at intersections – but there seemed nothing in those days to be afraid of.

When the message came at last from Charlie Beltane it was disappointing. There was no contract for Rocky and at the moment no prospect of one. What he could offer in the meantime was some work. War movies were going out of fashion and Westerns were coming back. A studio wanted some regular back-up men who could ride horses, look mean, break balsawood chairs over one another's heads, and sling guns. They might get a line or two of dialogue. They weren't just extras, but they weren't on salary. They bought their own costumes and they were paid when there was work.

'You want to make me into a Gower Gulch cowboy,' Rocky said.

'It's better than that,' Charlie insisted. 'No one's asking you to hang about the streets waiting to be picked up when there's work. You'll be on their list. And these are going to be top-class Westerns.'

Rocky talked it over with Arlene. He was sober and they were both depressed. Next day she took a long lunch-break. They met at a little restaurant called Oblath's and ate a good lunch and drank some wine. Across the street they could see the Paramount Studio entrance with its double columns on either side of an arch and its beautiful wrought-iron gates. When they'd eaten and drunk enough to feel cheerful they walked a hundred yards or so down the street to the Western Costume Company and Rocky was fitted with a gun-belt, leather leggings, boots and spurs, a check shirt and scarf, a leather jerkin, a big hat.

Arlene felt as if she'd come in with her child to buy a costume for a fancy-dress party. Rocky probably felt worse.

'Before you go to work in all this,' the salesman advised, 'you better find a nice big patch of dirt and roll in it. If you come in looking all shiny they'll think you're a greenhorn.'

Rocky nodded. 'Sure pardner,' he said, and drew his six-gun.

As they walked back to the car he said, 'Rocky Tamworth. I chose myself this stupid fucking name and now I'm going to have stupid fucking work to go with it.'

'Hey cheer up,' she said. 'It might be fun. It might lead to something.'

She drove him back to Santa Monica, dropped him at Pacifica Street with his gear, and returned to the studio.

When she got home that evening there was a note on the kitchen table in large unsteady letters: GAWN TO A LYNCHIN PARTY. She looked for the cowboy outfit and couldn't find it anywhere in the house. But when she took some food scraps out to the alley she found it there, stuffed into one of the bins. She took it out, dusted it off, and put it away in a high cupboard in the second bedroom. When she went to bed that evening Rocky was still out and there had been no message from him.

In the morning she found him asleep on the couch in the living-room. She kissed him as she was leaving and he half woke. 'I'm glad you're not going to do it,' she said. 'When you make your first Western you'll be wearing John Wayne's boots and Gary Cooper's hat.'

'Sure, Captain,' he said, in a husky voice. 'Keep the Southern Cross flying.' And he fell asleep again.

Recalling that time in her life many years later it seemed to Arlene the excitement of being in Hollywood, working in a studio, seeing the stars at work and at play, must have been overshadowed by her worry about Rocky. There had been a first few idyllic months when they were still getting to know one another and when they had no reason to believe that Charlie Beltane wouldn't be able to open the necessary doors. In those months they'd gone about trying to take in the fact that they were in Hollywood – the dream factory, the mythical place. But even then it was difficult. It was as if the 'real' Hollywood was somewhere else, as unreachable as ever. You could only get a sense of it by going to the movies. Day-to-day Hollywood even then was a dingy suburb in a sprawling shapeless city. Some of the big studios were there; others were in other parts of Los Angeles. And if many, or even most, of the stars and directors and producers made their millions in Hollywood, at the end of every day they got out of it. The real Hollywood was not a place; it was a state of mind. You couldn't put your feet on one piece of the earth and say 'Here I am at last'. Or if you could, it would have to have been some place like the forecourt of the Chinese Theatre, with the hand- and foot-prints of the stars, and the leg-print of Betty Grable, and the nose-print of Jimmy Durante, pressed into wet cement.

She spent some part of every day with Jesse Fischer, and sometimes all day. She got used to moving about the studio with him, or sitting in a chair at one side of his desk, notebook and pencil ready to record what he wanted recorded. She was becoming his memory bank. He often asked her opinion, sometimes when there were rushes to be looked at, sometimes when there was a problem with a piece of dialogue in a script. They seldom talked about anything but work, except when something made it necessary for them to have lunch together away from the studio. Then there might be twenty minutes or half an hour when he relaxed and talked as he had at the Formosa Cafe. But she felt all the time that she grew closer to him just by working alongside him. She thought of their relationship as side-by-side. There was very little eye contact, and so the communication between them, which undoubtedly was there, seemed peculiarly subterranean, secret and vaguely exciting.

One day they were on one of the sound stages watching O'Donoghue direct his latest thriller. A businessman who was a minor suspect in the case had to come into the annexe occupied by his secretary and ask for a file, which she found for him. The actress sent by General Casting to play the secretary was a stunning blonde with a charming breathy whisper of a voice, big blue eyes, a broad mouth, a large bosom, a wasp waist, and long well-shaped legs. She was a nice young woman doing what must have been one of her first assignments since she'd joined the studio. O'Donoghue did the shot again and again. The actress was anxious. She had trouble controlling a nervous tremor in her chin; but she was patient and she worked at it. After a take that looked better than the others had been O'Donoghue sat thinking. Then he thanked the actress and said she'd been very co-operative, and that would be all. It was almost lunch-time, but when she'd gone he told the crew and the other actor to wait. He turned to Jesse Fischer. 'Why can't they send me someone who looks like a secretary? Why do they all have to be goddesses?'

Jesse laughed. 'I've never heard you complain about pulchritude before.'

Arlene winced. Pulchritude was a favourite word in Hollywood in those years.

O'Donoghue shook his head. 'I dunno Jesse. She doesn't look right. Does she look right to you?'

'She looks just great. What do you think Arlene?'

'She looks great. That's the problem isn't it, Dennis? She looks like a star.'

O'Donoghue nodded. 'She's gonna be a star. You can bet on dames like that. Stellar quality, Marvin calls it. You can pick it a mile off.'

'So why complain?'

'Because . . .' O'Donoghue looked helpless. He wasn't good at talking. 'She's a red herring.'

Jesse turned to Arlene. 'D'you know what he means?'

'It's the audience, isn't it? They're going to expect her to turn up again in the picture. She's so stunning they'll think she's important.'

O'Donoghue nodded. 'She's a red herring.'

They were silent for a while.

'See – I've lost my fix on it,' O'Donoghue said. 'I'm dazzled by blonde.'

Then, after a moment: 'While we've got it all set up could we just go through it again? Arlene – get up there will you sweetheart. Be the secretary.'

She frowned. 'I can't act.'

'Don't act, baby. Just do it for me will you? Get the boss his file. I need to look at it.'

So she got up and went through the motions, with the actor coming in and asking for the file. There was no thought in her mind that it would be filmed. After a couple of tries she relaxed.

'Certainly Mr Fronsett. It's right here,' she said, getting up and going to the open filing cabinet.

'That's what I want,' O'Donoghue said. 'Not too much ass. Just right. Isn't it right, Jesse?'

Jesse Fischer nodded, smiling. 'It's perfect.'

They were silent again.

'Couldn't she . . .' O'Donoghue said.

'I don't see why not.'

They turned to her. 'We're breaking for lunch,' Jesse said. 'After lunch Arlene, will you let them make you up?'

'For . . . I don't . . .' She didn't know what it was she wanted to say.

'Do it, lover,' O'Donoghue said.

'Let's have lunch,' Jesse said.

So they broke for lunch and afterwards returned to the set. Arlene was made up and dressed. They did three takes and O'Donoghue said any one of them would do. He had what he wanted. He thanked her and said he would see she got a cheque.

'Leave that to me,' Jesse Fischer said. 'I'll look after it.'

When she was getting ready to leave the office that evening he put his head around the door. 'Time for a drink?'

This was something new. He had a small cocktail cabinet in his office. He mixed martinis. 'To your first picture,' he said.

She raised her glass. 'The first and the last.'

But she was pleased. As she drove home thinking about it she began to feel excited. It wasn't that she thought it meant a great deal – certainly not that she would now become a screen actress. It was just a lucky chance. Everything that happened to her she felt happened by chance; and a good proportion of the chances were lucky. Now she was going to appear in a Hollywood picture. She was impatient in the rush-hour traffic, eager to get home and tell Rocky. But then, just before she reached Pacifica Street, a new thought struck her. It made her drive right on until she came to the ocean. There she parked and sat looking out across the sand to where the waves were rolling in. It wasn't so much a thought that had checked her as the sense of a dreadful irony. Rocky was trying so hard to break into movies, and now, without trying, she was going to appear in one. The longer she thought about it the more she felt it wouldn't be possible to tell him. Not yet anyway. Soon his luck would change and then it wouldn't matter.

# 6

Recently, I was walking with my wife Marion along the Auckland waterfront. Two people came towards us on bicycles, a man and a woman. The man had a shaven head and wore dark glasses. He looked quite unfamiliar. Then as they passed he called, 'Bill. How are you?'

I turned and waved and called back, answering him by name.

Last time I'd seen him, five or more years before, he'd had shoulder-length hair and a beard. It was the voice I recognized, not the face, and four words were enough, not because there was anything odd about the voice but because I have that kind of ear. When I turn on the radio I know instantly which newsreader, or announcer, or politician is speaking. It's the same when I answer the phone. This is something I inherited from my grandmother.

That's why it only needed the secretary in the movie to say to the businessman, 'Certainly, Mr Fronsett. It's right here,' and I knew it was Edie. And I knew my grandmother would know, though she wasn't with us that evening. But I didn't say I was sure, even after the whole family, together and apart, had seen the picture three or four times. By then feelings in the family were so intense and so explosive, we all drew away from one another. We became like politicians, weighing our words, never giving too much away.

Our mother was the problem. Her tendency to hysteria had increased since Edie had left. Now Edie's appearance in a movie, and the uncertainty whether it was her, unsettled her even more. Sometimes she would weep at the thought that Edie could so ungratefully go off, become a Hollywood star (interruptions of 'Mum, she's hardly a star!' didn't help) and forget her family. Other times she would snap at the suggestion that it was Edie, denying it flatly. Edie was somewhere in Auckland, or not far away; and when she got over 'the bee in her bonnet' she would come back to us.

My father never made it clear what he thought. Everything he said on that subject was designed to calm his wife, so he often contradicted himself, and she was quick to point it out. If she wasn't present he would say he was pretty sure it wasn't Edie, though he admitted the likeness. I don't think that's what he believed. He just wanted the agitating subject to go away.

It was true that by appearance alone you couldn't be certain. Edie's hairstyle had changed; her accent was Americanized; and anyone looks different made up and filmed in black and white under studio lights. So I suppose the family, those who hadn't inherited the grandmother's ear, were in doubt. I think Ellie and Cassie wanted it to be true – wanted to have a sister in Hollywood – and that meant they tried to believe it but probably secretly found it incredible.

Meanwhile my own life was going on somehow separate from the family and all its drama. I was what was just then beginning to be called a teenager. I lived as much of my life as was possible – and a lot was possible – off the family turf. Summer weekends were spent at the tennis club. Winter Saturdays were taken up with football. I learned chess, joined a club, and played it fanatically. The years of boredom were over. My photograph of Edie remained in the sock and handkerchief drawer. It had a special aura about it – more so now she'd put in that fleeting and enigmatic appearance in a movie – but I didn't look at it often. For real excitement I kept three pictures of Hollywood stars – Betty Grable, Ginger Rogers, and Susan Hayward. 'Grable, Rogers and Hayward,' I could have said, echoing the Biblical text, 'and the greatest of these was Grable.' But as it happened the sexiest picture I had was one of Ginger Rogers in a shimmering low-cut gown.

Hollywood was receding as a force in my life, but I still went to the pictures – everybody did – and there are movies from that period that were to stay fixed in my consciousness. One was *Casablanca*. The love agonies of Bogart and Bergman, renouncing one another for the greater Good, combined with the excitement of a thriller set in an exotic place (Warner Brothers' back lot, gone Moroccan) – it was irresistible, as was Claude Rains's elevator eyebrow, and the line 'Round up the usual suspects'. I've seen *Casablanca* since, more than once. But I remember almost as clearly another picture I haven't seen again, in which Danny Kaye played a dreamy milkman in love with the agonizingly beautiful (or so she seemed to the teenage Bill Harper) Virginia Mayo. I remember a scene in which Kaye, thinking of her over breakfast, confuses the toast with a pack of cards and begins to shuffle the slices.

I didn't love movies any less, although I needed them less. They stayed right where they had always been in my mental landscape. But something else had come into that landscape. It wasn't only Keats, and poetry. It was the notion of art – even of 'High Art'. And I didn't, not then, and not for a very long time, think that movies were art; or if I did, they were low art. The Hollywood package was so familiar I don't think anyone noticed how much art sometimes went into it. The good, the bad and the sludge poured out of Southern California in a constant familiar stream. We knew our likes and dislikes, and that was enough.

Hollywood was glamour and it was money. It was still the world capital of popular entertainment. So whether your daughter was there embarking on a career as an actress, or whether she was not – this was a question of some consequence. And my mother's wildly erratic responses to the uncertainty were more than my father could manage. I was forced now to recognize that she had always been prone to hysteria and he to violence, and that each bad quality promoted the other. My job was to close the windows.

My mother usually started the rows. She had a strong line in unsubtle innuendo. The Hippo might suggest that Cassie should come to lunch when she was called, or that it was ill-mannered of Ellie to read at the table. My mother would seem to let it pass, but then she would offer some thundering generalization to no one in particular. 'Some people,' she might begin, 'have to be always laying down the law and then they wonder why their children run away from home.' Everything followed from that in due sequence. If it was Saturday lunch you could see the pattern stretching away ahead, laying waste to the weekend. My father might let her first salvo go over his head; but he would glower and sulk. The next from her might take the 'Some-people-just-can't-be-spoken-to' line. Once his anger broke through his restraint he at once turned it personal. 'And you can't open your silly mouth without having a go at someone.'

After that the verbal gloves were off. The battle would rage, die down, flare up again. I shut the windows because it embarrassed me to think the neighbours heard the rows; though once those two began shouting I don't suppose windows were enough to contain the racket. The question was whether the violence would become physical. Sometimes it did. My mother in battle used an old-fashioned rhetoric – something which might have come out of Hollywood. Having goaded my father, heaping scorn and contempt on him (and verbally she was much the more agile) she would shout something like 'Strike me then. Go on. Strike me. I know you're just dying to lay hands on me.' Sometimes he obliged. When he hit her he either screamed, or she subsided in a sobbing heap. I feared the screams. They were like the collapse of a whole civilization.

I was never able to talk to anyone about these quarrels – not then, nor later when I left home. It was partly embarrassment; it was also because I knew there were two ways of presenting them – comic and tragic – and neither seemed entirely truthful. My parents' rows were absurd, they were grim, they were bitter, they were sad; and they were all those things at once.

As for embarrassment: there have been times when I've accused myself of shallowness. How is it that even now, so many decades later, I can sometimes wake in the morning, recall some awful detail, and groan aloud. It happens before I've quite woken, so my own groaning wakes me. Isn't embarrassment, I ask myself, an emotion of the ego, which wants always to be seen in a favourable light? The answer is yes. But then I think of Johnny Keats whose poems and whose life were so full of blushing ('Full of the true, the blushful Hippocrene', he says in that first of his Odes to come my way). Aren't sensitivity and egotism twins, and almost inseparable? Aren't they even the incestuous parents of art?

And in any case embarrassment wasn't all that I felt. I might as well come clean and admit that in the short time remaining while the last vestiges of Sunday schooling still clung to me and prayer seemed, if not efficacious, at least still worth a shot, I prayed always and only for one thing: that these two, who both loved me, and loved one another, should stop tearing one another to pieces.

I always took my mother's part. In retrospect it doesn't seem fair. But I'd been brought up to believe that women were weaker, and that any man who laid a finger on a woman (there's the old rhetoric again) was a coward and a cad. And besides, I'd always been closer to her than to him. As I got bigger I began to protect her physically. She played on that, and would sometimes get in her worst verbal thrusts while I stood between them deflecting my father's angry blows.

The things which remain clearest in my memory are, of course, the most spectacular. I've forgotten a great deal, or almost forgotten; and in fact I think I must have spent my early adult years deliberately putting all that pain – Edie's departure, the quarrels, the family wreckage – behind me. I can't say now exactly what formal steps were taken to trace my sister. I know at one stage the police were briefly involved. I seem to remember they pointed out that Edie was a grown woman, that there was no evidence, or even a suggestion, of foul play, and that therefore the matter was none of their business. But of course once she'd appeared, or seemed to appear, in a movie, that must have suggested ways of finding her. The problem, I think, was that no one in the family would quite admit that it was really her. We denied it, or shrugged it off, because that seemed the best way to calm our mother. And then there was the fact that no one knew much about Hollywood. We knew its products. I suppose we all knew it was a suburb of Los Angeles. And my grandmother was a mine of information from gossip columnists about who was dating whom, and who had given a party where, and who was being paid what for which. But did anyone understand, for example, the studio system, or how pictures were made, or what kind of contracts people worked under? I doubt it. Hollywood was glamour and therefore it was mystery. It was a big neon sign, or an exploding star, in the far distance. Its edges were blurred. To write to Hollywood must have been like writing one of those letters children send off to Santa Claus care of the North Pole.

But I know my mother did write at least once. One Saturday morning I went down to the gate to collect the mail. As I was looking through it my father loomed up behind me, holding out his hand for it. At the same moment I saw a letter with an American stamp, addressed to my mother. It was typewritten and her name was misspelled, so I knew it hadn't come from Edie. Stamped at the bottom of the envelope was the monogram of one of the Hollywood studios – I was sure that was what I'd seen, but at that moment my father snatched it away from me.

I half protested. 'It's for her.'

'I can read,' he said, and turned away to go back up the path.

Back indoors there was something like a silent battle of wills between us, which he won. I was sure he hadn't given the letter to her, but I didn't quite dare to bring it up for fear of the consequences. He looked at me across the room with a bold stare that challenged me to open my mouth. I kept it shut.

It wasn't until many years later that I saw the letter – in fact there were two. It was when my father died and I was going through papers in his desk. Mother must have been uncertain which studio had made the picture, *Out on a Limb*, so she'd written to ones whose names she knew, asking whether they could give her the address of an actress called Edith Harper. MGM and Paramount had written back saying they knew of no actress of that name. I still have those letters. One is headed 'Paramount Productions Ltd / 5451 Marathon Street, Hollywood, Calif / Telephone Hollywood 2411 / Cable Address Famfilms.' The other is headed 'Ars Gratia Artis' in a curve over the head of the MGM lion. Below that it reads simply 'Metro–Goldwyn–Mayer Studios / Culver City / California.' I stare at those letterheads. Even now they seem to come, not from a geographical location, but from somewhere fabulous and remote. If Edie was there, they must have felt, she was beyond call. I don't think any further letters were written.

The rows at home got worse. Always and endlessly they circled around the subject of Edie. No matter how far they went back into the past, or off at a tangent, they came back to her. It was my mother's obsession. Either it was driving her mad, or it was the point of focus her madness had chosen. Though I was still half in love with Edie, the other half of me would gladly have wished on her a less than Easeful Death. Why didn't she at least write to us? But then I could see that even that might have made things worse.

I lived as much as possible off the premises. I won a cup at the tennis club for the most improved player. At soccer I moved from right wing to inside right and finally to centre forward – striker, as it's called these days. I represented my school and was allowed to wear the rep. pocket on my blue-and-gold blazer. At chess I played a fast aggressive game, favouring the queen's-pawn gambit. There were no girls at the school, and the ones at the tennis club were mostly older. My sex life went on with Betty Grable of the marvellous legs and with Ginger Rogers of the plunging neck-line.

But I couldn't always avoid the fights at home. One day it was worse than usual. I did a quick circuit of the house, up one side and down the other, shutting windows and doors. I turned on the radio and turned up the volume to scramble as far as possible the voices and what they were saying.

My father at that time was particularly tense. Something was coming up in the Labour Party – some internal election on which he counted a good deal. At the same time he knew he was being talked about in the neighbourhood, and that some of it was getting back to the local party branch. Those were the days when he was only to be approached with caution.

The fight blew up like a forest fire. My grandmother sailed forth in defence of her daughter and was picked up bodily by my father who carried her back to her bedroom, dumped her there, and slammed the door on her. At that my mother ran shrieking from the house, down the path and across the street

to a sympathetic neighbour. Resident Hippo must have been
out of his mind. He went after her and caught her at the
neighbour's door. He grabbed her from behind, around the
waist, and heaved her, screaming and kicking, back across
the street. She was shrieking 'Edie. Edie. He's murdering me.'
Why in this moment she should call on Edie, whom she had
never got on with, needn't be asked. The cries must have been
heard all over the suburb. 'Edie. Your father's killing me.'

As it happened he was much closer to killing himself. She
was no lightweight. He was overweight, and a smoker as well.
When he got her back indoors he collapsed, purple and heaving.
There was no need to defend her. If she'd set a pack of gangsters
on him to beat him up they couldn't have done a better job.

# 7

The room in which they held their story conferences was long and narrow, with cream-coloured walls, black leather chairs and couch, a long table and a coffee machine. Along one wall was a series of six coloured sketches from some years back, each labelled 'Costume for Miss Davis'. No one seemed certain whether the Miss Davis had been Bette or Joan.

When Arlene came in Sarah James and Jock Bateman were already there. They were two of the studio's highest paid writers. She was a novelist from somewhere in the east. He'd had some small success as a playwright in New York before coming out to Hollywood.

They exchanged good mornings. Sarah was drinking coffee, and offered Arlene a cup. 'Where's the great white father?' she asked.

'No sign of him yet,' Arlene said, accepting the coffee.

'Brother Bateman's reading enemy dispatches.'

Arlene recognized the copy of *Hollywood Reporter* Jock had spread on the table in front of him. Rocky always read it along with *Daily Variety*. That way you knew what pictures were being made, who was starring in them, who had a new contract, who'd been dropped, who'd been seen at Chasen's or the Mocambo.

'The cold war's getting to us,' Jock said. 'Since Thomas came to Hollywood it's like even Roosevelt's a word you can't use in the presence of a lady.'

J. Parnell Thomas was chairman of HUAC – the House Un-American Activities Committee. HUAC was holding closed hearings on the influence of Communism on the film industry. Now it was rumoured there might be open hearings in Washington later in the year.

Jock's hands shook as he turned the pages. He was an alcoholic – a bout drinker. Just now he was dry. There was a story about him sitting drunk in a caravan on the studio lot typing a script all day to keep ahead of a shooting schedule. As they were finished the sheets were re-typed and rushed to the director and the actors. It was said to be the best script Jock had ever written.

'Maybe it's time to run away to sea,' he said.

Sarah said she would like to go out on the Dorothy Parker line. 'You know she's supposed to have thrown open one of the upstairs windows in the writers' building at MGM and shouted down to people in the street, "Let me out of here. I'm as sane as you are."'

Jock nodded. 'She called it Metro-Goldwyn-Merde.'

Salka Viertel had come in. She was an older woman, a German refugee who had come to Hollywood in the 1930s and written scripts for Garbo. She wasn't on the studio staff but Jesse Fischer had got her in to help with the story. 'They won't let you run away if they decide you're the wrong shade of pink,' she said. 'It took me so many years to get my American citizenship and now they won't let me have a passport to visit my son in Paris. You make such an effort to get in and then you find this America – it's a trap.'

'I'm starting to think of the war with nostalgia,' Jock said. 'One thing Hitler did for the world – he made the Left respectable. But it hasn't lasted.'

Jesse Fischer came in. 'Sorry I'm late.' He threw down his bag and stretched out on the black couch. 'Now everybody listen. Something's clear that wasn't clear before. We're going to make this picture in the studio.'

There was a puzzled silence. Jesse Fischer closed his eyes, concentrating. 'I'll explain. Let's go back to the beginning. I want a thriller, a murder, a detective story, and I want it straight. The public have to look at it and say "I know what this is. I know where I am." But I'd like it to be something better than just a B-grade formula product. As I see it there has to be a single central image we can keep coming back to. Something that will hold it all together. Story's no problem.

I can rely on you guys for that – and we've made some progress.'

He opened his eyes and looked around. 'What I've got to throw into the ring this morning isn't exactly an image. It's more like a pun. A verbal pun but it could be a visual pun as well. The pun is shooting. Just that. Shooting. What I'm suggesting is this. Suppose we keep on exactly as we did yesterday, working towards a conventional detective picture. A murder, a victim, suspects, cops, a private eye. But we pick up the whole thing and transpose it from suburban LA to a movie studio. Most of the characters are employed in the studio. Let's say we're going to film what we know and we're going to use what's lying around us – sound stages, back lot sets, movie crews, directors, writers, actors, the whole box of tricks. They're going to be in the picture. The murder probably happens somewhere in the studio, and a big part of the story happens there. What do you think?'

Salka Viertel and Sarah James looked enquiringly at one another. They were interested.

Jock Bateman was first to speak. 'We like it.'

'It makes a lot of things easier,' Sarah said. 'And more interesting.'

Mrs Viertel tapped a pencil lightly on the table top. 'It's so obvious,' she said. 'Why hasn't anyone thought of it?'

'Aren't the good ideas always obvious,' Jesse said. 'They're the ones you don't notice until you trip over them.'

Sarah looked across the table. 'What about you, Arlene?'

Arlene smiled. 'She likes it,' Jesse said. 'It's her idea and I'm buying it.'

Arlene had been working seven or eight months for Jesse Fischer. One afternoon, two or three weeks before the first of their story conferences, he'd asked whether she could come to his house in the evening to look at a picture the studio was making about the Civil War. It was being done by one of the studio's most talented directors. Marvin Major had opposed the idea and Jesse Fischer had helped push it through into production. Now Mrs Nightingale, their best cutter, was showing signs of doubt. She said it was all looking pretty static.

62

'I've looked at it so often,' Jesse told Arlene, 'I can't see it any more. I need a fresh eye on it. Can you make it?'

She said she could. He sketched a map for her showing how to get from Pacifica Street via Sepulveda to Mulholland Drive.

It wasn't quite dark as she drove up into the hills that evening, and for a moment she stopped and looked over Santa Monica to the ocean where the sun was just setting among a heap of fiery clouds. Looking the other way she could see the darkening hollow of the San Fernando Valley and the peaks of mountains still alight on the farther side.

The Fischers' house was set back and above the road. There was a long drive through a garden. Several cars stood in a turning circle at the front of the house. The door was opened by a maid, and Arlene was taken through two or three beautifully furnished rooms, each hung with paintings she recognized as Mrs Fischer's work, to the projection room.

'We're just about ready to go,' Jesse Fischer told her. He introduced her to his wife, Judith, and to the children, Danny, Delores and Doug. Mrs Nightingale she knew. Also the projectionist whom everyone called Bobso. The three Ds were eager-faced and expert. They were very discriminating, especially if it was a straight question of which of three or four takes was best acted. Arlene and Judith Fischer offered opinions. But it was Mrs Nightingale who ruled the roost. She used a stop-watch. She would check a take and say 'Twelve seconds. Five's all it needs.' Or sometimes, less often, 'He cut it too soon. It needs to be longer – more lingering.' Then there were shots which she said made no sense at all. 'I can see why he did it – it looks so pretty. But it doesn't add anything to this picture.'

Jesse Fischer seldom disagreed with her but he worried about the director. 'John's in love with that shot. He'd die for it.'

Mrs Nightingale shook her head. 'Cut it and don't tell him. By the time he discovers what you've done he'll be in love with something else.'

When this part of the work had been dealt with Mrs Nightingale excused herself and left. The kids were packed off to bed and Jesse got Bobso to run through a rough cut of the picture,

as far as they'd got with it. Over coffee afterwards he asked
Arlene what she thought. She was hesitant. She said she liked
it.

'But something's wrong?'

She nodded. 'Something. It's hard to say what. Maybe it
needs a basket.'

'A basket?'

'A container. It has the feel of a lot of good things being . . .
You know. *Spilled*.'

He looked at her, then looked away, thinking. 'Maybe a
voice-over?'

'Or the book,' Judith Fischer suggested. 'Doesn't it come
from a book? You know – you kick off with a shot of the book
being opened and the first sentences being read.'

Jesse nodded. 'Marvin might go for that. John would hate
it.'

He rubbed his eyes. 'I'm tired of patching up other people's
work. Or maybe spoiling it. It's crazy. I came into the movie
business because I wanted to make pictures. It's like over-
shooting the off-ramp on the freeway. Before you know it
you're half way to San Diego.'

Judith Fischer reached out and patted his hand. 'Be patient,'
she said. 'You'll get your chance. One day you'll be head of
the studio.'

Arlene looked from one to the other and was silent. When
she was leaving he went to the door with her. It was a beautiful
clear night. 'Come and look at Los Angeles,' he said.

He led her up a path to some high ground at the side of the
house. From a paved platform with stone seats there was that
view again – one way over Santa Monica to the Pacific, the
other over the valley. The lights in both directions were clear
and sharp. A moon was low over the ocean. They stood
watching it. Somewhere not far away a bird let out a succession
of harsh sounds. Tchack tchair-tchack. And then the same
phrase again.

'It's a mocking bird,' Jesse said. 'They're not night birds but
sometimes in spring and early summer they seem to get up in
the night.'

She said, 'There's a bird I keep hearing around our house. It makes a sound like "Do it, do it, do it". I used to think it could be the motto for Southern California.'

She could just hear his laugh. They were standing side by side, as usual, looking away into the distance. After a moment she said, 'I think your wife's wrong. If you're patient you won't get your chance. You'll just get to be head of the studio.'

He didn't reply and they walked back together to the car. She got in, closed the door, and wound the window down. 'I'm sorry. I don't know why I said that.'

He leaned over her. 'You said it because it's true.'

She switched on the engine. He asked did she know her way back and she said she did.

'Drive carefully,' he said. 'And thanks.'

It was after that he began to work towards making a picture of his own. He didn't have a clear idea, but now he wasn't prepared to sit around waiting for one. He would do a detective picture and see what he could make of the convention. Marvin Major grumbled but he couldn't prevent it. It was in Jesse Fischer's contract. Jock Bateman and Sarah James were called in from the writers' building; and Salka Viertel was added, because Sarah and Jock had other scripts to work on at the same time. Arlene sat in on the story conferences. At first she thought she was there just as a recorder. But she was as inventive as they were, and by the end of the second session she seemed to be accepted as part of the team. It reminded her of games children play which always begin 'Let's pretend . . .'

What they seemed to be talking their way towards would probably be good of its kind; but Arlene couldn't see how there was much in it to satisfy Jesse Fischer's ambition to make a picture that was in some way out of the ordinary.

On the morning after their second full-scale ideas session Arlene woke early. The birds were noisy on the roof and in the trees that lined the street. She began to think about the studio, and then about their picture. It was then the idea came to her to set the story in the studio.

When Jesse Fischer arrived that morning she went straight

into his office. He told her to sit down but she stood in front of his desk while he leaned back in his chair and listened. As she elaborated on the basic idea she grew more excited by its possibilities.

'Imagine a chase down a city street and then you pan back and it's a movie set. A real chase down an unreal street – except that in another sense it's all unreal. Or someone runs up some steps and through a door and there's nothing on the other side. Or a suspense scene when all the lights get turned off in one of the sound stages. All those cables and all that movie gear – people tripping over it and climbing around it. Or say the private eye breaks in when a scene's being shot and you get two kinds of shooting. Could we call it Shooting? My God – wouldn't that be good? Maybe real cops in uniform get mixed up with extras dressed as cops – or is that too Keystone?'

She stopped because he was holding up a hand.

'You don't like it?'

'I love it.'

'Was I shouting?'

'Probably. But that's OK.'

'Then what?'

'Go away. Now. This instant. Shut yourself up in the back room and type it up. Then come and offer it to me. For sale.'

'For sale?'

'Do you know how much an idea like that's worth?'

She shook her head.

'A lot.'

'But I work for you.'

'Sure you do. And now you're working as part of the team that's supposed to produce a story, and ultimately a script, and you're getting paid secretary's rates. D'you know what those guys are getting?'

She nodded. 'A thousand a week?'

'More like two. So if the studio buys this from you you'll be getting your share of the cake.'

'I don't want you to buy it just so I'll get my share of the cake.'

He got up and walked around his desk. 'Arlene I want to

66

buy it because I want to use it. Now do as I say. Get it down as an outline. Put "Copyright Mrs Arlene Tamworth" at the bottom of the page, and bring it to me.'

'But there's no story yet.'

'Don't worry too much about story. Just set out in as much detail as you can the idea of putting a conventional detective story in a Hollywood studio. Use just basic plot outlines and concentrate on the possibilities that kind of treatment opens up. You sell us that idea and we'll match it with whatever story the team puts together.'

So she went. As she typed, she thought about what Jesse Fischer had said. She took her time through the morning, and the idea expanded as she set it down.

Around one in the afternoon she went down to her car. It had been standing in the sun. She wound down all the windows, turned on the radio, and drove out through the studio gates. She wasn't driving anywhere in particular, only thinking at the wheel. She went down through Hollywood, made a right turn, and coasted on looking as she went at the tall palms, and the trees that hung over the sidewalks from beautiful gardens, half listening to the music, letting her mind take its own course between the possibilities of the movie she now thought of as *Shooting*, and how she might make the most of Jesse Fischer's enthusiasm for it. Beverly Hills, Bel Air and Brentwood came and went. Through Pacific Palisades she felt that cool breath that comes up off the ocean. Finally she'd driven all of the ten or twelve miles Sunset Boulevard runs from Hollywood to the sea. She parked the car, got out, and sat on a rock. In her mind she saw a map of America, the curve of its western coastline, the vast downward bend of the Pacific into the southern hemisphere, and away down there the two islands of New Zealand. Facing south and west like this she was looking homeward across thousands of miles of ocean, and a phrase came into her head, 'Look homeward, angel', not because she knew the poem it came from, but because she'd seen it as the title of something, a movie or a book. She felt nostalgia, and at the same time, contradicting it, relief at being so anonymous and so far from home.

Late that afternoon she went back to Jesse Fischer's office. This time she sat down. He ran his eye over the pages, nodding from time to time. Once he lowered the sheets, looked at her over them, winked, and went back to reading. Finally he threw them down on the desk in front of him. 'It's a winner, sweetheart. We've got a great picture here.'

This was Hollywood talk but she felt sure he meant it. It was an idea he needed, and knew how to use.

She didn't reply. She just leaned forward, waiting. 'I can't name a figure until I've talked to the money-man,' he said. 'But we want it.'

She told him how much it would cost to clear the mortgage on the little house in Pacifica Street.

He nodded. 'It's worth all of that.'

'I thought I'd make that my price,' she said. 'And . . .' She hesitated, then said it firmly. 'And a small part for Rocky.'

His face hardened. He went to speak, then didn't. He got up and walked to the window. Looking out he said, 'I don't want to be hard on you Arlene. But when I offered you this job I made a rule. Don't try to break it.'

Now she felt combative. That helped her get her breath. 'I'm not breaking any rule.'

'An agreement. We made an agreement.'

'I said as your secretary I wouldn't ask you to do anything for my husband. I'm not asking as your secretary. In fact I'm not asking. I'm just telling you my price for those sheets. Whoever buys them – that's the price. If no one pays, they're not for sale.'

He pushed the window open and half-sat on the sill. 'Arlene, sweetheart . . .'

She knew he thought he was being very patient with her. She met his eye. A kind of intuition was at work – an instinct for survival. At this moment it was important to hold herself in a kind of neutral gear. Aggression or fear – both would be fatal to her purpose.

The silence continued. His fingers at either side drummed gently on the sill.

He became explanatory. 'I haven't told you this. I got hold

68

of your husband's tests. He can act – sure. And he's a big good-looking guy. He seems to have picked up Method since he's been here. It's not a style I like a lot, but it's fashionable. The problem with Method is the actor acts how he feels, and you can't feel outside your own native accent. If he was an old-style stager like Flynn he'd do something about it. Then we could think about a contract.'

She didn't want to be sidetracked into talking about Method acting. That was only one of the things Rocky could do. She said, 'I'm not talking about a contract. I'm talking about a small part in one picture.'

'Why?'

'It would be good for him.'

'Are you sure?'

'No. I'm not sure of anything. Maybe the best thing for him would be to go back to Australia where his acting's appreciated. But until he decides to do that, he needs work.'

Jesse Fischer didn't answer.

She stood up and gathered up the sheets. 'I'm sorry,' she said. 'I thought it was worth a try.'

She turned as if to leave. 'Hold your horses,' he said. 'I told you – I'd like to use your idea.'

She looked at him and didn't speak.

'I'm going to use it.'

That had the ring of a challenge – one that had to be met. 'OK. Fine. And I've told you the price.'

He stood up. Anger almost got the upper hand. She knew what it was he wanted her to understand – that he could take her idea without asking and without paying; that he was being scrupulous and generous in offering to buy it. But he didn't want to say all that, partly because it mightn't be quite true (the copyright question could be complicated), and also because he wanted her to think well of him. That was part of her strength. His interest in her wasn't neutral – she was sure of that. He didn't want to lose her. But now he didn't want to lose face either.

She allowed herself to seem to plead a little. 'It's not a big thing I'm asking.'

69

He shrugged. 'I guess not. What's the chance he'll stay sober?'

That question came at her like a blow. How much did people talk about them, and about Rocky's drinking? She took a deep breath. 'What are the chances with Jock Bateman? Rocky's a serious actor. Give him a chance.'

He went back to his desk. 'Let's sit down and talk about it.'

In the end they reached an agreement. A small part would be found for Rocky. Jesse Fischer mixed martinis and they drank to it. She could see he felt pleased with himself. He'd bought her idea, and he'd shown himself to be patient and generous. 'Isn't it time you called me Jesse?' he said.

She said she supposed it was.

'It's just my sort of luck,' he said. 'A nice-looking gal asks me to do her a favour and it turns out to be something she wants for her nice-looking husband.'

Arlene stared at her glass. Finally she said, 'I'm very grateful to you, Jesse. You've been generous to me ever since Bogie introduced us at that Laughton party. I don't know how I would have got on here without your help. But the fact is I didn't ask you to do me a favour. You told me I had something I could sell, and I named a price.'

'So it's a sale, not a favour.'

She nodded.

'Are you always so meticulous?'

'Meticulous? I'm not sure what it means.'

'It means . . . Well, it's like you won the war and now you're writing the history book.'

'I'm sorry. It's a kind of anxiety. I like to get things straight in my head. I spell it all out. It's very boring.'

'I'm not bored.'

'Can I just say . . .'

'Spelling it out?'

'Yes – I guess so. I don't feel as if I've won a war.'

'Well that's OK. I feel as if I lost one.' But it was obvious he wasn't feeling anything so simple. He was pleased with himself. He liked her – better now, probably, than before. But what most pleased him – she was sure of it – was the idea itself. Jesse Fischer really wanted to make a good movie.

Next morning was the story conference when he put to the team the general idea of shifting their story into a movie studio. As soon as he knew they all liked it, he began to elaborate, mixing his own ideas with those Arlene had set out in her proposal.

'Transposing the outlines we've established already – we've got a murdered young woman and two suspects, one who didn't do it, one who did. The one who's innocent – we've been calling him A – is the one the cops suspect. But we want the audience to feel on side with him, so they don't believe in his guilt. Just as a type, Bogart would be perfect. Or maybe Alan Ladd. I don't suppose Warners will let us have Bogart. And the trouble with Ladd is you've either got to find a woman short enough so he won't object to acting alongside her, or you've got to keep her sitting down when they're in the same room. Let's think of it as Bogart so we've all got the same image in mind. He's a bit too quick with his fists, he drinks too much, but the audience likes and trusts him. We contrive the story so he's in big trouble. He looks like the only person who could have done it. And he doesn't do much to help himself. Now if we're moving all that into the setting of a Hollywood studio, why not make him a screenwriter? As for the one who did do it – he's the one we've been calling X – I've had two types in mind. He could be suave – the kind of character an audience can easily be made to distrust. Claude Rains maybe. Or George Sanders. Or he could be more rugged, with a bit of gangster showing under the veneer – say Robert Mitchum or Kirk Douglas. I see him as some kind of executive in the studio, so maybe Mitchum and Douglas are too young. The point is he's been cheating the company. It really doesn't matter how. I mean, for example, he could be selling off land the studio holds which he happens to know – but the studio doesn't know – contains oil. Anything will do. Whatever we settle for, the young secretary finds out and so she gets murdered. She's not a major character. She's alive and then she's dead, and until late in the picture the audience doesn't know why. But it might come out that she'd had some kind of association with A – the Bogart character. That throws more suspicion on to him. And we're looking for suspense, not for big surprises. It doesn't matter if the audience feels pretty strongly right from the start that X is the killer. We don't want to pull a rabbit out of a hat. We want to make them anxious. Will A escape a rap, or will he be framed? Will X get cornered, and if he is, what will he do? We want four men – character A, character X, a senior cop and a private eye. We also want a leading lady? Have we a role for her?'

'The writer's wife,' Arlene said. 'They're either estranged or divorced – probably just separated, and they still like one another pretty much. His drinking's the problem. And his fists. He's an uncontrolled character – that's what puts him under suspicion. But won't we need to have her working in the studio as well?'

'She could be a writer too,' Sarah suggested.

'Or maybe some kind of technician,' Jesse said. 'Sound, or lighting. That would take us into the sound stage. She's working in there while shooting's going on. She has headphones and a clip-board. She's working alongside the director. They tell her there's been a shooting. She doesn't hear. Or she doesn't understand at first. She's confused by the pun.'

Jesse smiled and looked around at his team. 'I'm starting to see our picture.'

There was silence. They seemed all to be looking inward at what Jesse Fischer called his governing image.

# 8

Edie and Rocky are visiting a house in the Hollywood Hills.
It's all angles and slopes and roof-windows – very modern.
There's talk of 'open plan' and 'split level'. The decoration is
Mexican – cracked earthenware pots, ceramic wall-plaques,
blankets, woven rugs.

Two couples live there – Fred and Baby Daniels, and Moss
and Lee McConey. Fred is an Australian, a set-designer Rocky
knew in Melbourne, working now for the studios and for the
Coronet Theatre in Beverly Hills. Baby and Lee are actresses
– Baby from San Francisco, Lee from New York. They're like
Rocky – they have prospects but no contract so they work as
waitresses. Waitress/actress: they say the words are inter-
changeable in Los Angeles. On a good day all the waitresses
look like stars; on a bad one all the stars look like waitresses.

Moss McConey is from New York. He's writing a novel
and looking for work as a screenwriter. He lives off remittances
from his family who are, he says, 'big with the garment trade'.

Out in the steep street Rocky stands with Fred Daniels under
huge eucalypts. They pick up green gum-nuts that fall to the
side-walk, dig a thumb-nail into them, squeeze, and breathe
Australia. Their faces are contorted in exaggerations of nostalgia. But they feel it. These are the overpowering signals of
home.

Moss and Lee call them into the garden. They have a bag of
unshelled peanuts. There's a pair of scrub jays on the roof. Lee
says 'Watch' – and she holds a nut up over her head, loosely
between thumb and forefinger. One of the jays swoops and
takes it. The other isn't so bold, Moss throws a nut into the
air and the second jay catches it in flight.

Rocky has been taking lessons with Salka Viertel's acting class. She tells them to forget about movies and contracts and think about the art of acting. He likes to quote Shakespeare, imitating and exaggerating her accent:

> Age cannot vizzer her nor custom stale
> Her infinite variety; ozer vimmin cloy
> Ze appetites zey feed, but she makes hongry
> Vere most she satisfies.

Or he imitates Charles Laughton inviting him to come and look where his cliff has fallen to the road below: 'Come and see may disastah, deah boynh. Aim just an old Laimy ham. Don't maind if Ai put an arm around you. That's what they're saying, you know. Just an old Laimy ham.'

It's Sunday afternoon. On Sundays that house is open to friends. They bring beer and wine and talk about people who have 'sold out' to the Industry. Moss likes to reel off lists of American playwrights and novelists who were destroyed by Hollywood. He tells how Scott Fitzgerald and Nathaniel West died within twenty-four hours of one another – Fitzgerald of booze, West in a desperate car crash – and how the same train carried their bodies back east.

'So why are we all here?' Arlene wants to know. 'Why don't we run away?'

Moss says because in the fairy tale someone always gets away with the loot.

Arlene sticks to her guns. 'But why is it whoring for one person and not for another?'

'I guess,' Lee says, 'it depends on the product.'

'As long as you haven't got a product,' Arlene says, 'it's easy to be sniffy.'

The doors and windows are open. A light breeze is blowing through, but it's warm, and getting warmer as more people arrive. Now the talk is about J. Parnell Thomas and the House Un-American Activities Committee hearings on Hollywood. Arlene describes the seedy little federal marshal arriving to serve Jesse Fischer's subpoena. It was a pink document telling

Jesse Fischer 'by authority of the House of Representatives and the Congress of the United States of America' to attend the HUAC hearings in Washington and not to leave until he has permission. 'Herein fail not,' it concluded, 'and make return of this summons.'

The Sunday afternoon shadows grow longer. Someone has put on a record and Lee and Moss and Baby are doing a wild dance – a sort of jitterbug-for-three. Fred is drumming on a brass tub. Rocky is flat on his back on the floor. Arlene has gone out into the garden. She's squeezing the juicy gum-nut and breathing the eucalypt scent deep into the back of her nose. She wants to cry. She cries, and can't stop . . .

# 9

Every year, late in the summer, there was a big fancy dress party at the Fischers' house on Mulholland Drive, and that year, 1947, Arlene and Rocky were invited. It was there that Rocky blew his first chance of getting into a movie.

He went as Carmen Miranda, wearing a long red dress with a slit up one side, and a hat that was a pile-up of artificial fruit. Arlene wore Rocky's cowboy suit, modified to fit, with a sheriff's badge and the hat slung by a string at her back.

Double doors were open from the main rooms of the house to the patio and pool. Beyond the pool, on lower ground, there was the marquee from which came hired waiters carrying food and drink. Everyone was there, including Louella Parsons in something pink and so strange Arlene suggested it might be a HUAC subpoena.

At first – and for most of the party – Arlene enjoyed it. She ran into Humphrey Bogart who dug her in the ribs, called her sheriff, and asked her was she keeping his sailorboy sober. She found herself standing beside Louis B. Mayer while a combo played and her boss and Dore Schary of RKO got up on a little stage on either side of Danny Kaye and sang 'Meet me in St Louis, Louis', 'Moonlight Bay', 'Ain't She Sweet', and finally, very sweet and plangent, 'O the Moonlight's fair tonight along the Wabash'.

The party was winding down – it was just beginning to get dark and some people were leaving – when Danny, Delores and Doug started running around telling everyone a movie was just about to start in the projection room. Arlene saw Rocky heading indoors, so she followed. She sat with Jesse Fischer near the back. Up near the front she could see Rocky removing his Carmen Miranda headgear. Bobso called 'Ready to roll' from the projection box, the lights went down, the studio symbol came up on the screen (cheers from the audience), followed by 'Executive Producer Jesse Fischer' (more cheers) and 'Director Dennis O'Donoghue.' Then the credits and the title. It was *Out on a Limb*.

'Oh Christ.' Arlene put her hands up to her face. It was common enough for pictures to be shown at the end of a Hollywood party. It hadn't occurred to her that it might be this picture.

Jesse leaned over to ask her what was the matter. She told him Rocky hadn't seen it – didn't know she had played the part of the secretary in that single scene.

'Does it matter?'

She shook her head. 'I don't know.'

The opening shot was a long one of Santa Monica Boulevard with its tall palms against an evening sky. Footsteps. A shot of a man's shoes, well-shined, walking, stopping. A shot of him lighting a cigarette, flicking the match away, walking on.

'Why didn't you tell him?'

She shook her head again. 'I don't know.'

The man was walking on down the street, which seemed to be empty of people. A large black car cruised slowly alongside him. A window at the back wound down and a man in a heavy coat, hat pulled down shading scarred, pock-marked cheeks, looked out. 'Goin' somewhere, pal?'

Arlene said, 'I think I wanted him to get his contract first.'

The man walking picked up his pace but the car stayed with him. 'Get in,' Scarface said.

'I don't think I can watch this,' Arlene said; but she stayed where she was.

Jesse patted her knee. 'Don't worry. It'll be OK.'

There was the sound of a gunshot, then two more. The man fell to the sidewalk. The big black car sped off into the Los Angeles dusk.

When the picture was over Arlene stayed in her seat. Rocky came towards her slowly, carrying his hat by one of its bananas.

She could see he wasn't perfectly sober. Jesse was still beside her. Rocky was smiling. It wasn't quite a smile – more a faint precarious grin. 'Certainly, Mr Fronsett,' he mimicked. 'It's right here.'

'Don't,' she said. 'I was just filling in for them.'

The three of them walked out together into one of the living rooms. 'One for the road,' Jesse suggested.

While he mixed martinis people were waving from the door, saying goodbye, telling him it had been a lovely party. Judith Fischer was seeing them out. The three Ds raced in and out helping the butler and the maid find coats and bags. In the next room a group who weren't ready to leave were settling down in chairs and on cushions. Scarface from *Out on a Limb* was there; also Dennis O'Donoghue and Mrs Nightingale.

'Why didn't you tell me?' Rocky asked.

She said nothing. Then, as if finding an excuse, 'I was embarrassed. I didn't want you to see me making a fool of myself.'

He stared at her. He stared so hard it made him sway forward. He checked himself, and blinked.

'Rocky, are you sober?' Even as she asked she thought it a stupid question.

Jesse was back with their drinks. 'A good slug,' he said.

He stood beside her. She had the feeling he wanted to protect her. She wished he would move away.

'Like our picture?' he asked.

Rocky looked from one to the other. 'Certainly, Mr Fronsett,' he said. 'It's right here.'

Arlene put her drink down. 'Come on Rocky,' she said.

He turned away from them and wandered to the window, downing his drink and looking out towards the pool. It was dark out there now. There were strings of lights in the tubbed trees, and lights under water in the pool. The gin bottle was open on the bar. Rocky picked it up and sloshed more into his martini. 'My little wife's an actress. Let's drink to that.'

Jesse looked anxious. He raised his glass. 'You'll be in my

next together. Husband and wife.' He searched Rocky's face for a sign of recognition. There was none.

Arlene turned away. 'I haven't told him.'

Jesse did his best to make light of it. 'I talk too much. Spoiled a surprise, have I?'

'Talk on, brother,' Rocky said. 'If people are making plans for me, I'd better know what they are.'

Jesse didn't have much choice but to fill the silence. He explained how the picture that was to be called *Shooting* had developed. He wanted to use a few big-name actors for the major roles and for the minor roles get people working around the studio to be themselves. He'd persuaded Arlene to be the secretary again.

'She has just a couple of brief scenes. Nothing difficult. Then she vanishes. Later her body's found under Santa Monica pier. Meanwhile someone – husband, brother, we haven't quite decided, but that's you, Rocky – you're demanding to know where she is. And you have to identify the body. That's about all.'

'Stone the crows.' Rocky took another swallow of his drink. His Carmen Miranda makeup was smeared and he was having trouble moving his legs inside the long red dress. 'Don't you think it might be a good idea to ask?'

Jesse said he thought Arlene had. 'It was her idea to have you in the picture.'

Arlene didn't speak. She hadn't told Rocky about *Shooting* because she wanted it to come as an official offer through Charlie Beltane.

Rocky finished his drink, looked at his empty glass, then out into the night. 'Can we just get it straight,' he said. 'My wife might be an actress and a screenwriter – it's news to me. I don't know why I have to be the last to hear about it, but anyway that's OK. It's just fine. Good on you, Arlene. But so far as I've heard she's not an agent – are you sweetheart? Or anyway she's not my agent. If you want me in your picture, call Charlie. But just don't think you can drag me in by the apron strings.'

Arlene could see Jesse was beginning to be angry. 'If you

79

'don't want to be in it,' he began, but Rocky wasn't listening.

'Because I'm interested in acting,' Rocky was saying. 'If you've heard of it. It's that thing actors do.'

'Rocky, please . . .'

'I've got a talent for it.' He laughed. 'I might be doing it now. How would you know?' And then serious again: 'I have the talent. I have the temperament. I work at it. I believe in myself. I also have an agent.' He took an uncertain step towards the bottle. 'D'you mind?'

'Help yourself,' Jesse said grimly.

Rocky splashed gin into his glass and drank it neat. 'I have more talent than any six Marvin Major stars wrapped up in one tacky Hollywood package. Much more. I . . .'

'Oh Rocky. Please.'

He turned on her. 'Please what? What's your problem Miss New Zealand? Embarrassing you, am I? Putting on a bad show in front of the boss? Certainly Mr Fronsett, it's right here. Shit. Where's here? Between your legs?'

'That's enough.' Jesse took the glass out of Rocky's hand.

Rocky stared at him. 'Just get my name off your cast list until you've got my permission.'

'I will.'

'And that won't be until you've got something an actor wants. Actor. A-c-t-o-r. Keep your handouts for the ones who haven't got anything to offer.'

He walked out. Arlene went to follow. She turned back to look at Jesse. He was angry, but when he looked at her his face softened.

'I'm sorry,' she said.

He shook his head. 'I'm sorry. I didn't know you hadn't told him.'

'It's not your fault.'

He took a step towards her. She was afraid he might want to give her a consoling hug. 'You don't understand,' she said. And then, 'I'd better go.'

'What is it I don't understand?'

'I'd better go,' she said again. 'Rocky can't drive in that state.'

'Arlene.' There was something Jesse Fischer wanted to say.
She looked at him. There was that look of sympathy again.
She turned from it and headed for the door.

# 10

Early morning, not even a sign yet of light in the eastern sky. Arlene pulled the hose over the grass that felt springy underfoot, watering the bougainvillaea, the hibiscus, the lemon, the strelitzia, the bamboo and the banana. All foreigners like herself. Nothing belonged where it was except the soft brown blowaway soil that would not stay. Even the water was piped from far away.

Lights from kitchen and back porch shone out into the garden. She wasn't sure Rocky would water it while she was away.

Indoors, she carried her bag to the front door and put it out on the top step. She checked her watch, went back into the bedroom. A light from the bathroom shot a streak across their bed.

'Rocky. The car's due any minute.'

He stirred, grunted, rolled over and woke. 'Is it . . .' He tried to look at the clock. 'All packed then?' His voice was hoarse.

'Yep.' She did up his pyjama buttons and pushed the hair back from his eyes. 'Don't get lonely while I'm away. Fred wants to see you. Let Baby look after you. And the McConeys.'

He nodded, yawning. 'I'll be OK.'

'What have you got planned for today?'

'They want me down at the theatre.'

'That's good. And I want you to stay . . .'

'Sober?'

'Dry might be better.'

'OK.'

'Promise?'

'Promise.'

She kissed him. They lay there for a while. A quiet car pulled up outside. A door opened. Footsteps. The engine stayed running. She kissed Rocky again. 'See you Friday.'

He held on to her. 'How much do you like me – out of ten?'

'Eleven.'

'Not enough.'

'I'll work on it in Washington.'

When she came out into the darkness her bag was already in the car – a big studio limo, chauffeur-driven. Jesse was in the back seat. She got in beside him. They spoke quietly to one another. There was something lovely about driving through the dark streets. The gardens seemed to breathe. The air was cool and fresh. All her perceptions seemed sharp and clear.

They were heading for the airport. She had never flown before and she was apprehensive, but excited too. Since her arrival in the United States she had never been east of California.

As they took off, Los Angeles was still dark. She could see the pattern of the street lights, green at intersections of small streets, orange on highways and freeways. Westward the ocean was dark. As the plane banked, climbing, she could see the sun just pushing up through cloud beyond the eastern mountains.

In the month since the Fischers' party Hollywood had talked little else but politics. Newspapers and gossip sheets were full of the coming hearings in Washington. Louella Parsons and the Hearst Press were enthusiastic. Communism would be exposed in the Industry; then, if Hollywood didn't act to eject the guilty from its community of workers, it would only have itself to blame for the consequences.

On the other side there had been big rallies and meetings to protest against the hearings. A Committee for the First Amendment had been formed to argue that it was unconstitutional for Congress to enquire into the political beliefs of American citizens. Some of the biggest names in Hollywood had joined, including Bogart and Bacall. A group would be flying to Washington to support the nineteen witnesses designated in advance as 'unfriendly'.

The witnesses heard in the week before she and Jesse flew to

Washington were all 'friendlies'. Listening on radio, reading transcripts in the *Los Angeles Times*, Arlene alternated between anger and contempt. Gary Cooper, Adolph Menjou, Ronald Reagan, Robert Taylor – they were famous names and famous faces, and they insisted that Communism was strong in Hollywood. But when it came to particulars they found it hard to name pictures, point to scripts. Ginger Rogers's mother had done her best before the hearings ever reached Washington. Didn't the line 'Share and share alike – that's democracy', which her daughter had been required to speak in one of her pictures, show a Communist influence? A screenwriter, Ayn Rand, suggested an MGM movie called *Song of Russia* had been Communist propaganda because it showed Russians smiling, looking prosperous and happy; and Robert Taylor apologized for his part in it, saying that if there hadn't been a war going on in which Russia was America's ally, he would never have agreed to make it. He said he believed Communists must be at work disrupting the Screen Actors' Guild because its meetings, 'instead of finishing at ten o'clock or ten-thirty when they logically should', ran on until one or two in the morning.

'It's a farce,' Arlene said. 'No one's going to take this seriously.'

Jesse wasn't so sure. 'It's a farce. But you don't know America. We live by our farces. We live up to them. It's the American way.'

She thought he was needlessly anxious; but she felt protective. As they flew through that long day, landing and refuelling along the route, she tried to keep his mind off Washington. She told him about New Zealand, her childhood, her rift with her family. They did crosswords together. They dozed, ate, talked over their script, even solved one or two small problems. When they landed in Washington it was dark, the air was cold, there was a feeling of autumn Arlene hadn't experienced since she'd arrived in Southern California. A terrible nostalgia washed over her. At the hotel they ate a late meal together and she went to bed with a paperback she found she couldn't read. She lay awake in the big hotel bed with the curtains apart and lights shining in, longing for a phone call from Los Angeles, or even one, which she'd made sure could never come, from six thousand miles further west and away to the south.

During the next few days she did a little sight-seeing – she saw the White House for the first time, and the Lincoln Memorial – but mostly she sat in on the hearings in the Caucus Room of the House Office Building. It was a huge room, and crowded. People queued and scrambled to get in, most of them eager to see film stars. Because Jesse was a witness seats were reserved for him and his lawyer and Arlene, near the front. There were sometimes thirty or forty newspaper cameramen, and close on a hundred journalists. Arlene counted nine news-reel cameras. There were floodlights, clusters of microphones, rows of control panels for broadcasting and recording equipment. Uniformed guards tried to keep order.

On the second day the group of stars representing the Committee for the First Amendment arrived. Two rows were reserved for them at the back. Arlene saw Bogart and Bacall with Danny Kaye and Gene Kelly standing on benches to get a better view. She waved to them and Bogie put his finger to his temple and shot himself.

As those few days went by the tension mounted. She watched one after another of the 'unfriendlies' refused permission which had been granted to the 'friendlies' to read preliminary statements, denied the right to cross-examine witnesses who had named them, and finally dismissed from the stand, or dragged from it, under charges of contempt. The point at issue was always whether the Committee had the right to demand that the witness answer whether he'd been a member of the Communist Party. The 'unfriendlies' claimed the First Amendment of the Constitution protected them from having to declare their political allegiance. When they refused to answer they were cited for contempt.

'Why don't they just answer?' Arlene asked. She and Jesse were having dinner in the evening at their hotel. 'If they're members, so what? Who cares? It looks worse if you hide it.'

'It's not that simple,' Jesse said. 'The next question is "Name people who were Party members with you". If you don't answer that one, you're cited for contempt.'

'Well then why don't they just deny it? Say they were never members – even if it's untrue. Why be bullied?'

'Because if the FBI can bring evidence that they are in fact members of the Party, or have been, they can be cited for perjury, and that's worse.'

'So what does a citation for contempt mean?'

'If Congress backs up the Committee it means jail.'

'Jesus.' She put down her knife and fork. 'I thought this was just a sideshow.'

'It's a sideshow with consequences. People are going to lose their jobs. People are going to jail. The studios are going to turn into manufacturers of cake and candyfloss.'

'That's pretty much what they make now.'

'Worse cake. More candyfloss. The new realism can pack its bags and go back to Europe.'

She had another thought. 'You've never been a member, have you Jesse?'

He laughed. 'Of the CP? I'm a Democrat from way back.'

She looked reflectively into the far corner of the room. 'I used to think I was a Communist. My father and I used to argue about politics. I never got around to joining.'

He looked to see if anyone nearby had heard. 'Take it easy, Arlene. This is America.'

Next day the tension in the Caucus Room got worse. The Chairman, J. Parnell Thomas, a squat bald man who, it was said, was sitting on two telephone directories and a cushion so he could be seen over the bench, banged his gavel and shouted, while the 'unfriendlies' asserted their rights until they were led or dragged away.

The last of the 'unfriendlies' was the German playwright, Bert Brecht. Smoking a cigar he told the Committee that as a foreigner he couldn't claim the protection of the Constitution of the United States and so would answer all questions put to him.

'Is he being funny?' Arlene whispered. She was wondering what protection the Constitution had offered those who weren't foreigners.

As the questioning continued Bert Brecht assured the

Committee he had never been a Communist ('No-no-no-no-no-no-no,' he said in answer to that question). He described the path of his own retreat across Europe from Hitler's invading armies. He admitted visits to Moscow and explained how they had come about. He corrected what he said were mistranslations of his poems so the Committee would see how innocent the originals were of radical thought. He was so polite and obliging the Chairman thanked him for his co-operation and released him.

'A psychiatrist examined by a panel of monkeys,' someone said as they filed out at the end of the session.

That evening Jesse had to consult with lawyers. Arlene waited in her room working over a few scenes of their picture script. It was almost nine before he called to say he was finished. He would be waiting for her in the restaurant downstairs.

They sat at their usual table, in a far corner out of sight. At first Jesse seemed agitated. He wasn't happy with the way the 'unfriendlies' were conducting themselves. Turning it into a shouting match, being dragged away – it was embarrassing for the people who'd come to support them. Bogie was said to be ready to go home. Only Betty was holding him.

'It's the evidence the FBI brings in after each of them testifies. Their party cards. Meetings. Membership of front organizations. It looks bad.'

Arlene shook her head. 'I can't understand what the fuss is about. This is supposed to be a free society. An American's political allegiance is his own business. It's supposed to be protected by the Constitution.'

'Sure. But it starts to look as if the Committee for the First Amendment is really the Committee for the Protection of the CP.'

'Well if people can't make that distinction . . .' She shook her head. 'And anyway the Press is pretty much on the side of the unfriendlies.'

'So far. And if you don't count the Hearst papers. I just don't know how long it's going to last. If they'd all been as wily as Brecht . . .'

'He was able to say he wasn't a Party member.'

Jesse nodded. 'That was a surprise. And they didn't produce a card to prove he was. I guess if he ever was, it would have been in Germany.'

They lapsed into a silence which lasted a long time. They'd worked so much together, and such long hours, there was no strain in being silent. It wasn't necessary always to talk.

Their orders were brought to the table, and a bottle of wine. They commented on the food, watched guests arriving and leaving, listened to the band that was playing at the far end of the room above a small square of dance floor. There were moments during that meal when Arlene felt that Jesse was on the point of saying something personal, and that without thinking about it she was heading him off.

When they'd finished eating they got up and danced. It was that old crooning-style foxtrot music, very soothing. Jesse moved easily, he was easy to follow. Sometimes he sang the words of the song into her ear in a voice that was somewhere between Bing Crosby and Danny Kaye, soft and mournful, with occasional swooping notes. She felt herself to be floating, physically, but inwardly too. In the course of the past few days her image of herself in relation to Jesse had changed.

They went into the bar for a drink, then back to the dance-floor. It can't have been quite so wordless as her memory of it afterwards suggested; but whatever was said was just noise on the surface.

So after the dance floor, and the bar, and the dance floor again, everything that happened continued to seem part of drifting with a lazy current. For him it might all have been much more purposeful – probably was, she thought. For her it was simply compliance with the moment.

They went up together in the lift. He took her to the door of her room. He came in with her. She turned on the frilly-shaded lamps on either side of the big bed and they danced again, humming one of the songs the band had played downstairs.

'I don't want to make a big pitch about my feelings,' he said.

'Don't,' she said.

They continued to dance. Their bodies felt comfortable together. 'You know I'm scared of you,' he said.

'No. I don't know that. It's not true.'

'Not of you. Of your mind. It's all those story conferences. I might give myself a bad line and you'd chop it.'

She smiled and kissed his cheek. 'You'll just have to be careful then, won't you.'

It wasn't easy dancing on the carpeted floor. They kicked off their shoes. 'What about a waltz,' he said. He began to sing 'Meet me in St Louis, Louis', and they waltzed to it, around and around in a very small circle, clockwise, then reversing it.

'Are we going to bed together?' he asked.

'I think we are. Yes.'

So they did, and each stage seemed to follow easily from the one before. There was a moment when she felt something like a doubt, or a fear, but it was crowded out by everything else. At the last moment he wasn't Jesse Fischer, he wasn't anyone, he was just a body her body wanted, and she took hold of him hard, harder than she'd ever taken hold of anyone before. And then as they surfaced slowly from what had happened she began to feel he'd done his work, done it well, and she wanted him out of her bed, out of her room. She suppressed the feeling; and when it persisted, she hid it. They lay there murmuring things to one another, Jesse dozing and waking; but when she felt enough time had passed she persuaded him to dress and go back to his room. Almost as soon as the door closed behind him, she fell asleep.

She must have slept heavily for three or four hours. What woke her was something inside herself that felt like a pang of grief. At first she didn't know where she was. Then she remembered. Even long afterwards she wasn't able to understand her own behaviour. The recollection of what had happened with Jesse made her jump out of bed. She began walking up and down the room, groaning and weeping and running her hands through her hair. She didn't feel anything so exact as guilt, or anger. If she felt regret it was only regret that she'd done something which was now causing her this pain, this panic.

She tried to calm herself. She washed her face with cold water, then sat at the window looking down into the chill

deserted Washington street, and smoked one of her rare ciga-
rettes. She said to herself 'I need a formula. A form of words.'
No sentence which included Jesse's name seemed right; but
neither did any which included Rocky's. 'I don't know who I
am,' she told herself. And she repeated it, putting great empha-
sis on the second 'I'.

She and Jesse met, as usual, over breakfast. She didn't want
to see him but she hid her feelings. To go to bed with a man
at night and treat him coldly next morning was something
she thought of as teenage behaviour. She was embarrassed at
herself; and she was enough of an actress to look pleased when
he came in. This was the day when he was to appear before
the Committee. He'd been growing apprehensive as the time
approached, but now, over breakfast, he seemed more relaxed
and confident than she'd ever seen him. His face, freshly washed
and shaven, looked smooth. The flesh seemed plumper, the
skin glowed. He smiled at her and his eyes shone.

'You're a handsome man,' she told him. She said it as if she
meant it, because she did mean it; and he was not to know she
registered it as a fact only, one that didn't alter her feeling that
she wouldn't have cared if he'd vanished for ever, at the
moment of her saying it, into a hole in the ground. She
also knew that her aversion, whatever its cause or its source,
wouldn't last. And this certainty that she was registering the
complexity of the moment and that it was passing him by,
gave her a sense of power. She remembered telling herself in
the night, 'I don't know who I am.' Now she said to herself
silently, as she dug into her grapefruit, 'Whoever it is I am,
she's not lacking in guts.' This statement, with its peculiar
grammar, pleased her so much she laughed.

He smiled across the table at her, full of a bland certainty
about her and about them both. 'Come on – tell me the
joke.'

She shook her head. 'I couldn't. I was just remembering –
us, you know.'

He nodded, smiling. He understood.

Jesse's call to take the stand came early in the afternoon. The
first questions were factual ones about his name and date of

birth, his present residence and work, his career. Arlene was surprised to discover the man she'd been to bed with was eighteen years her senior. Long ago, when they'd first met, she'd been aware of the gap. Now it seemed to have vanished, to be meaningless.

Mr Stripling, the Grand Inquisitor as he was known among the liberal faction, asked whether Jesse was a member of the Association of Motion Picture Producers. Jesse affirmed that he was.

'And you don't mind answering that question Mr Fischer?'

'Not in the least.'

'We've had witnesses in the past few days – you may have heard some of them – who've objected to questions by this Committee as to their affiliations.'

'I think they had political affiliations in mind, didn't they?'

'There were objections to questions as to membership of, for example, the Screen Writers' Guild.'

'I have no objection.'

'And politics?'

'My politics are no secret. I'm a Democrat.'

'But if I asked you whether you were, or ever had been, a member of the Communist Party . . .'

'The answer would be no.'

'I'm sure it would, Mr Fischer, and that it would be an honest answer. Would you agree that no loyal American would object to such a question if he had nothing to hide?'

'No. I wouldn't agree with that. There's a principle at stake. I don't think it's a question this Committee should be asking. I'm just not willing to risk a charge of contempt. I have the greatest respect for those who've taken the risk.'

In the momentary silence which followed, Arlene clapped. It set others off. There was a round of applause. The Chairman banged his gavel. 'I've said before, we'll have no demonstrations for or against what witnesses have to say.'

Mr Stripling continued his questioning. 'In your work as a director and producer, Mr Fischer, and in your earlier work as a screenwriter, have you had any dealings with, or knowledge of, Mr Dalton Trumbo or Mr Ring Lardner Jr?'

Jesse said he had – with both of the men named. 'They're among the very best writers in Hollywood.'

'You've heard these gentlemen refuse to answer questions about their membership of political parties?'

'I have.'

'And you've heard FBI and other evidence that they are, or have been, members of the Communist Party?'

'I've heard no evidence that seemed to me conclusive. It was all hearsay, and the witnesses weren't cross-examined.'

'I didn't ask whether the evidence was sufficient to seem conclusive to someone of your obviously cautious disposition, Mr Fischer. I asked whether you heard it?'

'I don't think you can assume . . .' Jesse frowned. 'I might have been asleep.' He appealed to the Chairman. 'Mr Chairman, am I to be questioned about what I have or have not heard in this room?'

The Chairman looked uncertain.

'I was taking a short cut, Mr Chairman,' Stripling said. 'But let's go the long way round. Let me inform Mr Fischer of what I think he's already perfectly well aware. Evidence was put before this Committee that Mr Trumbo and Mr Lardner have, or have had, affiliations with the Communist Party. It was evidence of a kind which I believe this Committee and most loyal Americans will accept. But let us suppose for a moment that the evidence was sufficient even to convince you, Mr Fischer. My question is this: would you then employ either of those men to write movie scripts for your studio?'

'If either of them was right for the particular job, and if the studio allowed me to, yes. I would.'

'So you're not concerned about any programme they may be engaged in to undermine the American way of life?'

'I think the American way of life can look after itself. I think it includes them. I'm interested in making pictures.'

'At any cost?'

'We look at budgets very carefully.'

There was laughter. The Chairman banged his gavel. 'Very good, Mr Fischer. You got your laugh. Hollywood usually does, doesn't it. But the American people might have the last laugh, don't you think?'

'I'm sorry Mr Chairman, that's a mite too deep for me.'

The Chairman waved his gavel at the investigator. 'Proceed, Mr Stripling.'

'These hearings, Mr Fischer, arise from a concern that Communism may be infiltrating the movie industry. Doesn't your answer to my question lend weight to the evidence of Mr Menjou and others that the concern is well-merited?'

'No it doesn't. These men write good scripts. I don't care if a script is written by a monkey. If it's a good script, I want it. If the monkey starts advocating free bananas and bananas are irrelevant to the picture, I tell him so and he either writes it again or I engage another writer.'

'But if you were not directing matters, Mr Fischer. If some other director – Mr Dmytryk, for example . . .'

'Mr Dmytryk is answerable to a producer, and to a studio. The point is these hearings are not an objective enquiry. They're set up in a particular way to produce a particular effect. You have a handful of obsessive people saying there's a Red under every bed. And you have another handful of people who have reasons for not wanting to answer questions about their political pasts. You bring them together in Washington and you say to the American people "This is Hollywood". Well it's not Hollywood. It's not the Hollywood any of us who live and work there recognize.'

Towards the end of this statement Chairman Thomas had begun to bang his gavel, attempting to cut it off. Now he was banging harder at the applause it received. When something like silence had been restored he addressed the witness. 'If what you say is true about these hearings, Mr Fischer, can you explain why we invited you here? Or Mr Emmett Lavery? Or Mr Dore Schary?'

'I suppose even you make mistakes, Mr Chairman. Three out of forty-five – that's not bad going.'

There was laughter. The Chairman hammered his desk. 'Mr Fischer, you are dangerously close to contempt.'

'I think I am, Mr Chairman, and I apologize.'

The questioning continued, but not for long, and the Committee looked relieved when the session closed..

As the room was clearing Jesse came over to where Arlene was standing waiting. She put her hand on his arm. She didn't know quite what she'd expected of him, but she hadn't expected anything like this. Maybe he hadn't expected it himself.

'You were good,' she said. 'You were bloody stupendous.'

He took a deep breath and smiled. 'I don't know what got into me.'

'Are you OK?'

He nodded. 'I'm just fine.' He looked down the room where photographers were waiting. 'Let's see if we can get out by a back door.'

As they turned to go someone said 'Have you heard the news? Bert Brecht flew out of New York last night. They say he's on his way to East Germany and he won't be back.'

# 11

I had known, it seemed from a very early age, that if I had anything that could be called a character, it was lumbering, blunt, laborious. Now I was discovering there was, not often, but sometimes, a second character in me that might be capable of some kind of cleverness, or grace. But there were not just two characters. There were three, there were six, there were a great number. Keats helped me understand how this could be. I was reading his letters as well as his poems. I liked especially the dense, compact sayings he cast off in the heat of the moment, things which seemed marvellous and truthful at the same time that they were almost impenetrable. In my cupboard beside the plunging neckline of Ginger Rogers I pinned up something copied from one of his letters: 'The Genius of Poetry must work out its own salvation in a man. It cannot be matured by law and precept, but by sensation and watchfulness in itself. That which is creative must create itself.' Sometimes as I rode my bicycle through the suburbs on my way to tennis or to a soccer match I would say over, 'That which is creative must create itself.'

I liked the letter he wrote to the woman he loved, Fanny Brawne, in which he told her an oriental tale of a city where all the men were melancholy because each had found his way into a Garden of Paradise, the home of an incomparably beautiful woman. As each man went to kiss her he was told to close his eyes, and when he opened them, found himself descending to earth in a magic basket. I thought this story must have set him writing the poem he called 'La Belle Dame sans Merci', in which the knight finds a beautiful woman, takes her on his horse, rides through the countryside with her, is told that she

95

loves him, kisses her, sleeps, and wakes to find himself alone on the cold hillside – after which he wanders melancholy like the men in the oriental story. Both the poem and the story made the same kind of journey as the Nightingale Ode – from the mundane to the marvellous and back to despair. It seemed like a warning about the narcotic powers of imagination, but also an advertisement for them. And I liked it that having told the story of the melancholy oriental men, Keats became incoherent trying to see Fanny Brawne as identical with the magical lady, but different. He wanted to say that she too was magical; but he didn't want the story to end in despair.

It must have been in 1948 that our English teacher decided he would take the whole form out for an evening at the pictures. His name was Mr Pearl, and we called him Pansy Pearl, I thought at the time because he dressed well and wore a different tie every day, but there may have been other reasons. We were to meet at the Embassy Theatre in town, which stood where the Auckland City Library is now, and I remember getting off the tram and running down Wellesley Street, a few minutes late, conscious of my grey flannel trousers and my blue and gold school blazer with its rep. pocket and school monogram – a gold lion rampant over a scroll that read 'Per Angusta, Ad Augusta' – through hardship to glory.

Mr Pearl had let us vote on what picture we wanted to see. We thought it pretty decent that he would pay for us all and that he hadn't insisted on something 'educational'. In those days, before television, the pictures that did well were seen by just about everyone, and the newest one people were talking about was called *Shooting*. Humphrey Bogart was the star, and that was the picture we chose. A few of the boys had seen it but they didn't mind seeing it again. They were warned that if they let out who the murderer was before the end of the screening, they would be thumped.

Bogart played the part of a Hollywood screenwriter, a man famous as a thriller writer, who drinks too much and is too quick with his fists. He's having trouble finishing a script. His studio needs it, and he needs the money. He's friendly with a secretary. Sometimes he exchanges a word with her in an office where he goes to pick up his mail, and sometimes in the studio restaurant, which is called the commissary. She's rather shy. He's kind to her and makes jokes about her boss who seems unpleasant. Then one night he runs into her as she's leaving the studio. He asks her to help him. He tells her he has a deadline and a bottle of whisky. The whisky will help him meet the deadline, but he needs a typist. If he dictates, will she type for him? She's surprised, and a bit apprehensive, but it's obvious she likes him, admires him, she's a bit in awe of him, and she's flattered to be asked. So she says yes. He takes her to a nearby diner for a hamburger and then they go back to his office and get down to work. There are shots of them working on into the night. His jacket is off, his tie is pulled down, his top button open, his hair roughed up. He looks more weary and less sober as each shot dissolves into the next and the hands of the clock move around. But the typist keeps on typing, and Bogart, glass in hand, keeps dictating. These shots are all silent, seen from outside through a window, and in the last the two of them are smiling at one another and shaking hands. The job is done.

Now it's morning. We cut to a long shot of a beach and a wharf, or pier. There's something pale lying just above the water-line among the wharf-piles. The waves wash in and swirl around it and pull back. The shot closes in. It's a body. Closer, we see it's the secretary, lying there very dead and very beautiful, with seaweed in her hair and around her legs.

So the movie develops from there. Did Bogart kill her? The cops think he did. He already has convictions for crimes of violence committed when drunk. Of course we, the audience, don't think he did it, but it's possible.

Did her boss do it? We don't like her boss, but then the movie-makers may just be playing tricks on us, making us dislike the boss when really someone else is the murderer.

Then there's Bogart's estranged wife. She's one of the studio's top artistic directors and she seems too beautiful and too accomplished to be guilty of murder. But she still loves Bogart, and she's said to be capable of passion and jealousy. And we soon discover she worked late that night, and on

97

her way to the carpark must have gone past the window of the office in which Bogart and the secretary were working. Could something romantic have developed after the dictation was complete – something which the wife looked in and saw?

And then, to complicate it further, suspicion also falls for a time on the secretary's husband (played by Lloyd Nolan). But the husband is also a private eye, and he's the one who finally solves the crime.

There's a lot more to the story, and no need for me to go into it. If you're old enough you probably saw it at the time. Or you may have seen it replayed on television. My interest in it here is only, of course, in the role of the secretary. Right from her first appearance I knew it was Edie. I should explain that it was a very small part that didn't involve much acting. There were just a few brief scenes in which you saw her exchange a word or two with her boss, or with Bogart. And in the late night scene, because it was all shot from outside, you heard nothing of what was said. Almost everything about the secretary emerged after she was dead. The role wasn't important and it wasn't listed in the credits, which only named the half dozen stars. But I didn't need anything to reassure me. Edie was changed, she was older, her hair was different, her accent was altered, but she was still Edie.

But now I had a problem. I walked home that night, all the way to Mt Eden. I was bursting to tell someone. I wanted to celebrate. Edie was becoming a movie star. But I knew I wouldn't dare say a word to anyone. I was already inventing another movie I would say we'd seen. I would try to avoid the subject; but if I was asked I would say that some of the boys who had seen *Shooting* said it was boring and we'd gone instead to one called *The Ghost and Mrs Muir*, with Gene Tierney and Rex Harrison.

Within a few days I was sure my grandmother had seen *Shooting*. She became silent and purposeful, hobbling off every afternoon without saying much before or after. When questioned she pretended, as I did, to have gone to *The Ghost and Mrs Muir*. One night I took her by surprise in her room. The door was ajar and she didn't hear me come in. She was sitting in her chair in the dark, her back to the door, looking out through a big open window into the garden. The crickets were very loud. I stood in the doorway and a faint glow reddened and faded as she drew on her cigarette.

'Gran,' I said. At once the cigarette spiralled away into the darkness. 'You'll burn us all down one day.'

She didn't look around. She knew who it was. 'What are you talking about?'

'Your cigarette.'

'What cigarette?'

I abandoned that. 'Gran,' I said, still talking to the back of her chair. 'You've seen it haven't you?'

She didn't answer at once. Then she said, 'Five times.'

'It's her isn't it?'

'Yes.'

'What should we do?'

Another brief silence, and then: 'Just keep our fingers crossed and our traps shut and hope it goes away.'

But it didn't go away. It was doing good business, and my parents weren't going to miss a Humphrey Bogart movie. They went to see it – I'm not sure how long they stayed. I had the impression that our mother had a fit of hysterics at seeing her daughter lying dead on a foreign shore. My recollection, though memory may have pushed two or more days together, is that she came home distraught and a doctor was called to calm her down. He said she was suffering from anaemia which made her weak and exhausted and lowered her resistance to emotional things. She would need a course of injections to get her red blood count back to normal.

While the doctor was with her in the bedroom, Resident Hippo was striding up and down in the next room. He was insisting the actress, whoever the silly cow was, wasn't Edie. He was furious with her for looking like Edie and upsetting people. He was also furious with Edie for running away and disappearing so it was possible for people to imagine she was now a Hollywood actress. Finally he was furious with his wife for believing that the actress was Edie, and worse, for seeming to believe that a person lying dead on a beach in a movie was really dead.

All of this happened at a bad time for our father. He was preoccupied with political matters, and deeply anxious. A Member of Parliament had just announced his retirement from one of the Labour Party's safest Auckland seats, and as local President our Dad was in the running to become the Party's new candidate. His chief rival was a trade union secretary. I had the impression that a lot of skirmishing and lobbying was going on. But the final decision would be made by what was called a selection ballot. In this, each of the would-be candidates would have to make a speech to assembled Party members, and then a committee of six, three local, three from Party headquarters in Wellington, would choose.

What was needed was peace at home. The Hippo needed it so he could concentrate his mind; and he needed it for the sake of his reputation. Neighbours were talking about the screaming and thumping issuing from the Harper household. Was a wife-beater the sort of man you wanted to represent you in Parliament? And even if you took his side, as some did, still a Member of Parliament needed his wife beside him, and if she was putting on a pretty fair imitation of a mad-woman, that too ruled him out. Either way he couldn't win.

Maybe none of these things were said. If they were, how did they get back to me? As I raced around my circuit of the house closing windows, I seemed to pick them up out of the air of the neighbourhood. It was as if I could hear the voices saying, 'There goes the Harper boy shutting the windows again. They must be getting the gloves on over there.'

And my father did seem to be going to pieces. He'd bought a big second-hand car with olive-green leather seats and I remember the day when we turned out of Queen Street into Shortland Street. On the hill there was a terrible grinding and bumping, the car lurched to a stop and smoke came out from under the long snout-like bonnet. I got out with my father. He unclipped the bonnet on one side and lifted it. The engine seemed to have slipped its moorings and to be dragging along the street.

When anything like that happened now, my mother wept. She wept copiously. She couldn't be stopped. As if to find an excuse for her tears she would begin to talk about Edie – even about the sight of Edie lying dead on the beach. It drove the Hippo to despair, and for him despair and violence were near relatives.

That day I couldn't take it. I left them there and climbed on to the first tram that came along. When the conductor came to take my fare I found I didn't have any money. I got off and walked the three miles home.

There were many bad scenes at that time. I will describe the worst. It happened, of course, one weekend. Somehow I hadn't managed to escape. A quarrel had blown up. My father was attempting a new style of calm rationality, superficially plausible, but really alien to him and therefore about as durable as a house of cards. He was trying to explain to our lachrymose progenitrix that the person she'd seen in a certain movie was not her daughter, and that if she insisted on believing it was, she might at least take comfort from the fact that when people in movies lay about in the water pretending to be murdered they were not in fact dead. As soon as the scene was over they got up, dried themselves, and went off to spend a fortune on lunch.

At the words 'murdered' and 'dead', mother wept. Her distress was real – as real as the tears that flowed down her cheeks, and my sympathy was stirred. I couldn't stand seeing her so grief-stricken. But I felt sorry for him too. I shared his sense of helplessness and frustration. Our mother wasn't insane, but she was letting herself appear to be. It was as if she was stubbornly determined to be irrational, and to inflict on us all the consequent disruption and embarrassment. I didn't know why, but I felt she was punishing us.

Now she was blaming the Hippo for driving Edie away. At this, his reasonable tone vanished. The house of cards collapsed. He told her, with his usual colourful verbal flourishes, that she was the one responsible because she'd always treated Edie as a rival instead of as a daughter.

The argument went on from room to room. At some point

they withdrew into that front bedroom where I imagine all of us, Edie included, had been conceived. The door was shut, the voices were raised even further. And then it began – my mother was screaming. It was a sound that killed sympathy dead and made you want to wipe out its source. Then it stopped. It didn't stop because it was completed. It was a scream cut off in its prime. The scream had been bad but the silence was worse. My legs went soft with fear. In a moment I couldn't stand it. I burst into the room. He had her down on the double bed and he was holding a pillow over her face. I grabbed him by the shoulder and pulled him off her. He fell back against the wall and slid down to the floor, gasping for breath. The moment the pillow was removed the scream began again. That was good. She wasn't damaged if she could make such a racket, but how could it be stopped? I felt I was taking command. I remembered what they did in movies. When a woman became hysterical the hero usually slapped her face, not too hard, but briskly. In the movies the woman always stopped screaming and appeared to wake, as if from a trance.

It was a hard thing to do. It went against everything I'd been taught. I did it in a spirit of desperate courage. I slapped her face. She screamed louder. I slapped the other cheek. It wasn't working. Was Hollywood wrong? I slapped her a third time. It made no difference. Now it was Ellie's turn to rescue her. She pulled me away. I was glad of it. She had a cup of water. She sprinkled it over that glowing face, speaking soothingly. 'Don't worry. Quieten down. Everything's alright.' It worked. The scream died a natural death. It turned to sobbing. I dragged myself away, out into the back garden, and banged my fist against a flat rock, as hard as I could make myself, until the knuckles were bleeding.

Next day mother's cheeks were streaked with broken blood vessels. This was what I had done to her. I was ashamed, humiliated, contrite, dismayed. She was calm and forgiving. She didn't seem to blame me. I suppose she blamed the Hippo. She seemed almost glad of these signs of brutality. She walked down to the local shops and let her face be seen.

All of us were shaken up. I slept long hours and had terrible dreams which I couldn't remember but which stayed with me as an atmosphere and an oppression.

It wasn't long afterwards that my father had to face the selection ballot. As usual we went as a family. I'm sure my mother was as keen as the rest of us that he should succeed. Her face was almost back to normal, and she was able to conceal any lingering marks with make-up.

My father's rival, the trade union secretary, spoke first. He had a loud voice, a hectoring manner, and a north of England accent. The world was an evil place. Money was power and power was used to oppress the working class. Labour had saved New Zealand from the great depression, and would keep on saving it. The sticks could be broken one at a time, but never the bundle. Solidarity was essential, especially at this point in time when the forces of reaction were regrouping. America was being rabble-roused into a war against our brothers in Russia. What Hitler had failed to do, America thought it could accomplish – the defeat of the worker state. But that would never be the case while the world's workers remained united. Workers needed to be in Government. At the moment Labour in New Zealand was under threat from within as well as from without. There were middle-class men, money men, who saw their way to power on the backs of the working class. They pretended to speak for the workers but they could never do that. Their hands were soft, their collars were white, their language was impeccable, but their loyalties were divided. They didn't know how to handle themselves when the chips were down. They were too ready to compromise on long-established leftist principles. Labour had to keep its roots deep in the soil of the common man. He had toiled, he knew what it was to toil, what it was to stand up to the bosses on the factory floor. As a Labour MP he would never forget his origins or be confused about where his loyalties lay. When he spoke in Parliament he would give voice to the aspirations of his mates . . .

And so it went on. A lot of it was familiar, but the old rhetoric I had grown up with was being given a special twist in the hope of excluding President Harper. And the union man had his mates along. They applauded, they cheered, they hammered the floor with their heels.

When my father got up to speak he looked nervous. He put a written speech on the table in front of him, but he began speaking off the cuff, warming himself up, and then I could see he wasn't able to switch from that casual manner to the sentences he'd written for himself. There was an awkwardness – I felt it like something tangible in the air, and I felt him losing points. But then he began to think on his feet. What his rival had said gave him something to take hold of and argue with. He said the previous speaker had used the traditional workers' federation image of the sticks that could be broken one at a time and the bundle that was unbreakable. That was all right as far as it went. But did anyone give any thought to the fable about the willow and the oak? The oak boasted of his strength and looked down on the skinny willow. But a huge storm blew up, an unprecedented storm, and the oak split and fell while the sinewy willow flipped about in the winds and survived. There were some pretty strong winds being whipped up against Labour just now. He didn't deny that. And he didn't deny their principal source was the United States of America. The question was this: was the Labour Party going to stand mono-lithic and inflexible like the oak, and risk being snapped and broken? Or was it going to show a little flexibility, a little adaptability? Wasn't politics the art of the possible? Of course that dictum could be used to argue in favour of any and every compromise. It could be the rationale for a sellout of principles. He did not, and would never, advocate any kind of sellout. There was always a line to be drawn, and if that meant defeat, so be it. But short of that line, well short of it, there was a variety of options and possibilities. There were times for radical action and times when the population recoiled from it. A politician had to have a nose for the possible – that was his skill. He had to know what he wanted, and what they wanted and marry the two. Labour had traditional ties with the union movement and no one wanted them broken. They could never be broken. But the party in New Zealand that won an election always won by keeping its hold on the middle ground. You came from the Left or from the Right, but you won or lost in the middle. That was where Labour at this moment needed to fix its sights. It was a moment of danger for New Zealand and for the World. The whole of the Western World was being panicked about the Red Menace, and New Zealand wasn't exempt from the panic. We didn't have to believe in the Red Menace, but we did have to believe in the panic. If we in the Labour movement didn't face up to present political realities and modify our image, we were done for. And then what? New Zealand might be swept along by that international panic into something much worse than compromise. It might mean war. It might mean the death of democracy as we'd known it and fought for it. 'If we value New Zealand,' he concluded, 'don't let's hand it to the other crowd on a plate. Let's fight for it with the most effective weapons we have – our brains.'

It wasn't only the Harper family who applauded. No one cheered or stamped but his supporters weren't the noisy type. I thought he'd maybe gone on too long about compromise, but I felt he'd done well. I was sure he deserved to be chosen. I was sure he would be. But in the interval before the choice was announced he was depressed. He said he thought the decision had been made before the speeches had even begun.

People stood about drinking tea and eating sandwiches. It was painful waiting. My father looked pale, with dark rings under his eyes. My mother looked flushed. She was strangely still and silent.

We were called back into the room where the speeches had been made and a man from Central Office made the announcement. The union man had been chosen. There was applause. He stood up and made a short speech in which he ran his main slogans out again, like a string of flags. My father went across and shook his hand. Then my mother stood up. She asked if she could say a brief word. The chairman looked apprehensive, but he said she could.

I remember the physical sensation of my embarrassment. I bent almost double in my chair and my body twisted involuntarily away from her. I groaned. I could hear Ellie saying, 'Mum don't. Sit down.'

I thought we were all going to be sluiced from the room in a flux of tears and a gale of anguish, but my mother's voice came forth surprisingly dry and precise, almost as if it belonged to someone else. She said she was resigning from the Party and she wanted to do it here and now so members would understand why. In one sense it didn't matter who was chosen today. This was a safe Labour seat. We could put up any fool in it and he would be elected. But the choice mattered because it signalled how the Party saw itself. We'd heard first today from a man who learned his politics 12,000 miles away in a society as different from New Zealand as chalk was from cheese, and who thought Bradford's slogans of the 1920s and '30s would be good enough for Auckland in the 1940s and '50s. Then we'd heard from a man who knew and understood this society, here in the South Pacific, at this moment in its history, and who didn't have any ready slogans, thank God, because we hadn't been in this place at this time before. 'No doubt he'll stay with the Party because he's loyal,' she said. 'But I'm leaving. Labour has signalled today where it's going tomorrow – downhill. Labour will win this electorate but it will lose the election – and all the elections that follow until it learns the lesson that man – my husband Jim Harper – could have taught it.'

She sat down. There was no applause. Everyone was embarrassed. The chairman thanked her for her comments, said he understood her feelings, and hoped she would reconsider her resignation from the Party. It was a sad aspect of these occasions that there had to be a winner and a loser.

'Yes, and Labour is the loser today,' my mother said.

'Tell the old hen to pipe down,' someone shouted.

The meeting was declared closed. I walked out, avoiding every eye. I waited downstairs, away from the door. People came out slowly, talking. The crowd thinned. Soon there was no one. I went back up the stairs. Ellie and Cassie were in the outer room reading magazines. 'Where are they?' I asked.

Ellie picked up a sandwich. 'In there.'

I went to the door. They were sitting alone together in the

big room. They weren't talking. She was looking at the ceiling, he was looking at the floor. They were holding hands. I went back to the sandwiches and waited with my sisters.

# 12

She was aware of sunlight coming in around the holland blind
but she was asleep and dreaming. Jesse had a present for her in
a big round hat-box striped pink and blue. He said, 'It's your
birthday present but you can't have it yet.' She jumped up and
down. She was quite small. She said, 'Give it to me. Give it to
me.' Jesse said, 'First, Edie, you must answer some questions.'
She noticed he called her Edie. He hadn't done that before. She
couldn't tell whether that was a good sign or a bad one. He
asked, 'Where do monarch butterflies migrate to?' She said,
'Mexico.' 'Right,' he said. 'And why did Cecil B. De Mille
wear gaiters?' 'Because he was afraid of snakes.' 'Right again.
Happy birthday.' He kissed her. It was a long kiss. She wriggled
free. Now she was opening the box. Inside there was a white
pigeon. It was beautiful. She ran her fingers over its smooth
hard feathers. It made pigeon noises. 'It's lovely,' she said. All
at once it flew up out of the box, past her face, its wing-tip
flicking her eye, and towards the window. But the window
was shut. The pigeon crashed into the pane and fell to the floor.
He picked it up. It was dead. 'It's dead,' she said, and she began
punching him around the head and shoulders. He reeled back,
still holding the dead bird. 'It's dead,' she said. 'You silly
American drongo, you fucking bastard.' And she woke.

She opened her eyes, registered where she was and that
Rocky wasn't in the bed beside her, and dozed again, remembering the dream. She seemed to bring it up with her from the
deeper waters of sleep. A minute or two later her alarm clock
sounded. She rolled over and reached out to turn it off. She lay
there for a moment, then called, faintly, 'Rocky.' There was
no answer. She got up. Rocky was asleep in the next room,

propped among pillows on the floor rug. The television was still switched on. She stepped over him and turned it off. She bent down and touched his shoulder.

'Rocky.'

He stirred and turned on his side. 'Hang on.' His voice was a mumble. 'In a minute.' He was still asleep.

She went into the kitchen and got her breakfast together on a tray – orange juice, cereal and yoghurt, toast and coffee. When it was ready she took it back through the big living room and out on to the patio. Under an awning there was an outdoor table and chairs. Already it was hot out there. She turned on the sprinklers. Little jets of water sprayed out from nozzles planted in the grass. Two more taps set sprays of water jetting, turning in an arc, up the bank that rose behind the house. That seemed to attract the blue jays. They swooped through arcs of water. Two squirrels came down into the lower branches of the biggest tree at the bottom of the bank and began to quarrel. They made angry squeals, attacking and retreating around the base of the trunk. One drove the other away up the steep bank, but it returned a few minutes later and the fight started again.

Under the awning there were hanging baskets of flowering plants, and there were more in big earthenware pots around a barbecue fireplace set into the bank. The lower part of the bank was terraced and planted in flowering shrubs. Further up were pepper trees and eucalypts, until the bank turned into a crumbling hillside of brown grass and chaparral.

Through the three summer months since she and Rocky had moved from Santa Monica she had sat out there every morning having breakfast. Though the house wasn't on the floor of the San Fernando Valley, it was much hotter on this side of the hills. She missed the breeze that came up Pico from the sea and cooled the little Spanish house on Pacifica Street. But here there was a sense of openness. She could climb the hill behind the house and look out across a still largely wooded, or at least scrub-covered gully. There were houses among the trees. The suburb, Sherman Oaks, was growing all the time. But she had a feeling of escape as she drove down from Mulholland to her own space where in some degree plants and birds and animals still obeyed their own rules. Gophers ruined the lawn. Deer wandered down the slope in the early morning and chewed flowering shrubs. There were coyotes in the hills. Mocking birds cackled and shouted down the chimney when she was trying to concentrate on a script. The sun wrecked the roses someone had planted at the front of the house; and the hot dry wind from the mountains spread fires that started when the oily chaparral ignited spontaneously in the summer heat of the gullys. She feared the fires and she didn't much like the coyotes; but all the rest she liked. It made her forget herself, and Rocky, and everyone. She loved her hillslope and her garden and the house she'd bought. There was a mortgage on the house – what she'd got for the one in Santa Monica had paid half the price of the new one. But she was now officially a scriptwriter, no longer a secretary, and with the money that brought in, the place would soon be paid off.

While she drank her coffee a hummingbird came into the garden. It hovered around the flowers hanging in baskets, taking nectar, then vanished. When her eye found it again it was hovering around the red bottle-brush flowers on the terrace.

On her way to the shower she stopped a moment. She went to the room where Rocky was still sleeping. She stood in the doorway looking around. He must have fallen asleep watching television. Somewhere . . . She climbed over him and felt underneath the couch. There was a bottle of bourbon, still more than half full. As she pulled it out he struggled to wake. He reached out vaguely after her. 'Don't . . .' Then he woke, enough to remember their agreement and to realize he'd been caught out. He pretended to sleep again; or perhaps he let sleep, still strong in the provinces of his body, re-invade the capital. That way he escaped a confrontation, an admission, another promise.

She took the bottle with her to the bathroom and up-ended it. The bourbon ran away into the lavatory bowl. When she came out again, showered and dressed, Rocky was curled up tight on the rug like a dead, dishevelled foetus.

She went back into the kitchen and dialled Jesse's home

number. He must have been waiting right beside the phone because he answered at the first ring. 'Is that Jackson's Superstore?'

It was meant to be no more than a signal to him, but this morning he answered, 'No darling. It's not.'

'What do you mean "darling"? Where is everyone?'

'Judith's down the bank. The kids are off to school with Brendan.'

'Down the bank' meant that Judith had gone to her studio to paint. It was behind the house, down the hillslope. It had big windows looking out over the valley and towards the far mountains. It had no phone. When Judith went 'down the bank' it meant she wasn't to be disturbed. And Brendan was the Fischer's Irish chauffeur — a little freckled man with a drooping ginger moustache. He'd brought his brogue to Hollywood hoping to act in movies and hadn't made it, but he liked to recite, to dance an Irish jig, and to sing Irish ballads in a high lyric tenor.

'What about you? Where's Rocky?'

'He curled up with his girlfriend last night.'

'His . . . ?'

'Miss Kentucky Dry. He's still asleep on the floor.'

'Miss Kentucky Fried?'

'Dry, darling. Not fried. He's fried. She's dry. Bourbon. That stuff you don't drink.'

'Out cold is he?'

'Oh no. It's not as bad as that.' She could hear the note of sympathy and concern in Jesse's voice. She didn't want that. It made her feel disloyal to Rocky. Infidelity was one thing, disloyalty another. She knew — or she felt — that Jesse liked to be told of Rocky's excesses. It meant he, Jesse, was some kind of protector. It helped to excuse what went on between them. Jesse wasn't an easygoing Hollywood lover. He was a conventional family man, afflicted with guilt. She didn't like his guilt because it seemed to define where his first loyalty lay — and that wasn't with her. Also she was beginning to be ashamed of Rocky, and shame felt like further disloyalty.

'I thought you said he wasn't drinking.'

'Well – occasionally. You know how it is. He's doing much better.'

As she said this her eye was roving over the bank behind the house. There were so many crannies and stones and thickets in which he could hide bottles if he chose to. There was no possibility that she could really police their agreement.

'I'd better get off this phone,' she said. 'Usual time?'

'Usual time. OK. *D'accord*. See you there sweetheart.'

He made kissing noises and hung up. She stood there, staring at the bank. The agreement she'd come to with Rocky had seemed good at the time. It was a relief to talk about his drinking and have him admit he was afraid of what it was doing to him. Now it didn't seem to have been a good thing at all. It was as if the responsibility for keeping him away from alcohol had passed to her. She was his keeper, his chief of police. He didn't have to discipline himself. That was her job. His was to out-fox her, to deceive, to conceal – and it was too easy. He was drinking more than ever. It was becoming a way of life. And it was odd – something she could never have explained to Jesse, or to anyone – but though she hated and despised it, there was something in it she admired, or envied. Rocky's life was becoming so complete, so self-contained. It was almost true that the bottle was his mistress. Arlene was beginning to recognize that all his waking hours were governed by the thought of when he might have his first drink, and how he might get it; and then how long he might hold out until his second – and so on through the day. He had small triumphs and he suffered huge defeats. Everything else was secondary. All his cleverness, all his strengths and his weaknesses, went into this battle with himself. She and Rocky weren't lovers any more.

But when she thought of that she knew it wasn't only because of his drinking. She didn't want him. She wanted Jesse. And as Rocky lost confidence his approaches became more tentative, more timid. It was easy for her to pretend she hadn't seen the weak signals he sent out to her.

She went back into the bedroom, passing again the door of the room in which he was still sleeping on the floor. She sat at her dressing table doing her hair, putting on make-up, thinking of Jesse up there on Mulholland in that huge house with its pool and its projection room. In her mind she went through it all – Judith and the three Ds; the butler, the two maids, the cook and the chauffeur; the two gardeners, three dogs and four cars. And then the studio entourage – Mrs Nightingale and Bobso and editors and directors coming and going. The charge account at Romanoff's and the holiday house at Malibu. Jesse was so pampered and surrounded – it was the same for him at home or at the studio. He was a success, a man of power – and now she'd become part of his team. She was no longer the secretary. She'd had, she thought wryly, a promotion. She was the mistress. Her role in his life was as particular as Mrs Nightingale's, or the cook's, or the wife's, or the chauffeur's.

She knew that wasn't all. Jesse Fischer loved her. It was possible he loved her more than she loved him, because she tried not to love him too much. She was afraid of how much she might love him. He had no need to be afraid of that – there was so much else in his life to keep her in her place.

But then how could she resent his power? It was part of what she loved. And he'd used it always to help her. It was never a threat. There was nothing of the bully about Jesse, nor the Hollywood slob.

She heard Rocky stirring. She hurried to get her things together – her handbag, her papers for the day. She didn't want to talk to him now. But just as she was ready to leave he was there in the doorway, one shoulder supporting him against the jamb. He looked so pitiful, so guilty, it made her angry.

'I tipped it out.' She said it brutally.

He nodded and licked his lips. 'Listen,' he said. 'Good news. Charlie called yesterday. He thinks I should go down to Monogram and get some work as an extra. No use hanging about for the big stuff. Get inside a studio and start small. He thinks I need to see a bit more of the technical side.'

This was a lie. Why would Charlie Beltane advise him to go to one of the Gower Street studios and pick up work as an extra? There was nothing in it for him. Charlie had probably forgotten Rocky Tamworth altogether; or written him off.

Rocky must have known she knew it was a lie. Or was he too fuddled even for that? She didn't want a scene. She said, 'I think Charlie's right. It's good advice. When are you going?'

He blinked. He didn't seem to have thought beyond the story of Charlie's call, which was to cover the fact that she'd found him with a bottle of bourbon. 'Probably this morning. I might call them first and find out what's going on.'

'Well, drive carefully. Good luck.' She kissed him briefly. 'Stay on the right side of the road.'

It was something they said to one another now they each owned a car, because they both came from countries where you drive on the left. But he took it as a hint that he mightn't be in a fit state to drive.

'Look, last night was . . .'

He wasn't sure what it was. Probably what he meant to say was that it was something out of the ordinary. But how could he say anything so absurd? She looked at her watch. 'Darling I'm running late.'

He heaved himself out of the way, mumbling 'I know you haven't got time for my problems.'

She was past him but she turned back, flaring despite herself. 'I had time while you were out cold on the floor. And when you start going out to work I'll be right here when you need me. And I won't be boozing all day. In the meantime someone has to pay the bills.'

He didn't answer. There was no answer. He looked crushed. She wanted to go back and say she was sorry, but that would set in train another exchange which would take them out of one thicket of recrimination and into another.

She went down to the garage and sat in her car trying to calm herself before pressing the switch that triggered the double doors. When she thought of Jesse – saw him as if from a distance – it was the orderliness, the control of his own life that she envied. Not the wealth – just the perfect management. She wanted control of her own life, as he had control of his. It was like trying to heave a huge boulder into place. It moved when she worked at it, but never quite as she wanted it to.

She drove out of Merivale Crescent and up Woodcliff Road

towards Mulholland. There were jacarandas, hibiscuses, flame trees, poinsettias, bougainvillaea, mimosa, flowering eucalypts. They hung over the street shedding their colours of leaf or flower. Though the gardens were different, they were like enough to make her think of home. There was a friend in Auckland, Veronica, a girl she'd been to school with, with whom she exchanged letters on the understanding that no one was to know where she was. So she got a little news of her family while they received none of her. The latest suggested her mother might be unwell. Not serious, Veronica said. Just anaemia and some kind of minor nervous collapse.

Arlene thought of her mother's life as one long nervous collapse – there was nothing new in that. What was new was her own feeling. She'd felt a kind of coldness towards her mother, but now it seemed to have gone, as if under the surface she'd never really lost her infant love. Even by thinking of those things she most disliked she couldn't bring back the old resentment. Now was the time when she might have begun to think about writing home, telling them where she was and what she was doing. She'd always intended to, when enough water had flowed under the bridge. But she'd imagined that by then Rocky would be a success. She'd thought it would be a kind of triumph, even a small revenge, to be able to write saying 'I'm married to Rocky Tamworth,' knowing that he was a movie star they would have seen or heard of. Now all she had to tell them was that she was working for a living in a Hollywood studio, married to an out-of-work actor who had a problem with alcohol.

Silence was better. It would be disastrous if a letter from her brought them over on a visit. It wasn't likely, but it was possible, and that was something she didn't want. She couldn't write to them, and that made her, almost for the first time, feel that she missed them, that she was lonely. She felt vulnerable. If she lost Jesse, what would there be in her life to hold on to?

He was waiting for her in the little gravelled area just off Mulholland where they met three mornings a week. She skidded to a stop in the gravel, jumped out and ran to his car, leaving the door swinging. She got in beside him and kissed him hard. Then she pushed his head away from her, stared at him, and kissed him again. His skin was so firm and smooth and brown. He was so healthy. There was something lovely about the skin of men in their forties, successful men. And there was the smell of cologne; and the quite particular, faint, deliciously human smell of Jesse Fischer. She made a purring noise in his ear. 'Edible Jesse,' she said. 'I'd like to fuck you right here.'

He craned his neck over her shoulder, looking around. 'Do you think we could?' His hand was under her skirt.

She closed her eyes and was quiet for a moment. 'Sometimes when I was still calling you Mr Fischer I used to imagine fucking you. It was always in a car – a great big one.'

He was wrestling with buttons and straps. All at once she stopped him. 'Jesse darling . . .'

He looked confused. She said, 'If a patrol car came . . .'

He nodded, pulling away from her, and sat for a moment with his head back, breathing. 'You're right. What a meal for Louella.'

'And my citizenship's pending.'

'My citizenship's erect. It'll pend in a moment.'

'Darling.' She took a comb out of his pocket and ran it through his hair, remaking the military parting. Then she smoothed his eyebrows and straightened his collar and tie. 'Darling is such a silly word. I should call you squint.'

'Squint.' He looked at his eyes in the rearview mirror. 'I don't have a squint.'

'No of course you don't. Don't be so literal. It's just the sound. *Squint*. It's how I feel about you.'

'Squint.' He repeated it, staring into the distance. He shook his head. 'I don't get it. How does it work?'

'I don't know how it works.' She thought about it. 'Squeeze. Cunt. I don't know. You shouldn't have to think about it.'

She kissed him again. 'Lavender and obscenity,' she said.

He smiled a half smile. 'Lavender and obscenity,' he repeated. 'You take the biscuit, sweetheart.'

A day later they were lunching together at Oblath's. Jesse

had never quite made it official like a timetable, but every week it was the same. Mondays, Wednesdays and Fridays they met in the mornings up off Mulholland. Tuesdays and Thursdays they lunched together and afterwards went to a room he'd taken permanently in the gardens of the Beverly Hills Hotel. It was an arrangement she liked and disliked. She liked it because it meant that although they no longer worked together they saw one another every working day. She disliked it because it was so predictable, so unspontaneous. She felt herself neatly parcelled into the framework of Jesse Fischer's busy life.

'Casting's going to be a problem.' He was telling her about his picture for that year – his own picture – the one that would follow on from the success of *Shooting*.

'This is going to be a classic Western,' Jesse told her, 'with a shoot-out at the end like you never saw before. In colour. Blue skies. Tawny landscape. A minimum of mock-up sets. I want it to look good and look real. Good acting. And good Jock Bateman dialogue, if I can keep him sober. Tough crackling stuff.'

She'd had clam chowder and now she was eating a spinach salad with ham and cheese and garlic bread. He refilled her wine glass.

'I'd like to get Widmark as the sheriff. The problem's going to be how to present the father and son on the ranch. They can't deal with the bad guys because they're fighting one another. There are two ways of doing it. We can either make it that the old guy's dyed-in-the-wool mean and cantankerous and the son's trying to live in the present. Or we can make the father a wise old owl and the boy a wild one who's trigger-happy and dangerous – trying to prove himself. We can't decide which way serves the story best.'

He smiled, watching her tuck into her salad. 'Are you listening to me?'

'Yes father.'

'Am I boring you?'

She shook her head. 'Keep talking. It's just that I'm hungry.'

'You're always hungry. Tell me what I just said.'

She put down her fork. 'I'll tell you what you should do.

Make it a bit of both. The old boy's a mite mean and conservative but he's wise too. And the son – he's wild, and out to prove himself, but he's not just a gun-crazy kid. Why make two clichés when you can have just one? And why make one when you don't have to have any?'

'But then you don't have a problem for the story to solve. If they're not warring they just combine and beat the bad guys. It's all over too soon.'

'No – they're warring. But fathers and sons lock horns without there being one right and one wrong. You said you wanted it real. Make it real.'

He began eating again. 'You may be right. D'you like Westerns?'

'Love them.'

'Truly?'

'Absolutely. Why?'

He shook his head. 'No reason. I just like to know what you like.'

'What about Edward G. Robinson for the old man?'

He frowned. 'He's not on contract to the studio.'

'He's not on contract to any studio.'

Jesse shook his head. 'Eddie's a gangster.'

'He's not just a gangster. Rocky read in one of the trade papers that Joe Mankiewicz is casting him as an Italian banker.'

'A crooked banker. But that's not the point. Marvin Major wouldn't have him on the lot.'

'That's because of the black list.'

'Who knows? Marvin's the boss. He doesn't have to have a reason.'

'But you know it's the reason.'

'If I had to bet on it I'd say so. Sure. But no one in Hollywood needs to explain why he's not employing an actor. You could say you didn't like his aftershave.'

'His aftershave was OK before J. Parnell Thomas got to work. If you want Eddie Robinson . . .'

He interrupted her. 'I didn't say I wanted him.'

'Just say for a moment you think it's a good idea. And then you rule him out because you think Marvin Major won't like it. You know what that means? It means you're operating the black list for him. Passively. He doesn't have to do it for himself.'

'So I should put up Eddie's name just to have Marvin veto it.'

'Of course you should. Better still, you should argue with him. Ask him why he's interfering.'

'All this is hypothetical.'

'Is it? There must be other people you don't ask him about because you know he won't want to employ them. Writers. Directors. No wonder he says there isn't a black list. His underlings are operating it for him.'

Jesse bridled at the word underling. 'Can I just remind you of something? You told me I should forget about being studio head and get on with making a picture or two of my own. Remember? I think it was good advice. It's what I'm doing. It's the part of my work I like best. But it means Marvin Major still has the final say on everything. I work around him as best I can.'

She didn't answer. She felt angry because since the hearings in Washington everything in Hollywood had got worse. The Red scare was growing. There was agitation for loyalty oaths. There was fear that threatened to become panic. No one was standing up for principle any more. Since his brave showing in Washington Jesse had retreated along with everyone else. He was letting the tide carry him. He'd gone from Washington to New York, and though he said he'd fought it tooth and nail, he was officially aligned with the Producers' Association Waldorf Astoria Declaration, in which they agreed that none of the studios would employ any of the 'unfriendly ten' unless they said publicly that they weren't Communists.

But she didn't want to fight with Jesse. He couldn't be held responsible for the state of the Union. 'Come on,' she said. 'Let's put politics to bed.'

Later she was waving goodbye to him in the grounds of the big rambling pink hotel with its balconies and orange tiled roofs. She'd decided to stay on there in the outhouse room they each had a key to. There was a script she would work on; but really she was in a mood to float, to drift. Sometimes that could be as useful as hard work; and if it wasn't, no one would question her. She had a reputation for turning in her scripts ahead of time.

Jesse's car turned out of the drive into Sunset Boulevard, hesitated a moment, accelerated away into the traffic. She watched it go, then crossed the street to a little park where she lay in the grass and stared up through the branches of the lower trees at the showers of phoenix palm fronds, and higher again, the heads of giant palms like Giacometti models moving just perceptibly against a soiled blue haze of sky. She felt relaxed, physically content, satisfied – her body almost ached with it. It was a good feeling. But it left her dangerously romantic. She thought swimmingly about Jesse. She thought she would like to live with him for ever. She would like to have his child.

For a few moments she fell asleep and when she woke her mind went straight, and with perfect clarity, to her script. She saw the outlines of a hard, sharp, no-quarter argument between her two principal characters. She jumped up from the grass, so abruptly it made her giddy for a moment. She brushed small sticks and dried grass from her skirt and made her way across Sunset, through the hotel gardens, and back to their room. She left the door open and sat at the small desk Jesse had installed with its portable typewriter. A light breeze blew in, stirring curtains. For minutes she sat staring at the keys, turning sometimes to look out at the hibiscus flowers and a strange cactus plant that grew at the door. Then she began typing, banging down the hard, clean, uncompromising things she wanted her two characters to say to one another. A page. Another page. A third. She pushed the machine away, spread the pages in front of her, and read them over, making changes with a pen. They were good. They excited her. She rested back in her chair and looked around the room, catching sight of herself in a mirror. Her makeup was gone. Her hair was somehow puffed out around her face, as if a small explosion had occurred inside her head. Her clothes were ruffled. She quite liked what she saw. 'You look OK,' she told herself in the mirror. It was good to have work. And she was a writer. It hadn't quite struck her in that way before. It had all happened by stages, as if by accident. That was Arlene Tamworth in the mirror, and Arlene Tamworth was a screenwriter.

# 13

We are still beside the pool, Edie and I. It's dark now. The pictures are still forming. Words into pictures. To me they're mostly black and white, as if those old stills and movies record the world as it really was.

I'm telling her about the 1949 election. I go to a party. It's meant to be a victory celebration but it turns into a wake. After fourteen years – most of my conscious years thus far – Labour has lost.

I go into the kitchen. There's a man standing on one leg with his arms spread out on either side. He tells me, 'I'm the man who stands on one leg.' He doesn't stand very steady. He's had a lot to drink.

His wife explains to me he was once an Olympic athlete. He posed for the big bronze statue over the gates of the Auckland Domain. His genitals are what you see first when you look up.

I walk home. It's a bit like the end of the war. I feel a vague apprehension. What will life be like without a Labour government?

The lights are on in the living room, the radio is on, still delivering election results. The election charts are spread out on the table. President Harper has been filling in the returns. There's no sign of him. I find him in the back garden. He's sitting there in the dark on a wooden seat under a jasmine bush. I don't know what to say. I know the electorate he hoped to stand for has been won by Labour. If he'd won the selection ballot he would be in Parliament now, a member of the Opposition, but an MP.

I stand on one leg and spread my arms out wide. 'I'm the man who stands on one leg.'

He stares at me. 'Have you been drinking?'

I tell him only a glass or two. He doesn't seem to mind. I tell him about the Olympic athlete who posed for the Domain statue.

He nods and goes on sitting there. He makes me think of 'grey-haired Saturn quiet as a stone' in the poem by Keats. After a while he says, 'You've heard the results.'

I tell him I have. 'Sorry Dad,' I say.

He gets up, sighing, and pats me on the shoulder. 'Every dog has its day,' he says. But I don't feel he's had his.

By the poolside, after a long silence, Edie says, 'I remember the Domain statue. It embarrassed us as kids. We wanted to look up at it but we felt we shouldn't.' She laughs. 'Those great big balls.'

I try to see her face in the dark. What does she feel about our father? She's so familiar, and yet I don't know her. I want to tell her about my adolescent dream of her, and the photograph I kept among socks and handkerchiefs, but of course I don't.

We talk about the Waterfront Dispute in New Zealand in 1951. I tell her how the Cold War settled over New Zealand, and how all the democratic freedoms were set aside by the Emergency Regulations.

1951, she tells me, was the year of the Un-American Activities Committee's second investigation of Communism in Hollywood. It was much worse than the first.

We sit staring at the lights stretching and marbling the surface of the pool – staring through them each to a different gloomy picture of the first year of the second half of the twentieth century. From under Edie's chair comes the sound of Kapai chewing on his stick. Some dogs have their day every day.

We go indoors. Edie puts on a record. 'Come on,' she says. 'Let's dance.' We've been dancing a lot these past few days, but it doesn't stop us talking.

Edie mentions the Rosenbergs – Julius and Ethel, the Jewish couple condemned to death as atom spies in the 1950s. I describe how I felt at the time – the indignation, the sense of helplessness.

We stop dancing and hold on to one another in the middle of the room. 'It was awful, wasn't it,' she says. She's fascinated to think we should have been so far from one another and so troubled and obsessed by the same event.

'Let's go have a Mexican supper,' she says, 'and I'll tell you my story about the Rosenbergs.'

# 14

It was after Arlene's return from Washington that the changes had been made – first at the studio, then the move from Santa Monica to Sherman Oaks. Her recognition as a scriptwriter had come from Marvin Major himself. *Shooting* had been a success; and Mr Major apportioned credit about half-and-half between Arlene's idea, around which the story had been constructed, and Jesse's skill in negotiating the loan of Bogart from Warners. He seemed to give little or no credit to Jesse's directing.

Marvin Major was broad, loud, silver-haired, with a moustache that didn't quite, Arlene thought, look American. It wasn't sufficiently disciplined. Events took it one way or the other across the line of his nose. But he smoked cigars and wore bow ties. He threatened, cajoled, bribed, blackmailed and bullied to get his own way. He was ruthless with his actors, even his best stars, putting them on suspension if they refused a script. He counted success in money and talked about it constantly. He harangued everyone, reminded them that he had made the studio what it was, pointed to the danger signs on the horizon that threatened Hollywood, and made it known that he intended to fight for what they had all worked to establish. But to succeed he needed their support, their devotion, their loyalty. He also needed constant praise and occasional sexual favours. In all of this except, perhaps, the exuberance of his moustache, Marvin Major was probably, for those times, an average studio boss.

Before she was moved formally to his scriptwriting team Arlene was subjected to an interview, or an audience, with the great man. In this and subsequent encounters she registered that there were certain key words in his vocabulary that had to be understood. One was art. Art, as he used it, was something dangerous. Marvin Major suspected that Jesse Fischer had suffered a mild infection of art, and had never entirely recovered. There was always the lingering possibility that the disease might flare up and take Jesse off – something that would be a tragedy, because Jesse Fischer had talent.

Talent was another key word. Mr Major revered talent. He liked to say that he abased himself before it. Without talent there would be no Hollywood. The Industry would die. Talent had to be wooed – and Mr Major gave his favourite stars fur coats and diamonds or, if they were male, gold pens, watches and engraved cigarette cases, when they finished a picture to his satisfaction.

Then there was realism. Realism was something European, like art. It wasn't American. It brought ugliness into movies where there ought to be beauty or entertainment. It brought darkness where there ought to be light. Sometimes art, realism and Communism went together, especially in the script-writing department. Mr Major hadn't been pleased with Jesse Fischer's performance in Washington. There was no point in getting legalistic in defending the rights of the unfriendly ten. Their politics might be their own business, but he knew the kinds of scripts those people would turn in if they were given a free hand.

And anyway, Hollywood had to show a clean face to the world. Not that he was a sentimentalist. He didn't want to make weepies – leave that to MGM. Tough stuff, punch-ups, shoot-outs and good clean murders were proper grist to the Hollywood mill. It was only that you had to draw a line between real life and pictures. People had to know this was entertainment. Pictures were not the real world and they shouldn't try to be. These weren't times for taking risks or sailing close to the wind. Did Mrs Tamworth know (she did but there wasn't a moment in which to say so) that Hollywood profits had slipped in the past two years from 90 million to 55 million? Attendances were down. Television was gaining ground. Anti-trust laws (unjust laws, Mr Major called them) were threatening to take distribution out of the hands of the studios. Was this a time to be defending a few Reds who were giving the place a bad name? No. It was a time to be seen ruthlessly and publicly pushing them out into the streets where they belonged so America would trust and feel safe with its greatest, most innovative industry.

While he said these things Mr Major moved about his office which was large enough to give him room to walk and wave his arms. Arlene wasn't called upon to answer. She wouldn't have answered – or not more than in the most neutral way – if she'd been invited. This was not a man to argue with. It was a phenomenon to be observed. It was a performance to be remembered even if, as she supposed, it was one he gave often. She felt privileged, she felt awed, she hugged herself, she stored it up.

Marvin Major didn't show a lot of respect for the writers he employed. When he bought a property, as it was called, or simply an idea to be worked up into a story, he usually assigned two writers to do a treatment. If they had trouble, he assigned a second pair, and sometimes, later, a third. The first pair weren't always told that the second had been engaged; the third pair might be called in to gut the best of what the first two had done, and add something of their own. When his writers complained Mr Major liked to quote an old joke about what Hollywood does to its writers. 'We treat you like dirt, ruin your best ideas, turn your characters into cardboard and sprinkle sugar over your dialogue – and what do you get for it? A *fortune!*'

He liked Arlene because she'd learned to write in the studio. She hadn't been spoiled by university creative writing courses or by literary magazines that were read only by the people who wrote for them. And she was good at her work. He told her the studio writers who complained most about what happened to their scripts were always the ones who couldn't survive as writers on the open market. Of course there were studio writers with talent. Those were the ones whose contracts were renewed, whose salaries climbed, and who occasionally even received the diamonds or engraved watches usually reserved for the stars. The rest, the ones inclined to be arty or difficult, came and went. Arlene was on a kind of undeclared probation. She knew that. But she also knew that Mr Major believed she had talent. So she found it hard not to like him; or anyway she found it easy to be tolerant of his extravagant manner, his loud mouth, and his habits of work.

He had a boyish love of story conferences. Sometimes he attended to take part in working an idea up into a plot. Other times he just listened. Often the conferences were held in his office where he could practise his golf shots up and down the carpet while listening to his team rolling ideas around. When he took part himself he became excited, shouting and inarticulate, but full of ideas, one in ten of which might be good and usable. At those times he stopped playing the studio boss. You were allowed to treat him as an equal – in fact you were required to. It was like a party game; or a party. You were encouraged to let your hair down, let your mind rove free, play with words, make jokes. Creative was one of Mr Major's positive words. You could be creative without being arty. There was a kind of electricity he generated. Everyone felt it.

But you had to learn that when the session was over, jackets were on, ties straightened, and the office returned to its usual order, Mr Major was once again boss of the show, ruler of the roost. Directors who had slapped his back exchanging jokes and insults with him returned to being at least respectful and more usually sycophantic. He would lay down the law about what had gone wrong with a picture and the director would say 'Of course Marvin. Yes. *Now* I see. Now it all becomes *clear.*' Marvin Major could raise his voice at anyone at any time around the studio; if you raised your voice back you might find yourself out on the street.

But he was no fool. He was inventive and clever; and Arlene admired the way he could keep the shifting plots of half a dozen current pictures in his head without confusing them. A director might change what a minor character did or said, because it worked out better that way during shooting, and Mr Major would say 'I thought we agreed . . .' He seldom forgot a detail.

His working principle was that they were there to tell stories. An idea was OK as a starting point; but if it couldn't be worked up into a story, there was no picture. 'Every picture tells a story,' he told Arlene; 'and if it doesn't, I don't want to hear about it.' And he was good at working out what scenes had to be done in what order so information was released at the right time. He was a good story-teller himself. He liked to tell them – bar-room stories – over his desk, while chewing on a cigar. Arlene thought they were mostly pretty awful; but she admitted he told them well.

At the end of a picture he liked everything to be cleared up – no obscurities, no loose ends. And he hated Method acting because you couldn't hear more than two thirds of what an actor was saying. 'Mystery and mumble' was how he character-ized most of the post-war pictures that were winning awards. 'What are these awards worth,' he asked Arlene. 'The only award I want is the one the American public gives me through the box office. Receipts. They're my Oscar. All the rest – it's chicken shit.'

When Arlene was involved in the writing of a script she was often called in before a scene was shot, and again afterwards to see the rushes. In the morning she would go down to the sound stage and sit with the director and the actors going over a scene – the director wearing a baseball cap or an eye-shade to keep the lights out of his eyes, the actors in costume, already made up. If there was a line an actor found difficult or awkward or unconvincing, they would talk about ways of changing it. Then, with a few lights on, the actors would try it out, deciding where to stand or how to move in relation to one another. When that was done the director called for full lighting, and shooting could begin.

Mr Major liked to find time to watch the rushes, especially if it was a scene in which one of his biggest stars was acting. Arlene tried to avoid sitting beside him because he was such an active viewer. If there was a fight scene he jumped about in his seat, fists clenched, making jabs at the air in front of him and grunting 'That's it. Hand it to him, boy. Lay waste to the bastard.' Emotional scenes made him active too. He would chuckle to himself and talk to the screen. 'Pour it on, darling. That's the stuff. Wring it out of them.'

No one was in doubt if he was pleased. As the lights went up in the projection room he would grin and wink to left and right. Getting up, pulling a cigar from his pocket, he would say 'Money in the bank,' and head for the door. If he wasn't pleased he didn't say anything. He went to his office and thought about it. When he'd decided what was wrong, the director was called in and told what had to be done to get it right.

One evening Jesse Fischer phoned Arlene at home. He said carefully, 'This is a business call.' Once that was established he went on, 'There's a sneak preview tonight. It's the Castile picture. I think you should be there.'

It wasn't Jesse's picture and it wasn't one she'd had a hand in scripting. She asked where it was to be screened.

'Only Marvin knows that. He keeps it secret. Doesn't like the trade papers to get wind of it. We leave from the studio.'

She began to say she hadn't eaten. He laughed. 'Why don't you let me pick you up? There's no point in taking two cars. We'll stop somewhere for a hamburger.'

Rocky wasn't sober. He wasn't drunk either, but she knew if she left him he would be. She also knew he wouldn't object to her going. By this hour he would be craving a drink, and to have her out of the house would leave him free. She felt guilty – but she wanted to go, and she said she would.

'I'll pick you up in twenty minutes,' Jesse said.

It was strange going back to the studio at night. The crowd of children and tourists that hung around the gates all day waiting to catch an autograph from a favourite star was gone. But the whole place hummed quietly, like a factory working night shift. There were lights in some of the offices. Lab workers were processing film shot that day. A red light outside one of the sound stages signalled that shooting was going on. The commissary was open. Two studio trucks loaded with palm trees and cardboard rocks painted grey and black went down towards the back lot.

They gathered in Mr Major's office – Jesse and Arlene, the

director, assistant director, two principal scriptwriters, the chief sound technician, someone from wardrobe, and a small group of assistants and secretaries who were to hand out and collect the cards on which the public were to be asked for comments.

Marvin Major gave them instructions. 'Remember we like to tell ourselves when we're working that it's going to be a great movie. That's because faith helps, even if it doesn't always work miracles. But then comes the time when we have to ask our masters – the public – what they think. And our job is to listen to what they say. That means what they say by their actions as well as in words. So everyone, please, remember what a sneak is all about. I'm not taking you on an outing. You're not there to see a picture. You're there to see an audience see a picture. Watch carefully. Notice everything. See how they react. Do they laugh at the jokes? Do they laugh when there's no joke, and if they do, what are they laughing at? When are they sitting still, glued to their seats, and when are they restless? Someone will be at the door to count any that leave. Let's hope they give us the thumbs up.'

He put his hand on Jesse's shoulder. 'I want you to turn your big brain on this one Jess. There's one hell of a bucket of money gone into it.' And to the group, 'OK friends. Let's hit the trail.'

The cars were lined up downstairs. They crowded in and went off in convoy. Once out in the street they were told where they were going. It was a little cinema in Westwood Village. As they pulled up outside Arlene looked up. Over its art deco curved entrance there was no picture title – just a big sign, 'Major Studio Preview Tonite.'

The picture was set in Castile in the fifteenth century. The hero, a nobleman and soldier, is betrothed to a rich man's daughter but falls in love with a peasant girl. He falls foul of the Inquisition, who torture his father to death and imprison his sister. He kills the villainous nobleman who has brought this about and escapes on a ship which turns out to be that of Cortés, setting out to conquer Mexico. In the New World the love between the nobleman and the peasant girl is able to flourish. But the villain, who is supposed to be dead, turns up

again as a messenger from Spain. He has recovered from what
appeared to be a fatal wound. He represents the continuing
power of the Inquisition and the Old Order. But the last scene
still has the soldier-hero and the peasant girl together. They
are advancing with the victorious army of Cortés, poised to
complete its conquest of the Aztecs.

As the curtains closed there was a modest ripple of applause.
No one had walked out. Marvin Major turned to look at Jesse.
'I think they liked it,' he said. But he didn't sound certain.

'We'll soon find out,' Jesse said.

Out in the foyer the audience were filling in their cards,
asking one another what they were writing. They were mostly
young. The studio people stood about awkwardly, trying not
to appear anxious. But as soon as the last cards were in they
began handing them around. 'Good.' 'OK.' 'Stinks.' 'Lovely
colour.' 'Good.' 'Very Good.' 'Not bad.' 'OK.' 'A bit boring.'
'Too long.' 'Inconclusive.'

'Inconclusive,' Jesse repeated. 'Let me see that.' And he took
the card and read the more detailed comments.

Taken altogether it hadn't been a bad audience response;
but not a good one either. This didn't look like a box-office
knock-over. Something was wrong. In the detailed comments
almost everyone seemed to want to give with one hand and
take away with the other. If they liked the stars they didn't like
the story. If they liked the story they didn't like the way it
ended. If they liked the colour and scenery they thought the
dialogue was too old-fashioned.

'We need these analysed in detail,' Marvin Major said when
they got back to the studio. 'I'll have an exact breakdown of
responses in the morning. I think we've got a picture here that
could make a good return on our investment, but there's
something wrong. We have to find out what it is.'

The studio was still humming faintly when Arlene and Jesse
came out. They got into his car and he drove out through the
studio gates and away. At an intersection he stopped. 'Are you
in a hurry to get back?'

She shook her head.

'Let's talk about the picture while it's still fresh.'

He drove slowly while they talked, gradually putting the picture together, almost scene by scene. They drove to San Fernando, to Van Nuys, to Beverly, to the ocean. More than an hour went by. They seemed to have a hold on the picture. Some of the things that were wrong were obvious. It was absurd to kill the villain – have him run through in a sword fight and seem to die – and then bring him back into the story so much later without warning and without more than a perfunctory explanation. It looked makeshift, and probably was, as if the writers had changed their minds and brought him back without revising earlier scenes. It might even have been done after shooting had begun. And what had happened to the hero's imprisoned sister, and to his beautiful fiancée? They were left back in Spain, abandoned by the narrative. Either the picture had to make more of them, or less.

'But if you fix all that up,' Arlene said – and she hesitated, looking out into the dark street as they cruised along.

'If you fixed it – what then?'

They were in Santa Monica now. 'Somewhere down here,' she said, 'there's a little all-night cocktail bar.'

They found it. 'Let's have a little all-night cocktail,' Jesse said.

The place was dimly lit. Through windows they could see the pier, and waves breaking. They were silent a long time, sipping their drinks.

Arlene asked, 'Did Mr Major do his double-up trick with the scriptwriters?'

'Two and then two more? Sure. It's the Marvin method.'

'That's the root of the problem. Yes. I can see it.' She shifted in her chair and looked at Jesse. 'It's like this. Team one thought of the New World. Capital N, capital W. Freedom from chains. Escape from the Inquisition and the oppression of class distinctions. Handsome nobleman and beautiful peasant girl find freedom in the Americas. Love flourishes under open skies. Right?'

'Right.'

'Now wheel in team two – and my God yes.' She laughed. 'Team one are simple American storytellers. Team two are intellectuals. They're thinking about truth and history and what happened to the Aztecs. Cortés as the destroyer of an ancient civilization. Remember how brutal he starts to seem towards the end? That's why some of the audience comments seem contradictory. Was Cortés a hero or a beast? They weren't sure.'

Jesse nodded. 'Go on. I'm with you.'

'Well, the end's not only inconclusive, as that smart guy wrote on his card – I mean not only inconclusive in the story sense. It's also ambiguous. That last scene, for example. They're marching forward together. But are they beginning something new and beautiful, or destroying something old and beautiful?'

'I guess both.'

'Sure, but . . .' She shifted about in her seat, impatient. 'To say that sounds OK. It sounds great. But it's more – you know, *high-brow* than . . .'

'Than the picture?'

'Yes. The picture's one of Marvin Major's simple stories. At the end it has to be one thing or the other. That second pair of writers must have brought in the stuff about the Aztecs, I guess because it's true. It's history. But it's no good where it is. That final march is meant to be glorious and it just isn't. It's confusing.'

He nodded, smiling. He was convinced.

'Well?'

He just went on smiling at her. She smiled back. She felt pleased with herself.

He said, 'Even your intellect has sex appeal.'

'I'm glad.'

'It must be because you spent your first twenty years walking upside down.'

'It doesn't work in every case.'

'Are you going to tell Marvin what's wrong with his picture?'

'I should find a way to tell him so he can say he thought of it himself.'

Jesse laughed. 'He'd love you for that.' As they were walking out to the street he said, 'Why tell him at all?'

She leaned against the car while he unlocked the door. 'Well if I don't, someone will. It might as well be me.'

Jesse shook his head. 'It's possible no one will put a finger on it so exactly. So many people involved – it needs a very clear head to unscramble the egg.'

'Surely . . .'

'You mean you've never seen a Hollywood movie that was confusing?'

'Oh sure. I've seen lots.'

'OK. So this could be another.'

'Is that what you want?'

'No. Not really. Although I never mind the thought of Marvin stewing in his own juice.' After they had driven a few blocks he said, 'There's a sort of rivalry between Marvin and me, but I guess I'm a company man.'

'Oh.' She shrugged. 'If I go to him – if you think I should – if you think he'll listen . . .'

'He'll listen.'

'It won't be for the company.'

'What then?'

'Ego, I guess. It's good to be clever – I mean, to be seen to be. And it's just possible I'm beginning to be ambitious.'

They drove up Pico and then along Sepulveda towards the hills. As they were climbing to Mulholland he said, 'Did you mean what you said about wanting to make love in the car?'

Her head was on his shoulder. 'Try me.'

He parked in their usual meeting place and they climbed into the back seat.

'Like college days,' Jesse said.

'In a car this size?'

'I guess not.'

It was a warm night but the leather of the seats, at least for a time, felt chill against bare flesh. Jesse had trouble getting out of his clothes in the confined space. He climbed out of the car to complete undressing. 'There's a rug in the trunk,' he said. She lay back on the seat and watched him moving about out there. His pale body seemed to glow in the dark. Then he was back in the car and they heaved about, laughing, finding a secure position, while the rug he tried to keep over them slipped away. Slowly the laughter turned into something different. Arlene smiled and groaned and closed her eyes and reached up to brace herself against whatever was solid back there behind her head. She had never felt such physical rapport as she did with Jesse. He had an uncanny sureness with her, and she felt confidence in herself as she responded. It had been, with him, like the discovery of a perfect self.

For a time they slept, awkwardly wrapped around one another. When they woke a steel grey light was pressing up behind the farthest mountains, and the valley in between was entirely filled with a mist so thick it looked as if you could step out and walk across it. They dressed and he drove her down into the mist of Sherman Oaks and stopped at her gate. 'Will you be OK?' he asked.

She nodded. 'He'll be out cold.'

They kissed and he drove away. She let herself in by the side door, took off her shoes, and tip-toed into the living-room. The curtains were open. The pale morning light was beginning to invade. Rocky was sitting in a chair. She bent forward, expecting his eyes to be shut. They were open. He was sober. 'Where have you been?' he asked.

She felt an awful sinking in her stomach. All the languidness of pleasure turned in an instant into a lassitude of apprehension. She readied herself to tell the truth. She feared it dreadfully, but she wanted it.

'Well,' she said. She sat down in the chair opposite and began to tell him how the evening had passed. She described it in detail. While she talked it was getting lighter. Perfectly still and perfectly sober, Rocky sat listening. All the time she meant to bring the narrative to its conclusion in the little gravelled place off Mulholland. But she stopped short of it. It needed Rocky to ask the question that must be on his mind – 'Are you and Jesse lovers?' – or maybe he would put it more brutally than that. When he asked, she would answer truthfully.

But he didn't ask. As it grew light she saw there were tears in his eyes. She went over and crouched beside him. 'What is it, Rocky?'

He shook his head. 'Nothing. Everything. It's just that we came here so I could be in pictures and I'm not in pictures and you are. It feels like some kind of bad joke.'

They woke late that morning. The day was hot and still. She made tea and toast – a big pot of tea and toast in stacks, and they ate at the little iron table under the awning, watching jays and humming birds come and go among the flowers on the bank. They didn't talk. Rocky's hands shook as he lifted his tea cup.

She called the studio and said she wouldn't be in until the afternoon. She spoke to Mr Major's secretary and said she'd had some thoughts about the Castile picture – probably worthless, but she wondered whether he would like to hear them. Five minutes later the secretary called back to say that he would. It was agreed she would come to his office at five.

A couple of minutes before five that afternoon Arlene was outside Marvin Major's office. She expected what she liked to call Marvin's tycoon foreplay. He would be half an hour late. He would be fulsome and self-deprecating making his apologies. That way his authority and his charm were simultaneously registered.

But she was wrong. Exactly at five his secretary appeared at the outer office. Arlene was called in. Mr Major was on the phone. He put his hand over the mouthpiece. 'I'll be right with you Arlene.' And he waved her towards a chair.

'Sure I know your problem,' he said into the phone. 'You don't have to love her Jasper. Just make sure the public does.'

He listened. The little voice out of the instrument rattled on. He smiled at Arlene and rolled his eyes towards the ceiling in a sign of exasperation.

'Sure I'll tell you what to do,' he said. 'Don't give her too much dialogue. Keep it tight. Don't give her anything she can't handle. And cut to her face.'

He listened. 'Cut to her face,' he repeated. 'What are we paying for? Listen. Have her put on that injured innocence stuff. You know how she does it. "Who, *me?*"' He imitated the star's voice and laughed.

The little voice answered. It didn't sound quite so agitated.

'She may not be able to act,' Mr Major said. 'But she can react. She's great at that. You can make it work, boy. Just give me a dozen reels, a couple of songs, a couple of dance numbers, a bit of conflict between her and Gary, and some exotic backgrounds. That's all I ask. And you know why? Because that's all the public asks. You know that. They love her.'

There was a brief reply.

'That's my boy. You can do it sweetheart. You're the one around this place who can do it. OK? Go to it. We'll talk about a budget on Friday.'

He hung up. 'Troubles, troubles,' he said to Arlene. 'Now this Castile picture. Thanks for dropping by, Arlene. This one's a headache. It's a puzzle.'

He told her he'd had the details on the cards analysed. They were as confusing as they'd seemed last evening – full of contradictions. All you could say for certain was that reactions were mixed and there was no clear pattern. It was disappointing. There were a few things obviously needed tightening up, but no certainty that they would make audience responses significantly better.

Driving to the studio Arlene had planned an exchange in which she would gradually lead Marvin Major towards her own conclusions about the picture while leaving him free, if his ego required it, to claim he'd thought it all out for himself. Now, as they talked, she dropped that idea. She simply put to him her thoughts of the previous evening. He listened, eyes down, using a paper knife to roll an unlighted cigar around on the blotter pad in front of him. When she'd finished he went on sitting, silent. Finally he looked up and said, 'Rewriting's no problem. It's re-shooting. That costs. How far back in the picture would we have to go?'

Arlene thought about it. 'I need to see it again. I think all it needs is some cuts and then a rewrite and reshoot of the last ten minutes or so. And the scene where the villain gets killed has to be sorted out.'

'What gets cut?'

'Most of the stuff about the Aztecs. At this stage you've just got to choose between history and your picture. It's either that or start again from scratch.'

Mr Major smiled and began to light the cigar. 'Will you do the repairs for me?'

She was surprised but she didn't show it. She said she would.

# 15

It was 1949 and getting close to Christmas in Hollywood. It was 1949 and getting close to Christmas everywhere in the world. Arlene was driving towards the studio late on a Saturday morning. Not directly towards it. She was early for the lunch, and undecided. She drove towards it, then she drove away. She cruised in her car, waiting for her feelings to settle. Gradually she was getting closer, but there was still time to change her mind.

On Hollywood Boulevard there were tin Christmas trees, fifteen feet high, four to each intersection, like white cardboard cutouts. Everywhere tinsel icicles and cotton wool snowflakes resisted the sun. There were small pines in tubs, decorated with coloured balls. Coloured lights climbed in wires into tall dusty palms. Today there were people sitting in the sun in parks and down on Santa Monica Beach. All this was familiar. It was much like Christmas at home. But this was the northern hemisphere. Here it seemed wrong. It seemed dingy. She remembered the little German who called Los Angeles 'Tahiti in Metropolitan form'.

Having drifted all the way down to the ocean she made her way back now through Brentwood – Rolls-Royce and Bentley country – and Beverly Hills, where Lincolns and Cadillacs seemed to be favoured. There were still open spaces, surprising barren hills, empty glens, and green-brown canyons, but everywhere houses were being built, whole gardens planted, complete with trees and green lawns. If the Marzipan Kingdom was in danger of collapsing, as people said, there was no sign of it here.

By this roundabout route she came finally to the studio. She parked and went straight to sound stage number 14 where there was to be a lunch to celebrate completion of the Castile picture, *The Farthest World*. Inside, tables were set up under lights. A half-built set looked like some kind of prehistoric fortification. Builders were hammering a few last nails and gathering up their tools to make way for the lunch. People were milling around finding their places at the tables. Arlene found her name tag. It was beside Jesse Fischer's. She picked it up, did a cool swap with a name at another table, and sat down. No one appeared to notice. Waiters were pouring wine into glasses and putting out the first course, little strips of smoked pink salmon with brown bread, parsley and a round of caviar.

Most people were in their places when Marvin Major came in surrounded by his senior executives. Arlene thought it looked like the entrance of a Chicago gangster and his cohorts. Only Jesse Fischer looked out of place. It wasn't that he was more brilliantly intelligent – they were all clever in their way; but there was a kind of sensitivity about Jesse that showed in his lean face and alert eyes. He was looking around the tables. When he found her he smiled and winked. She returned the smile, but from a great way off, and she thought she saw him register that she was feeling distant, guarded.

As soon as they were all settled Mr Major stood up. Someone banged a fork on a wine-glass. Everyone stopped talking and turned to listen. He had a sheaf of papers in his hand. 'We're here to celebrate the completion of another great picture. I have here' – he waved the sheaf – 'first week returns from around the country. It's good news. All good. Box offices don't lie and they're telling us to drink up and have a good time.'

There was applause. Mr Major held up his hand. He read some of the returns from places far and wide – Denver, Seattle, Memphis, Birmingham, Wilmington, Akron, Tampa, Dayton, Atlantic City.

'Those are random samples,' he said. 'It's the same all over.'

There was another round of applause. 'Now you don't want speeches from me,' he said. 'You get enough of those. I'm here to say thanks to every one of you who worked on the picture.

And on the table in front of you there's a small token of my personal gratitude.'

There was a small, brightly-wrapped package by each side-plate – those for men wrapped in blue, those for women in pink. Arlene's was blue.

'But in addition,' Mr Major was continuing, 'I have to say just a few very special thankyous. First to our stars, Ty and Jean.' Everyone applauded. Mr Major walked around the table and handed each of them a special gift, shaking Ty's hand across the table, and giving Jean a generous embrace.

'Then there's something for our director, Henry, and our incomparable cameraman, Lee . . .'

As he went through the names he handed each person a gift.

'Finally I have something here for the little lady who was first to tell me what was wrong after we'd seen the sneak. You were all beating about the bush. It took Arlene to tell me what was needed – and then to get on and fix it.'

He'd reached her table by now. She took her present, and her hug, and waved a hand at the applause that came with them. She found it hard to smile. She wasn't in the right mood for all this.

She unwrapped the package while the people round about watched. Jesse Fischer came over to pat her back. Inside the wrapping she found a gold powder compact inscribed with 'Arlene' in italic engraving, and under it 'Thanks a Million. M.M.' She passed it around the table for people to admire.

'You're supposed to be at my table,' Jesse said.

She smiled without meeting his eye. 'Must have been some mistake.'

When it was over and Arlene came out into the sunlight, Jesse was waiting. He fell into step with her. 'Couldn't we go back the other way,' he suggested. 'We can't talk here.'

She turned with him and walked down towards the back lot. She waited for him to speak. He didn't seem to know how to begin. 'Something's wrong,' he said at last. 'You're avoiding me.'

'Christmas. I think it makes me homesick. I start to hate Los Angeles.'

'It doesn't seem real, does it.'

'Oh . . .' She shrugged. 'I know you're used to snow. It's not that. Where I come from we go to the beach at Christmas. It's not unreal. It's . . . Well, it doesn't matter what it is. I guess the trouble is me, not it.'

'You're depressed.'

'I'm tired. Maybe depressed too. Yes, probably.'

'Is Rocky drinking again?'

'That's none of your business.'

'I'm sorry. I'm concerned for you.'

'Don't be.'

'Arlene . . .' His voice sounded helpless and he fell silent. They were walking now through a familiar back lot street. It was familiar not because Arlene came down here often, but because it had been the scene of so many shots in so many movies. The buildings were what she thought might be called brownstones in New York, though she'd never set foot in that city. They were nothing like the buildings she'd got used to in Los Angeles. Steps ran up to the entrance of each, and down to a basement. Above the street there were three levels of windows. The façades were of brick or of stone, but if you looked closely you saw the stone wasn't real. There were also street lamps and telephone kiosks, mail boxes and public benches. There were signs in shop windows advertising bargains. In fact the street was 'dressed' for a contemporary American movie. In ten days' time it was scheduled to be redone as a street in Paris. It looked real except that there was not a person or a car in sight. And if you looked up you saw above the rooftops, scaffolding and railtracks for cameras and camera-crews.

The city streets came to an end. In a moment they found themselves in a village square. There was a courthouse, a post-office, some shops, some wooden frame-houses with verandahs and white picket fences and flower gardens. An oak tree grew in the middle of the square. There was a war memorial. The grass was being watered.

'Let's sit down,' Jesse said. He sat on a park bench and patted the space beside him. She sat.

'Tell me what's the matter.'

'I don't know.'

'Is it your work?'

She was silent, staring at the small-town scene. It reminded her of movies that had an awful artificial sweetness about them. 'I'm like this set. Fake.'

He tried to take her hand.

'All-purpose,' she said. 'Whatever's called for, Arlene's it. Even the name's fake.'

'Maybe you should get yourself an analyst.'

'Jesus.' She stood up and walked away so briskly she'd left the little town square behind before he caught up with her. 'I might be taking American citizenship,' she said, 'but I'm not an American. I'll never be an American.'

He looked offended. 'What does that mean?'

She shook her head and didn't answer. She felt tears welling up. She wished he would go away.

They came to a small forest and began to walk along a path that went through it, overhung by tall trees. Suitably worked on, these woods could be, and probably had been, Robin Hood's Sherwood Forest or Tarzan's jungle.

Jesse said, 'You should be celebrating. Marvin gives you credit for saving his picture. When a screenwriter gets a gift like that along with the stars . . .'

She pulled the compact out of her handbag and looked at it. There was the false name, engraved in the gold curve of the lid. 'Arlene.' And then that awful 'Thanks a Million. M.M.' She tossed it against the trunk of a tree. It broke open and fell, the puff fluttering behind it. Jesse dropped back and scrabbled in the grass for it. She could see him dusting it off but she kept walking. He caught up and held it out to her. She ignored it.

'It's gold,' he said, but she walked on.

'You're being hysterical.'

'Yes,' she said. 'It's my privilege as a woman. If you don't like it, get yourself a man.'

'Arlene . . .'

She didn't answer. She just walked on silently. It helped

her feel cool and independent. Jesse padded along beside her, resolute but silent.

'I love you,' he said, but she walked on as if she hadn't heard. They came out of the forest. They were walking back now along a studio street between rows of sound stages. She knew what he wanted. He wanted her to go with him to their room at the Beverly Hills Hotel, but he was too upset and uncertain to ask. In the car park he held the door of her car while she got in. She shut the door and wound down the window. He said, 'It's not all over is it?'

She pressed the starter. 'Where are you going for Christmas, Jesse?'

He blinked, looked away up into the near hills. He seemed so confused she felt sorry for him — but sorry from a great distance. 'I guess Malibu,' he said.

'With the family?'

He nodded.

She put the car into gear and began to move away. He reached in and touched her shoulder. 'Arlene, wait.'

She stopped. Before he'd decided what he wanted to say she said, 'Have I told you how much I hate your wife's paintings?'

His face set hard.

'And your children's names. How could you call three kids Danny, Delores and Doug?'

He took it grimly, saying nothing.

She let out the clutch slowly and moved away from him. As she turned to go through the studio gates she could see him still standing where she'd left him.

Next day, Sunday, she drove with Rocky to the house of their friends in the Hollywood Hills. Moss McConey was working now as a scriptwriter at MGM. His novel was put aside, but at the studio he had nothing much to do except read through screenplays and watch old movies made from them. This way he was supposed to be learning his craft. He shared a little office high up in the Irving Thalberg building which was referred to around the studio as the Iron Lung. He was full of gossip, frustration and anger. Lee McConey and Baby Daniels had been taken on temporarily in the chorus line of a musical in which Esther Williams was the star. They said they were learning to sing under water, just in case. Fred Daniels was still building sets. As a group they were prospering.

That Sunday there were just the six of them. The sunshine of the previous day had gone, there was a big wind in the trees, the temperature dropped and the sky darkened as the day went on. When they went outside to throw peanuts up for the jays, there was no sign of them.

The upper branches of the gum trees were heaving about. Long strips of bark trailed out in the gusts that raced up the hillslope. Then the wind seemed to ease just a little, and heavy rain began to fall. Arlene was excited. Rain. It was what she missed most. She wanted them all to go out in it and for a time they did, dressed in old oil-skins and sou'westers and carrying umbrellas they couldn't use because the gusts blew them inside out. They thought they were heading for Griffiths Park, but as the storm grew more violent they gave up and turned back towards the house. By now it was cold, and strangely dark. Fred and Moss made up the fire, and they sat around it drinking beer.

'Now is the winter of our discontent,' Moss said.

'Are we discontented?' Rocky asked.

'Moss is,' Lee said. 'He used to grumble that the studios didn't engage real writing talent. Now he's in there, he's still grumbling.'

Moss said, 'Inside MGM. It's my new vision of America. Where would you rather be? Inside the Iron Lung, or behind the Iron Curtain? What a choice.'

'It's not a choice anyone has to make,' Arlene said. 'But if anyone did . . .'

'I read old scripts and watch old movies and my novel sits at home pining for me.'

'Your novel can wait,' Lee said.

Arlene thought none of them quite believed in Moss's novel, though they all tried to be good about it.

'D'you know what my contract says? I can quote it, word for word. "The Author" – that's me – "The Author agrees that all material composed, submitted and/or interpolated by the

Author hereunder shall automatically become the property of the Producer, who, for this purpose, shall be deemed the author thereof."'

Arlene nodded. 'It's pretty comprehensive, isn't it.'

'You better save your best shots for your novel,' Baby said. 'Give 'em your cast-offs.'

Moss shook his head. 'Wouldn't do, Baby. If I don't get a screen credit in six months, the contract lapses.'

The rain was heavy. Gusts of wind slapped sheets of it against the sloping panels of glass. Arlene caught glimpses of the upper branches of a eucalypt whipping back and forth across a slate sky. 'Sometimes I feel I'd like to go home,' she said. 'It's hard here. But the rewards . . .'

'Oh sure.' Moss sighed. 'And every man has his price. So we let ourselves be pushed around by studio bosses who probably left school at twelve. Give me a happy ending. The public won't wear this. Remember the Hays Office. Cut this – it's too clever. I know I haven't started writing for them yet, but I hear that crap every day over there.'

'It doesn't have to be that bad,' Arlene said.

'You've been lucky,' Fred said. 'You've worked with Jesse Fischer.'

'I work for Marvin Major.'

'What's so good about Jesse Fischer?' Moss asked.

'Well he's some kind of liberal, isn't he,' Fred said.

'A liberal in Washington and a signatory to the Waldorf Astoria Declaration in New York. He'll have the black-list pinned up inside his skull, like all the rest of them.'

Arlene didn't want to defend Jesse. She wasn't even sure he deserved defending. But she allowed herself to say, 'He doesn't like the black-list any more than you do.'

'I'm sure he weeps crocodile tears over it. All the producers do.' Moss's face brightened. 'That reminds me of a story I heard about one of MGM's old stars when Thalberg died. I've forgotten which one. It might have been John Gilbert. Someone sees him weeping after the funeral. They say, "John, baby, I've never seen you weep like this." The star says "This is nothing. You should have seen me at the graveside."'

147

It was dark when they left. Rocky was happily, maudlinly drunk. Arlene drove. The rain was so heavy she had to lean forward catching glimpses of the road as the wipers swept the windshield clear for a moment. Brown earth was washing from gardens into the street. Branches were falling from trees. Banks were slipping. Rocky sang 'Show me the way to go home', his voice cracking into a falsetto.

Down Woodcliff and along Merivale it was the same. The gutters were rivers. The wind tossed trees about, wrecking gardens.

When they got home Arlene went out on to the patio at the back. Water cascaded down the bank to the lawn and on around the sides of the house to the street. Here and there loose soil was slipping towards the terraces. It was all so fresh and wild she felt excited. She went back indoors. Rocky had a glass in one hand and a bottle of bourbon in the other. She went up to him and held out her hand for him to give it to her. He smiled, touching the point of her nose with the lip of the bottle. 'Miss Liberty Bell,' he said.

'What does that mean?'

'Free country. Free man. Free drink. Have one.'

She turned away. She couldn't be bothered arguing with him. She went into the kitchen and began preparing a meal which she knew only she would eat.

Later that evening when the bourbon had taken Rocky off into a silence that might have been sleep, stupor, or death, she phoned Jesse at home. A maid answered. 'Who's calling, please?' she asked.

Arlene told her. Jesse came to the phone. 'I'm sorry to call you at home. I know I shouldn't. Can you pretend it's something urgent about a script?'

He said he could. He sounded nervous, guarded.

'I just wanted to tell you I'm sorry. I'm a bitch. I love you.'

He said, 'Can I check on that and call you later this evening?'

She laughed quietly. 'If you're not careful you'll win an Oscar. Yes. Call me when the coast's clear.'

It was almost midnight when the phone rang. He said, 'I'm

sorry I couldn't talk. I'm glad you called. I was feeling pretty slugged.'

'I roughed you up. I'm a bully. I'm sorry.'

'I deserve it.'

'You don't deserve it. You're the nicest thing in my life.'

'And you're the nicest in mine.'

'It's just that you're not in it enough.'

'In what?'

'In my life, dummy.'

'I know. It's hard.'

'And I don't believe I'm the nicest in yours.'

'You are.'

'Am I?'

'Of course.'

'Really?'

'Really and absolutely truly.'

'That sounds pretty good.'

'It is.'

'And I don't hate your wife's paintings.'

'Oh you're allowed to. They're not everyone's cup of tea.'

'They're lovely, Jess. Lovely colours. I'm just jealous.'

'Don't be.'

'I am.'

'Well stop. You've no grounds.'

'Sweetheart I have the best grounds in the world. She's the one you're married to. Remember?'

'And you're married to Rocky.'

'I know. Aren't you lucky.'

'You're not getting out the golden gloves again are you?'

'Sorry sweetheart. Goodnight. I love you.'

'I love you too.'

'Oh and Jess.'

'What?'

'I love your children's names. They're cute. That was silly and bitchy.'

'Stop apologizing.'

'Jess.'

'What?'

'Why don't you drive over here and fuck me.'

'D'you think I should?'

'Probably not. But I wish you would.'

'What about Rocky?'

'Out cold.'

There was a long pause. She held her breath. She thought in a sudden rush, if he says no that's the end.

'I'll be right over.'

She hung up and went to the door to look out. The storm was still raging. If he would come in this, she thought, he must love me.

She went and stood close to where Rocky was lying. In the pauses between gusts she could just hear his whistling breath. She closed the door on that room and turned on the outside light.

# 16

Auckland is a harbour city. It seems right to sail in and out of it, which is what we used to do, those of us who travelled, when I was young. My grandfather was a sea captain. When he gave up sailing he managed to build his house, which my parents inherited, out of sight of the sea. You looked from the kitchen windows towards Mt Albert and beyond to the Waitakere Ranges. From the front rooms and bedrooms you looked to Mt Eden and One Tree Hill. And from the back garden you could see what was left of Three Kings. But of course if you climbed to the top of any one of those volcanic hills you saw both harbours – the Waitemata and the Manukau. You got a sense of how it was that the weather – different weathers – seemed to sweep across the isthmus and vanish out to sea on the other side.

The boy who had been hooked on Keats became in due course a student at what was then the Auckland University College. He graduated, married a fellow-student, Marion, and won a scholarship that would allow him to do post-graduate work at a university in England. By that time his grandmother was dead, his father politically defunct, and his mother declining into permanent depression. In New Zealand there was still no television – everyone 'went to the pictures' as faithfully as ever. But it seemed Edie's career as an actress had ended as soon as it began. After her appearance as the body on the beach no one ever reported seeing her again.

So Marion and I sailed out of Auckland harbour, glad on the whole to be leaving it behind. Three days' sailing brought us to Australia. After Sydney came Melbourne, Adelaide, Perth – the whole southern sweep of the continent – followed by Ceylon, Aden, the Suez Canal, the Mediterranean, Naples, Marseilles. And after five weeks, that place the voices had come from in childhood. London. Years later when we returned it was by way of the Panama Canal. We had circumnavigated the globe. I had a PhD. I'd written my first book, *The Keatsian Poetic*. We hadn't set foot in America.

When we sailed out next we had our first child with us; and the time after, we had three. Perhaps we'd made a mistake. We'd bought a little house, as you could in those days, on Milford Beach. From our front windows we could watch the ships sail in and out past Rangitoto lighthouse. Sooner or later we had to admit to one another that we were spending more and more time staring out to sea.

In those days I had an exportable talent. It was easy to up-stakes and go. But we never sold the house. So we would find ourselves somewhere in the world dreaming about the little house on Milford Beach.

I didn't avoid America entirely. Once, in the early sixties, I was invited to a conference in New York. An airfare was offered. In those days there were no jets in and out of Auckland. You flew by turbo-prop to Fiji and picked up the Qantas flight through Nadi to San Francisco. Then it was on to New York for three weeks, and home by the same route. Did it cross my mind, landing in San Francisco, that I was setting foot in what had probably become my sister's home State? I must have thought of it. But next time we travelled it was once again by sea.

But that ship did take us through Panama and up the American east coast. Poking the aerial of my radio through the porthole I kept picking up Donald McLean singing 'Bye-bye Miss America Pie'. It was in the early seventies, airfares were beginning to compete with the cost of travel by sea, and I was getting tired of spending weeks rocking in a deckchair feeling vaguely unwell. When we came back that time it was by air. The route was London – Los Angeles – Tahiti – Auckland, and there was the question of an overnight stop. We decided against it. We spent a few exhausted hours in and around Los Angeles airport soothing the frayed nerves of our children, and boarded the jet for Auckland. But I'd seen Los Angeles. I'd smelled that peculiar smog-smell that hangs in the air and seems to loiter in those vast wide empty silent corridors of its hotels. I'd seen the palm-heads in long lines, and the big sun in an orange sky, and the cruising limos that move more like ships than like cars. I didn't like or dislike it. I simply felt its distinctness, its insidiously familiar strangeness, and got on my plane.

But now travel seemed to accelerate. I was invited abroad more often. I flew back and forth to conferences, or on leave, sometimes with family, sometimes alone. I tried going westward through Singapore and what Europe calls the East, but that seemed slow and laborious compared to the route over the States. So I stopped often at Los Angeles; but I didn't get to know it. I stayed usually one night at a hotel close to the airport.

Looking back I can't decide whether I was avoiding Edie's city, or the United States, or both. Maybe it was sometimes one, sometimes the other. Maybe it was neither. But if there was a pattern, it was a pattern of avoidance.

Of course I was still the Hippo's child and I went on being angry about American foreign policy and New Zealand's entanglement in it. That may even partly explain why England and Europe became so important to me. London especially felt like a second home. It was a place that welcomed me, that used and rewarded my talents, that gave me warm friends and clever colleagues. But it wasn't home. Home was Auckland city, and the little bungalow (getting bigger as we pushed out walls and built upstairs extensions) on Milford Beach, and the ships, mostly tankers and container ships now, sailing in and out of the Hauraki Gulf.

So I overflew the United States. I flew in and out of what I imagined to be Edie's city, which by an irony was officially designated a Sister City to Auckland. I got to know the airport hotels – the Hacienda, the Marriot, the Airport Hilton and Towers, the Sheraton Plaza la Reina, the Amfac. I sometimes took a bus into town on a route that passed through oilfields, the heads of the black pumps cranking up and down across brown hills and gullies, looking like iron horses. I found art galleries and a library, and a Spanish market. Once, tired from walking, I strolled into what appeared to be a perfectly ordinary movie theatre. I didn't care what was showing. I just wanted to sit down and rest. What I saw, in full colour and hugely inflated on the big screen, was my first X-rated movie.

Los Angeles was king-size hotel beds, and strange silences after thirteen hours of the rumble of jet engines. It was palm trees and smog. It was the diners I liked to find in the mornings, away from the hotels, where your coffee cup and ice water glass were filled as often as you emptied them, and you could order yoghurt and granola and rye toast and berry jam, or bacon and hash and eggs, or all of those things, and the Hispanic or black waitress was always charming and obliging. It was those oil wells and that X-rated movie. It was some beautiful modern paintings. It was a downtown eruption of fantastic skyscrapers that seemed to grow out of nothing, so you came very suddenly to the end of what felt like a great city, and thereafter the streets stretched away in all directions, dingy and vaguely threatening. I never thought of going to Hollywood, though bus tours were offered. I avoided Disneyland, which so many people came exclusively to visit.

Did I think about Edie? I must have, but I don't recall that I did. She inhabited a Hollywood of the mind. She was as far away as ever. I knew, but couldn't imagine, that it might be possible, if only I had the right information, to get into a taxi, give an address, and, at some considerable expense because the city covered such a vast area, arrive at her door. But I lacked that information. And after all, she might not be there. She might be nowhere. She might be dead.

Deaths made us think of her – deaths and weddings, those family occasions which brought us together and reminded us of her absence. It was difficult to believe, as the years went by, that we'd really seen our sister in those two old black-and-whites of the 1940s. And I think gradually, inevitably, and without always acknowledging it, we all came to think of her negatively. We felt rejected by Edie and we rejected her in return. We blamed her for the bad things that had happened in the family. I remember Ellie, after our mother's funeral, saying Edie had caused her death. I thought Ellie was overstating it. But it was true our mother had never recovered from the shock. She'd passed through her years of hysteria into a long slow decline, a depression from which nothing and no one seemed able to rescue her. She died of a broken heart was how Ellie put it; but when I remembered how little Edie and our mother had seemed to like one another, I thought there must have been at least some guilt mixed up in the heartbreak. And in any case, how could we know that her mental, and finally physical, health wouldn't have followed exactly the same downward curve towards extinction without benefit of Edie's absence?

As our mother quietened down during those final years of her life, so did the Hippo. As she grew more depressed, so did he. When she died he seemed inconsolable. He sat around at home listening to the radio, reading newspapers, smoking. He said he was waiting to die and I thought he wasn't going to have to wait long. Each time we visited he seemed worse. He perked up at seeing our children, or Ellie's, or Cassie's. Then he would sink back into silence and despondency.

But the wait went on too long. He got tired of waiting and decided to live again. He'd long since shaken off all political ambition and that helped to liberate him. He went back to being the fire-eating leftist he must have been in his youth. A paper tiger was how he described himself, but at least the paper was red. The Vietnam War gave him his object in life. He read everything there was to read about it. He knew more about it than anyone I met then or have met since. There was nothing anyone could say in defence of the American intervention there, or about New Zealand's contribution of troops, that he couldn't answer. He predicted always (I never believed him) that the Americans would be driven out. He waited for the day, but he didn't live to see it. In 1970 the American Vice President, Spiro Agnew (he was the one forced to resign even before Nixon went) visited Auckland. My dear old father joined the protest outside the Hotel Intercontinental. I'm told he was carrying a Viet Cong flag on a bamboo pole. The crowd was huge, the violence considerable. When it was over he was found clinging to the palings of Old Government House across the street. He was thought to be drunk, but he'd had a heart attack. In the ambulance on the way to Auckland Hospital he was muttering 'Make love, not war.' It was a slogan of the peace movement of that time, but when I think of the history of the Hippo's relations with our mother I can't help feeling that, as last words go, they were unusually appropriate.

So there was another funeral without Edie, and that seemed to close the book. My life went on as before. I travelled, and returned, and travelled again. Our children were growing up. My first book on Keats was followed by a second, *Keats and Belladonna*, much better, I thought, and less successful.

I can't say how or when it came to me that it was time to go looking for Edie. I suppose it must have had something to do with the passage of time. I reached a point where the painful past was so far off I could turn and look back at it. It was distant enough even to have about it a certain romantic glow. The decision didn't arrive in a blinding flash. It was just a thought that came to me from time to time, took root, and grew. Passing through Los Angeles all those times and not even enquiring about Edie seemed wrong, as if I'd been guilty of cowardice.

So when my next invitation to travel came I made plans to stop at Los Angeles on the way. I wrote to a Professor I knew there, a Keats expert at the UCLA. I said I would be passing through on my way to London, that I could stop off for a week or ten days, and if it would be of use to him I could give a few lectures to his classes on Romantic poetry. The Professor's name was Walt Ambrose. He replied offering a fee and saying he would put me up at his house.

Marion approved. She'd heard so much about the sister

who disappeared she thought it was time the mystery was explored. But when Ellie was told she pulled a long face and said, 'Why dig up the past? You must be some kind of masochist.'

# 17

Monday morning. Arlene working on a script. Or rather, on a treatment – it hadn't reached the stage of being a script. It was Marvin Major's idea and she was having trouble with it. I'm not a writer, she told herself. But she'd proved that wasn't true. When the idea was right – at least when it was right for her – her work was good. She was trying not to admit to herself that there was something wrong with the idea. She had to believe it had possibilities or she would get nowhere.

That morning she'd waited up on Mulholland Drive, but Jesse hadn't come. Now she didn't know whether he was in his office or at home. She didn't like to call and ask, but not knowing made her agitated and took her mind away from her work.

Marvin Major's idea was that they should do a picture about modern-day immigrants to America. He wanted something (he said) that would be a smack in the mouth for people who said Hollywood didn't make pictures extolling the American way of life. It would show these poor refugee folk escaping from poverty, disease, political repression, war, and coming to peace, plenty, and liberty. He wanted Arlene to do it because he was pleased with the work she'd done for him. And also because although she wasn't, as he put it, one of those 'schnooks' whose lingo sounded as if it came through a soup-strainer, she had come from another country to work in Hollywood. 'America has open arms and a big heart,' he said. 'That's what you've learned, isn't it? That's what they've learned. And that's what we're going to show.'

It was all very well for Marvin Major to assume that she felt as those immigrants felt. It wasn't so simple. And the more she thought about it the more she wondered whether it was simple for the schnooks either. She was more like them than she'd supposed. She too was a refugee of sorts. Her battlegrounds had been domestic and familial, but conflict was what she'd escaped from. And it was true – she'd found work, money, even a sort of welcome. But she didn't go around feeling grateful. Maybe she owed gratitude, but to whom apart from Jesse Fischer, who hardly seemed to her to personify the United States? In so far as she could think of the United States as a single identity she didn't like it much. At home it thought too well of itself; abroad it bullied and cajoled.

But those were negative thoughts. They wouldn't help her get her work done, and Arlene wanted to succeed. So as best she could she pushed them to the back of her mind. She thought of sweet old schnooks, and eager young schnooks, full of gratitude, glad to have left the bad old world behind. The trouble was she didn't believe in them; or if she began to believe in them, they began to have feelings and thoughts that didn't suit Marvin Major's plan. They began to show signs of homesickness for the bad old world. They began to be critical of the new – to feel that American society was harsh and raw and thin and soulless. Was that what she herself thought? The work was forcing her to look into herself and ask questions she would have preferred to leave unanswered. No immigrant could be fair to his new country. No new country could be fair to an immigrant. There was a story in that, but it wasn't the story Mr Major wanted her to tell.

She walked around her little office straightening the pictures. They were old costume and set designs, some from Marvin Major pictures, others that had been brought in by a woman who'd come over to them from Paramount. There was one that said 'Costume for Miss Lamarr.' It was from De Mille's *Samson and Delilah*. The seated figure wore a blue cloak with a red lining. Her bikini–bra and the thong around her waist were in fine stripes of red and silver. Her skirt was blue, very short at the front and long at the back. She wore gold sandals and a jewelled arm-band.

Arlene went to the window. Outside there was a dust-haze

blowing around the palm-heads. It was desert weather that came down from the mountains and refused to take seriously the gardens and sprinklers of Los Angeles. For the moment the ocean wasn't doing its job. No contrary flow of moist air was coming up to meet the dry air coming down.

She tried to think of Samson and Delilah as immigrants to America. It was no good. One cliché turned into another. Samson became a cowboy, or a prize-fighter, Delilah a bar-maid, his girlfriend. They didn't seem like immigrants. They seemed like good Americans. That was because she'd seen the movie. Victor Mature was Samson. All she could remember was that after Samson had killed the lion single-handed and without weapons, Delilah, excited, impressed, and won over from a recent sulk, had cupped her hands over Mature's big shoulder and batted her eyelids at him – at which he flexed his muscles, shrugging her off, and sneered, 'One cat at a time.'

Oh God! This was no good. Every picture was a new picture. It didn't have to be bad because so many others had been. And it didn't have to be bad because the assignment was difficult. There must always be a way out.

She was standing at the window looking down at the dingy street running away from the writers' building between rows of sound stages. Someone with a crew-cut was riding one of the studio bicycles over towards the commissary. The cut, and the shape of the head, reminded her of Bert Brecht. That was what she needed. Not an abstract 'schnook', a projection of Mr Major's idea, but a real one – not to be identified, but kept in the secret recesses of the mind as the model and the measure you went back to. Could she imagine Bert Brecht doing or saying this or that? If yes, then OK. If no, then think again. And alongside the immigrant character, two representative Americans – why not Bogart and Bacall? – again as a kind of secret measure, a way to project character and keep it consistent.

She felt she'd made a huge leap towards something that might be possible. She remembered Brecht telling her he was Charles Laughton's tailor. She'd been puzzled later to find he was a playwright. But what he'd said made sense. What was the use of being a playwright if no one knew your name? 'I'm a playwright.' 'Oh I'm sorry, I didn't recognize your name. What plays have you had staged?' 'Well – in America, none. Not yet. But I'm hopeful . . .' 'So where are your plays performed?' 'Well – they used to be performed in Germany. That's where I come from. But not any more. They're banned.' 'Banned! How interesting. Why is that?' . . . And so on. He must have had so many conversations like that. So instead, he told her he was Laughton's tailor. It was perfect. His words were the clothing the actor went forth in. And in fact for a long time many people believed Laughton had written *Galileo* as well as acted in it.

No one in Hollywood had known much about Brecht. It was said he lived for years off the payment he'd got for his part in a screenplay called *Hangmen Also Die*, though he'd been done out of the screen credit by a clever fellow-writer who knew the rules. It was also said he'd offered to work with Salka Viertel on a screenplay that would yield to all the Hollywood conventions and make them buckets of money. The central character was to be a young Frenchwoman whom the retreating Germans punished by shaving her head so when they were gone the French population would treat her as a collaborator. It was a great story, but Salka Viertel pointed out that no Hollywood actress would consent to play a whole movie with her head shaved. Brecht said she would have to. He wouldn't budge on that, and that was the end of the idea.

So Brecht was gone. He'd had his brush with the Un-American Activities Committee and left the United States for good, and now it was said he was one of the great modern play-wrights. Arlene didn't want to write about Brecht. She wanted to borrow his personality. Her character would have his kind of sly wit – but she would have to be careful. This was supposed to be a movie that showed America opening its generous arms to the world. What she needed now was to think of scenes – to put an imaginary Brecht together in a room with an imaginary Bogart and Bacall. Not a room, but a bar. (Bogart would suggest a drink, and Bacall would say 'You bet your ass!') And let them talk about America. But not directly about America.

About baseball, popcorn, chewing gum, hamburgers; about fights and racetracks; about New York and the Grand Canyon. Arlene's mind was ranging about impatiently, hunting for something. If she could get them talking in her head, that would be a start. A story might grow out of it. All she could imagine was Brecht saying New York should have been built in the Grand Canyon so you could stand at the edge and piss on it. That was good, but no good. She was laughing at her own joke when Marvin Major came in.

She straightened her face. Mr Major didn't waste words. They were going up to Mulholland. The limos were waiting downstairs. Jesse Fischer's mother had died at the weekend and he thought they should call. He seemed to be angry at the inconvenience but there wasn't any question they had to go.

Arlene didn't want to. She felt nervous at the thought of facing Jesse's wife. But Marvin Major was on his way out. 'Be downstairs in two minutes,' he said.

There must have been eight or ten of them crowded into the big black cars. Arlene felt, not for the first time, as if she had joined the Mafia. They swept out along Sepulveda Boulevard and up into the hills. From there, Los Angeles was blurred, vanishing in a smog that was getting worse as the day got warmer.

The Fischers' drive was full of cars and the house full of people. That was good. It made it easy to be inconspicuous. The door was open and they walked in without being announced. It was like a big subdued Hollywood party. The mirrors in the entrance were hung with black drapes. The Fischers were in the biggest of the living-rooms. Here and there among the comfortable chairs and couches were wooden boxes. The three Ds came and went. Judith Fischer was sitting on a box. There were a lot of people and a lot of weeping and unconcealed grief. Arlene caught sight of Jesse. He hadn't shaved, his hair was untidy, his eyes were red and moist as Marvin Major hugged him, patting his shoulder. There was something foreign about it all. Arlene felt disconcerted. Something coldly Anglo Saxon – the ancient English blood of the Harpers – rose in her. At that moment Jesse looked at her across the room. He seemed not to recognize her, and she felt she hardly recognized him. She wandered away through open french windows and down towards the pool. Mrs Nightingale was there lighting a cigarette.

'What's going on in there?' Arlene asked.

'Shivah.' Mrs Nightingale cut her conversation as severely as she cut Marvin Major pictures.

'Shiva?' Arlene was confused. 'Are they Hindus?'

Mrs Nightingale went as near as it was possible for her to go in the direction of laughter. 'Not Hindus, sweetheart. Jews. Shivah with an h.'

'I didn't know Jesse was a Jew.'

Mrs Nightingale glanced at her as if to check. 'That's one between the eyes for a bit of studio gossip,' she said.

Arlene didn't understand her — but she often didn't understand Mrs Nightingale. 'Jesse hasn't shaved,' she said.

'He won't for a week.'

'And the boxes . . .'

'Family sits on those. It's part of the drill.'

Next time Arlene saw Jesse he was clean-shaven. The week had passed. It was the following Monday morning and they were meeting as usual in their cars up on Mulholland. She'd missed him, but she'd had a good week. Her little refugee character and his two American friends were developing. A story line was starting to emerge. It was going to be a comedy — there was no other way she could do it. She just had to push on and hope that wouldn't conflict with Mr Major's notion of how it should be done. She'd even managed to give her refugee the line about New York and the Grand Canyon. But 'piss' had been changed to 'spit' — and it was just his little harmless joke.

'I'm sorry about your mother,' she said.

He nodded. 'It's all over now. All the tears and stuff.' He smiled and spread his hands in front of him. 'I'm dried like a fig.' He didn't look altogether dry. There was something precarious about the smile. She caught a glimpse of the Jesse she'd seen a week before, unshaven in the midst of lamentation.

'I didn't know you were a Jew,' she said.

'I thought everyone knew.' He smiled. 'Didn't you notice I'm circumcised?'

'So are all the little boys where I come from.'

'Really?' He looked at her, searching for something. 'So does it matter?'

She frowned. 'What do you mean?'

'That I'm a Jew. Does it change anything?'

'You think I might be an anti-Semite?'

He shrugged and grinned. 'Well – isn't everyone? Even Jews.' He told her about a German Jewish friend who had attended a Hitler rally before the war. 'He got so worked up – it was so exciting – he found himself cheering when Hitler said the Jews had to be eliminated. That was when he decided it was time to get out.'

She told him all she'd known about Jews in New Zealand was that there were some old families who'd come in the last century and ran some of the biggest businesses. And then there was a new wave came from Germany in the 1930s. They were mostly musicians and doctors and intellectuals. In childhood she'd somehow picked up that Jews and Scots were mean with money – that was about the extent of her training in prejudice. 'Then the war ended and the death-camps were opened in Europe. It was like lifting the crust off a cowpat.'

He didn't understand. 'They look nice and brown in the paddock,' she explained. 'We used to do it when we were kids. You lift the hard brown crust in summer and underneath there's a mush full of maggots.'

He winced and turned to look away across the valley. 'The trouble with being victim of an atrocity is you're somehow stained by it. It's like being pulled out of a sewer. Everyone's sorry for you but no one wants to come near.'

She ruffled his hair and hugged him. 'Stop whimpering. Look at me.'

He looked. They both smiled. She wanted to say his Jewishness mattered so little – so not at all – she would marry him at once if that were possible. But she stopped herself. It seemed to her he knew what was in her mind and why she'd stopped. They never talked about marrying, but she thought about it often. She tried not to, but sometimes, in weak moments, she drifted into a fantasy in which Rocky and Judith Fischer were somehow removed — Rocky usually by some resounding success as a movie actor, Judith by something like cancer, or a traffic accident — and she and Jesse became publicly a couple. It wasn't so much marriage she wanted; it was the removal of this secrecy, this duplicity and contrivance. She wanted them to be seen together — at Victor Hugo's and the Beverly Wilshire; at Chasen's, the Cock 'n' Bull, Ciro's, the Mocambo Club, the Trocadero. She wanted to get out of a car with him and walk through crowds to an Academy Awards presentation. She wanted them to be mentioned in the same breath by Louella Parsons, and Hedda Hopper, and Sheilah Graham. Or at least some part of her wanted that. Another part wanted to stand free. And anyway it was all dreamland. There was something in Jesse's eyes now which she couldn't quite interpret, but she read it as a warning that she should say nothing of these thoughts. If she gave free reign to them she might frighten him — she might lose him altogether.

Now it was her turn to look away across the valley. 'Time we went to work,' she said.

'Hey.' He was concerned. 'What's the matter?'

She shook her head. 'Nothing.' There were tears on the way. She could feel them pricking, and her throat constricting. 'Nothing,' she repeated, to his look of enquiry as she got out of the car. 'I've got a script to write for M.M. That's all.'

'I love you,' he said.

'Bullshit. Cowpats. Oh God — here we go.' She leaned in and kissed him roughly on the mouth. 'It's hard being a mistress. Just understand that.' She kissed him again. 'Now let's get on with this great enterprise. OK?'

He nodded, smiling. 'OK.'

# 18

Evening drinks out of doors again. Carlos is doing us a barbecue. After these Southern Californian days, 'in the cool cool
cool of the evening' means more than it ever did as the line of
a song.

Today we went for a long walk. Edie took me down Mabery
Road and showed me the house where Salka Viertel lived.
Rocky used to go there sometimes with his acting class. Once
Edie went to pick him up. She passed a tall thin German with
glasses and a moustache on the path to the door. He stood
back, raised his black hat, and wished her 'Gut eveninkʼ. It was
Thomas Mann.

'I've rubbed shoulders with some Oscar winners,' she says.
'That's the only time I got close to a Nobel.'

'I've got closer than that,' I tell her. 'I've read his books.'

As soon as I say it I think 'How defensive. How Kiwi.' But
we're beginning to spar, like brother and sister.

After Mabery Road we walked up to a park on the headland
overlooking the ocean. We sat on a bench under enormous
gum trees and drank cans of 7-Up.

Carlos is very fussy. He won't let us help. We sit at a
hardwood table and he spreads paper napkins, pours the wine,
and lays out the steaks and salad as if we were at a high-class
restaurant. Edie compliments him and praises him. Kapai has
been shut in the Buick to keep him out of mischief. He can be
heard whining occasionally, but he seems to accept it.

After the steaks, and a long contented silence, Edie reaches
over and grabs me just above the knee. 'New Zealand,' she
says. 'Tell me something, you know, *quintessential*. Put me in
the picture.'

I think I know exactly what she means. I feel I'm being tested and that I'm going to fail. Or New Zealand is going to fail. I think of things like race relations, the economy, the farming sector, the Pacific region, the Australian connection. What am I? Some kind of journalist? My mind's blank.

Then I begin to talk as if someone else were talking. This is what I tell her.

Marion and I have a bach up the valley from Karekare Beach, which Edie doesn't know, near to Piha Beach, which she remembers. From our bach the land drops, all in thick bush, then rises until finally it comes out on a grassy headland, about a mile away as the crow flies. Marion and I sometimes follow the road around – it's about three miles that way – until we can stand on the grassy headland and look across at our bach buried among tall kauris and rimus.

One day we took a walk and reached the headland just before sundown. It was one of those rare days when the ocean stretches away and there's not a cloud between you and the horizon – just a sort of fine haze which makes it possible to look at the sun. So you see it going down like a great golden coin sliding into a slot. We'd seen a French movie called *Le Rayon Vert*. The rayon vert was a flash of green light you were supposed to see at the moment when the sun disappeared below the horizon. We sat on the grass to watch and see if it was true.

It takes only a few minutes. One moment, there is the whole of that huge burning disc sitting at the edge of the world. Then down it goes – a third, half, two thirds, until there's just the final segment, sliding, accelerating it seems – and then it's gone – and yes, the movie was right, at the last instant there was a flash of green light, unmistakable, at the point where the sun had vanished.

We sat a while, then got up and headed back towards the road. We were walking uphill now, due east, with the last light and the sea at our backs, and ahead, a range of low hills, bush-covered, so you could see branches angled like arms against the eastern sky that was curiously pale and lit-up. Then as we walked towards it, up over the bush hills came another huge disc – a full moon, enormously enlarged as it is when

167

you see it come over the horizon. It was as if the two discs, sun and moon, were rotating on a single axis. So the landscape turned from orange and green to black and white, but remained strangely alight as we walked the three miles back.

Edie listens. I've nothing more to say. I've said it. Carlos has gone indoors. I hear a half-hearted whine from Kapai in the Buick. I feel a sort of embarrassment. I think if Edie's feeling scratchy she'll say something like, 'You know, Bill, I only have to walk to the end of the street to watch the sun go down over the Pacific.'

But she says nothing. Then she leans close to me. I think she wants me to kiss her, but when her face is close to mine it stops. She says, half whispering, 'You can't bully me, little brother. Nobody can.'

# 19

Rocky was drinking all the time now. She didn't seem able to stop it, or control it. She knew he depended on her to put some kind of brake on him, but she hardly tried any more, and that made her feel guilty. No one would blame her for her love affair. Everyone sympathized with her and blamed Rocky. She knew that wasn't fair. She felt she ought to be doing more for him. But it would have taken a stronger woman – it would have taken an Amazon – to do her work at the studio and look after Rocky as well. They had a Mexican woman in every day now to keep house, and her husband came once a week to do the garden. But that was probably bad as well as good. It meant Rocky had nothing to think about except his next drink. He no longer worked out, or practised with his voice. Sometimes he went to help out at the Actors' Lab in Hollywood, but it was beginning to look as if he wasn't welcome there. He'd had one charge for drunk driving and their lawyer had got him off, but there was another pending.

One evening when she got home the phone was ringing. Rocky wasn't there – his car was gone from the garage – and the Mexican woman had finished for the day. Arlene ran to the phone. It was Charlie Beltane. 'Arlene, sweetheart, it's Charlie. Where's that lover-boy of yours? I've been calling all afternoon. Couldn't get any sense out of your maid . . .'

'Her English isn't good.'

'Not good, honey. You can say that again. And her American's worse.' Charlie laughed at his own joke. 'Listen, Arlene. I think I got something for Rocky. Maybe big. Fox are scheduling an Australian movie. *Kangaroo*. Hasn't hit the trades yet, but it's definite. It's on. Now you tell your boy to get his ass over here in the morning.'

'Really! Oh Charlie, that's . . .' A wild wave of hope and excitement washed over her.

'It's good isn't it?'

'It's great, Charlie. It's . . .'

'That boy needs something. Right?'

'Right. He needs something. He deserves it.'

'He deserves it. That's what I've been saying. That boy deserves something. Well – didn't I tell him about waiting? Trust Charlie Beltane . . .'

'You told him Charlie, but it's hard.'

''Course it's hard sweetheart. Hollywood's full of wrecks who couldn't pace it.'

'People lose their nerve.'

'They do, sweetheart. They do.'

'Well thanks. It's great news. I'm going to sing "Charlie is me darlin'"' in the shower.'

He chuckled. 'You do that. And just call me up any time you want your back scrubbed.'

'I will. Thanks. And Charlie – what time in the morning?'

'Better have him here by eight-thirty in case they decide to make him up for a test.'

'They'll test him tomorrow?'

'They might, baby. We have to be ready.'

'Sure. I understand. He'll be there. And thanks a million Charlie.'

Her hands were shaking. After the excitement came the anxiety. Where was Rocky? What state was he in? She phoned Fred Daniels. Rocky wasn't there. She tried the Actors' Lab and the Coronet Theatre in Beverly Hills. She called Monogram Studios in Gower Street where he sometimes worked as an extra. They hadn't seen him. She got into her car and drove down to the Mexican housekeeper's little place in the valley. The woman spoke hardly any English, as Charlie had noticed. She said 'Meester Tamworth, 'e go out in 'ees car.' She added a few sentences in Spanish, but Arlene thought that was all the information she had.

When Arlene got back to Merivale around eight o'clock Rocky was sitting in his car out in the street, unable to get it into the garage. She got him out, helped him up the steps and into the house. She gave him coffee and coaxed him out of his clothes and into the shower. He sat on the floor of the shower, water pouring over him, rocking slowly back and forward and hugging his knees. She left him there, went down to the street and put his car away. Back in the bathroom she turned the hot water down. He began to shiver and complain. Finally he crawled out and she dried him as best she could.

'Listen,' she said. 'Charlie phoned.'

He said Charlie could go fuck himself.

'Listen to me.' She cuffed him around the head.

'Don't.' He waved his arm vaguely as if keeping off flies.

'Listen, Rocky. Charlie's got something for you. Fox are doing an Aussie picture. They want you for a test.'

He became very still. He didn't say anything. She wrapped him in a dressing gown, led him to the kitchen and sat him in a chair. She began by making toast and more coffee. She remembered now that she hadn't eaten either. She was hungry. Rocky sat, quiet. She put a plate of buttered toast in front of him and he began to eat, very slowly. At first he could hardly steer the pieces to his mouth. His jaw moved conscientiously. From time to time he stopped chewing, as if the effort was too much.

She made more toast and ate some herself. She hunted in cupboards and found a can of soup and one of beans. She put them into separate pans and heated them. Rocky went on eating what was put in front of him.

Finally he stared at her and shook his head. 'Fucking Charlie Beltane,' he said. ''Mazing.'

She was sitting opposite him at the little table. 'It's to-morrow. You understand that, don't you?'

He nodded, licking his lips.

'We've got to get you ready.'

He closed his eyes and opened them. 'Could use a drink.'

She cuffed his head again. 'Don't say that, Rocky. I'll kill you.'

'Don't.' He fended her off. 'Jussa joke.'

'It's not funny, darling. This is your chance.'

He stared at her.

'You understand that don't you?' she repeated. 'You've had a long, long wait. Now it's here. You've got to be sober.'

He nodded. He screwed up his eyes, thinking. 'Clarissa tied in the affairs of men . . .'

She wasn't sure what he meant.

'No hang on,' he said. 'Not Clarissa. Shit. Clarissa.' He laughed. 'Clarissa tied in the affairs of men.' He rolled about in his chair, banging the table top.

'Darling, just quieten down and have some soup.'

'Good toast,' he said. He dunked it in the soup and sucked it. 'Toast à la crème de tin.'

'Would you like some more?'

He was frowning. 'Therissa,' he said.

'More toast?'

'Therissa tide in the affairs of men. How's it go?'

When he wouldn't eat any more and couldn't take any more coffee she tried to make him drink water. She kept talking about the picture, and Charlie Beltane, and the screen test. Rocky dozed in his chair. When he woke he was much more nearly sober. But now sleep seemed impossible. He paced the floor, talking about everything and nothing, remembering his family, his successes in Melbourne. At midnight he was still wide awake. 'I'll sock it to the bastards,' he said. And he launched into Macbeth's speech about the dagger.

Is this a dagger which I see before me
The handle towards my hand? Come let me clutch thee.
I have thee not and yet I see thee still.
Art thou not, fatal vision, sensible
To feeling as to sight? Or art thou but
A dagger of the mind, a false creation
Proceeding from the heat-oppressed brain?

As he worked his way into it, his voice grew stronger. It filled the room. His whole body moved with the sense of the lines.

His eyes staring at nothing, his hand trembling and out-stretched, his voice thick with horror and disgust, he muttered

> I see thee still
> And on thy blade and dudgeon gouts of blood
> Which was not so before.

And then, flinging himself away from the vision, crouching, his hand over his eyes, he brought out in a growl that still kept each word distinct:

> There's no such thing –
> It is the bloody business which informs
> Thus to mine eyes.

Arlene was excited by it. She remembered how astonished she'd been, and embarrassed, when he'd first put on one of these turns for her. It had been at night on the beach at Mission Bay during those days he'd spent in Auckland before sailing to Los Angeles. She'd looked around, hoping no one was watching or listening from the shadows. But she'd been stirred by it, and she was again.

Now his voice and body movements had changed. The voice dropped. It was strong, fervent, despairing, authoritative. He was almost chanting the lines, as he did when he paced himself with the metronome.

> Thou sure and firm-set earth
> Hear not my steps which way they walk for fear
> Thy very stones prate of my whereabout
> And take the present horror from the time . . .

His drunkenness, and for the moment his uncertainty, seemed all swept away.

'Tomorrow, Rocky.' She took hold of his arm. 'This is what we came for.'

He looked down at her. 'D'you think so?'

'I'm sure. You'll knock them for six. There's so much that's fake in this town . . .'

'It's my turn, isn't it?'

'It's your turn, darling.'

But it wasn't Rocky's turn and he didn't get the job. She never knew exactly what happened. He wouldn't talk about it. She phoned Charlie Beltane but all she got from him was 'He came on too strong, baby. He needed to cool it.'

She dreaded going home when she heard the news. She feared some terrible scene, but there was none. It wasn't bad in the way she feared it would be. But in the way it was bad, it was worse. Rocky was sober. He was keeping on an even keel, retaining his dignity. That was what seemed so awful – the way he held himself together, hid his feelings, behaved as if it had been a disappointment, no more than that. And because his pride was at stake she felt she had to take her cue from him and act accordingly. She couldn't rush at him and smother him in kisses and weep, telling him not to despair.

That evening they walked down to the local movie theatre and saw a Western, *The Gunfighter*, with Gregory Peck. Years later Arlene still remembered how they'd walked back in the cool night air, an arm each around the other's waist. It was like old times, going to the pictures together. And they'd loved *The Gunfighter* which the trade papers said wasn't doing as well as it should because the public preferred Peck clean-shaven. 'That moustache,' someone from Fox was quoted as saying, 'cost us a million bucks.'

'Imagine having a million hanging on whether or not you shaved,' Arlene said. 'It's absurd.'

'Ridiculous,' Rocky agreed. And then, ruefully, so they both laughed: 'It makes my mouth water to think of it.'

In the weeks that followed she kept working at her script. Rocky remained subdued and thoughtful. He drank less. He was absorbing his disappointment – she was sure of that – but he never spoke of it.

One day over lunch she talked to Jesse Fischer about it. He listened and didn't say much. She accused him of being unsympathetic. He denied it. Then he qualified the denial. 'I guess I just don't have enough sympathy in the bank for all the people in Hollywood who deserve it.'

She couldn't quarrel with that. It was reasonable – in abstract. But for her Rocky wasn't abstract. He was living and real and she felt responsible for him.

But at the same time she had a mounting sense of excitement because she was sure her script was going well. It had left Marvin Major's original idea some way behind, and that worried her. But her German immigrant and her two Americans were developing such distinct characters, getting into such interesting and funny situations, and saying such witty things to one another, she just had to go with them. She would worry about Marvin Major later on. She'd never before had such a sense that the writing was looking after itself, developing a momentum of its own. It was like being on a runaway tram; and she used that as her working title, *The Runaway Tram*. The tram was America. Her problem was how to bring it to a stop.

But that problem resolved itself too. She finished her script, left it with Mr Major's secretary, and waited. A week passed. A fortnight. She was beginning to lose confidence. She had time now to stand back from what she'd done and see how it could have been better. She began to think of a completely different treatment that would have gone much nearer to meeting what she'd been asked to do.

It was well into the third week when she got her summons. This time he did keep her waiting. When she was called into his office he was sitting at his desk tapping a paper knife on the script of *The Runaway Tram*. He didn't look pleased; but he didn't look displeased either. His face was neutral – deliberately, she thought. She sat down and he went on tapping the knife on the script. He looked at her as if it was for her to speak first. She put on a bland, willing expression, and met his eyes. He flipped the script open. '*The Runaway Tram*,' he said.

She nodded and smiled.

'There's no tram,' he said.

'It's a working title.'

'Where's the tram?'

'The story's the tram.'

'The story?'

'Call it *The Immigrant*. Call it what you like.'

'I like *The Runaway Tram.*'

'You like . . . That's good.' And after a pause. 'You mean the title or the script?'

He flipped over a page or two. 'Why does this kraut want to spit on New York?'

'It's just a joke. He's that kind of character.'

Mr Major shrugged. 'It's a good line.' He took out a cigar. 'What happened to our idea?'

'I've been thinking about that. There's a way it could be done, if you don't like the tram. It needs a different . . .'

He shook his head. 'Hold your horses, honey. Let's talk about the tram. You know what we're going to do with this script?'

She sighed. 'Hang it in the john?'

'Is that what you think?'

She shook her head. 'I don't know, Mr Major.'

'Call me Marvin.'

'I don't know, Marvin.'

'We're going to make it, baby. We're going to make it big.'

'Really? You mean it?'

'I mean it.' He picked it up. 'It's a peach.'

Later, when they'd talked over some of the things he'd noticed in the script, he asked what she'd meant when she said there was a way his original idea could be used. Because as far as he was concerned that idea was still a good one.

She told him she'd been thinking about her housekeeper and her gardener. They came from Mexico. Los Angeles had so many Spanish speakers – people who had come up from Central America.

'When Hollywood thinks of immigrants it thinks of them sailing into New York harbour and saluting the Statue of Liberty. But they're pouring in here from the south. Isn't there a picture in that! And it's right here under our noses.'

'Hispanics.' Marvin Major turned down the corners of his mouth. 'Forget it, Arlene baby. Those roosters come over the border without passports.'

'They're good settlers,' she said. 'They're escaping from poverty and oppression. Wasn't that the idea?'

He shook his head. 'You stick to your tram. Pictures about coloured folk, Jews, Hispanics – leave that stuff to the studios that can afford the risk.'

That night she told Rocky her script had been accepted. She hid her excitement. She didn't tell him it would be her first solo screen credit, nor that Marvin Major wanted her to be around at every stage, from casting through to shooting and cutting.

A few days later she came home and couldn't find Rocky in the house, though his car was in the garage. Then she heard him calling from the hill at the back. She stood out on the lawn and looked up. 'Can you scramble up here?' he called. 'Come and look at the view.'

She took the path up through the terraced garden and on through trees until she came out on the steep crumbling slope beyond reach of the sprinklers. There was brown grass and bare patches with clumps of chaparral in the hollows. Rocky came down to meet her and they sat on the ground looking across the gully. Rocky quoted

> For God's sake let us sit upon the ground
> And tell sad stories of the death of kings.

Directly below was their house and garden. On the other side of the gully there were houses here and there, surrounded by gardens like their own. Between the houses there was bare hillslope with its sparse natural vegetation. On the hilltop, or just beyond it, a line of palms stood up against a very blue sky.

'What are you doing up here?' she asked.

He held her hand. 'Thinking.'

She laughed. He said, 'When a bear of very little brain goes in for thinking, he takes himself off to a quiet place.'

'And what does he think?'

'He thinks it's time to throw in the towel.'

She looked at him. She didn't answer.

'I think we should go back,' he said.

'Back?'

'To Melbourne.' His voice became positive. 'I'm known

there. People haven't forgotten me. I still get letters. I write back pretending I'm doing well. I even tell them about this house, as if it's all my doing. I can't go on deceiving people back home much longer. They haven't seen me in a movie and they're not going to. This Fox movie about Australia will come out and I won't even be in that. I'll be forgotten. If I go back now I can start more or less where I left off. I belong in the theatre. This Hollywood stuff – it was just a dream.'

She didn't say anything. She held his hand and stared at that line of palms against the sky. She thought of the palms as Hollywood.

# 20

There was a woman called Edie Harper and there was a woman called Arlene Tamworth and they were the same, and different. One was fading, the other becoming more distinct. But it wasn't a matter of life and death – more a question of which was visible. Edie Harper might have lost her public presence but she was alive and well in there, still critical, still articulate. She didn't like America in those years, liked it less and less, while Arlene Tamworth did her best to have no opinions about it, only to get on with the job.

They were the years of the Korean War, McCarthyism, the Red scare, the black-list. The House Un-American Activities Committee returned to the investigation of Hollywood, but this time, 1951, there were no heroes, no Unfriendly Ten, only yes-men and beaten dogs. Arlene Tamworth kept her eyes on her screenplay. Jesse Fischer made his Western and thought about a musical. Marvin Major looked at box-office receipts and told himself that Hollywood was heading for its Little Bighorn.

Sitting on the hillslope above their house in Sherman Oaks, her hand still held firmly by Bruce Burns who was also Rocky Tamworth, Arlene had said only 'You'll have to give me time to think.' And then, minutes later, 'It's a shock. I wasn't expecting it.'

It was surprising how quickly it grew dark. But even when the light seemed quite gone, she could still pick out that line of palms distinct against a velvet sky.

'Melbourne's not home to me,' she said.

'No.' He acknowledged that. 'But you'd like it.'

'Give me a day or two,' she said.

As they scrambled down the slope in the dark she wondered whether there was much professional theatre in Melbourne. But she didn't ask. It hardly mattered. If there wasn't much, now was a good time to go there – to be in at the beginning. And she thought Rocky was right – he should go back. He should drop the name he'd taken in Hollywood and be Bruce Burns again. He should be an Australian actor in Australia. He wasn't an Errol Flynn, and why should he want to be? Why should Australia go to the world? Let the world come to Australia.

A sort of excitement came with these thoughts, but she suppressed it – or at least she didn't express it. Because her life had changed. Once she would only have thought of what was good for Rocky. That was why they were here. But now she was succeeding in her own right. She seemed to have a hand and a foot firmly on the ladder. Already the money was very good, and promising to be better. And more than anything she'd begun before, she wanted to finish *The Runaway Tram*. She wanted to complete a shooting script that satisfied everyone, including herself. She wanted to be on the spot to discuss the cast list. She wanted to be around when it was being shot. She wanted to be alongside the director in the cutting room. She wanted what Jesse Fischer had wanted – enough control so the picture that emerged finally had on it the stamp of her own personality. It would be a team effort, because that was the nature of motion pictures; but it would be hers.

That mattered much more than the money. It mattered almost more than anything. She wanted to be author of a motion picture as a writer is author of a book.

A couple of days passed. She couldn't keep Rocky waiting long. He said nothing but she could feel his impatience. They were sitting over a meal in an Italian restaurant in Sherman Oaks when the time seemed right to talk about it. She told him exactly what was being offered at the studio. It was something new. Marvin Major usually put writers on in pairs and treated them like operators on a production line. Instead, Arlene was doing all the writing and rewriting on *The Runaway Tram*. He was promising her a hand in every part of the production.

She wanted to do it – to see it completed before they left Hollywood. Then she would be prepared to go.

'How long?' Rocky asked.

'It's hard to say. Maybe six months.'

Really she knew it would be longer. But he seemed satisfied. He was still excited at having made such a radical decision. He was happier than she'd seen him for a long time.

'There's one other thing,' she said.

He waited for it. There was that fright she often saw in his eyes these days.

'I'm not going back to Melbourne with a drunk.'

She hadn't meant to put it so starkly. He winced. But he didn't argue; and having started, she went on. 'If my picture takes six months, that's how long you've got to sort out your problem.'

There was a long silence. They were between courses and he was fiddling with his fork, turning it over and over, eyes down. Finally he looked up and met her eyes. He was smiling, but it wasn't a warm smile. 'Is that long enough for you to sort out yours?'

She wasn't sure what he meant, and she didn't dare ask. Maybe it was just a shot in the dark, but if it was, it hit the target.

'Those are my terms,' she said.

The waiter returned and Rocky made a show of discussing wines with him. Nothing more was said that evening about Melbourne.

It didn't seem a promising start, but there was a change in Rocky in the weeks that followed. He stopped trying. It was as if he'd turned his back on Hollywood, and almost at once things began to happen. He got a part in an Arthur Miller play at the Coronet Theatre; and before that was over, Charlie Beltane found him a small part in a Western being done at Paramount. Rocky was to be one of a gang of tough cowboys who were making trouble. He had only a few lines of dialogue. There was a fight scene in a bar in which he broke a chair over someone's head and threw someone through a window. Finally the gang was on the run. Rocky was to disappear from the picture when he was brought down by an arrow that came out of nowhere, signalling to the gang that they'd wandered into hostile Indian territory.

Arlene was working hard on her shooting script. But in those months Marvin Major's behaviour was changeable so she never felt quite safe with him. He had unpredictable rages. He altered plans. He forgot things and blamed his secretaries. Sometimes he disappeared from his office.

And he liked to have steam baths. It was his new fad. He'd had one installed in the studio and he recommended it to his senior staff. He said you sweated out the poisons. Sometimes he held important discussions with his producers in the steam room. They sat naked, swathed in white towels like Roman senators, panting and discussing policy. Jesse Fischer hated it. It made him breathless and left him feeling weak, but if Marvin insisted, Jesse would go in with him. One day the two were in there discussing the future of the studio and the pressure that was coming from New York to 'trim the fat'. The money men were saying the studio couldn't afford any expensive flops in the coming year. It had to show a healthy profit.

While they talked Marvin kept turning up the steam. He prided himself on being able to stand it better than younger men. It seemed to prove to himself that he was durable. Jesse complained. 'Wait till your pores open,' Marvin told him, chuckling. 'You'll feel better in a moment.'

Jesse splashed cold water on his face but he didn't feel any better. 'We're going to have to go on with this in your office,' he said. 'I'm not up to it today.' He didn't hear what Marvin said in reply. In the adjoining room he dried himself, dressed, and went back to his office. The morning went by and Marvin Major didn't call him.

That afternoon the boss couldn't be found. His secretaries phoned his home, his favourite restaurants and bars, even the hotel where it was rumoured he sometimes took compliant female stars. It was some time before the puzzle became a panic and the panic was reported to Jesse Fischer. Jesse went back to the steam room. It was almost impossible to see in there, the steam was turned up so high, but he found Marvin Major on the floor. He'd had a heart attack or a stroke. He was lying flat on his back staring up into the false clouds, his arms crossed over his chest. Someone said he was a lapsed Catholic and that the crossed arms meant he'd made an act of contrition. He'd been dead some time when he was found.

The funeral was big. He'd left instructions including a sketch of a double tomb in white marble, so there would be a place for Mrs Major beside him 'when her time came'. She was his fourth wife, a beautiful woman at least twenty-five years younger than her husband, and no one supposed that 'when her time came' she would still be Mrs Major; but Jesse went ahead and arranged for the construction, the cost to be charged against the estate. Because of the tomb that was planned, the burial couldn't be at Forest Lawn. It was in the Hollywood Memorial Cemetery, not far from the Douglas Fairbanks tomb and reflecting pool. While the burial service was being read Arlene could see, beyond a line of tall palms, the water tower of Paramount Pictures where Rocky was engaged every day making his Western.

There were stars weeping at the graveside. Speeches were made about the end of an era and the last of the greats. Crowds pressed around the gates to see celebrities. When they got clear of it Arlene and Jesse headed for their room in the hotel gardens.

They were subdued. They'd spent a lot of time cursing Marvin Major, or making jokes about him, but now they both felt they'd liked him and owed him a lot.

Already the bosses had been out from New York. Jesse was to be head of the studio. 'I don't mind,' he told Arlene. 'It's a relief in a way. I've had my shot at making pictures. I enjoyed it – and the pictures were OK. They're respectable, and they didn't make a loss. But they're ordinary. When I started I thought I could do better than that.'

'They're not ordinary,' she said. 'They've got your special flavour, Jess, and they don't die on you. That's rare.'

He smiled. 'Don't try too hard for me.'

'And you made them in the teeth of M.M. We should remember that when we're being nice about the old sod.'

Jesse was pulling the cork on a bottle of wine. It came out

with a good cloop. He poured her a glass and filled his own. 'Let's drink to our new partnership. I'm going to need you, honey. You haven't lost your freshness. You'll have to be the sharp critical eye on everything we put out.'

'Oh my God Jesse. I'm not drinking to that.'

'It's a promotion.'

'I don't want promotion. I just want to get on with my picture.'

'Sure. That too.'

'Not that too. That only.'

'Look sweetheart, you've got to face it. Everything's on hold while New York does its review.'

Arlene sat up in her chair. 'Jesse you wouldn't. I'd kill you.'

'Take it easy. You'll make your picture. You might have to wait, that's all. Things will be slow for a while.'

'How long?'

'I don't know. I don't know anything until they've finished. Just be patient. Hold on to your hat. You're on the way up.'

She had an uneasy feeling that as studio boss he might want her to be to him what he'd been to Marvin Major. She didn't want that. She said, 'I mightn't have much time.'

She smiled when she saw the expression on his face. 'It's not terminal, Jess. More . . . well, geographical.'

He held out his hand. 'Darling, do you have to be so indirect?'

'Rocky wants to go back to Melbourne.'

He withdrew his hand. He looked disbelieving. 'You won't go.'

'I've told him I want to finish my picture. And he has to stop drinking.'

'But . . .'

'But what?'

'But us. What else? I don't live in Melbourne.'

She closed her eyes. 'Do you want a frank response to that? Or do we just let it pass?'

'Arlene.' He was serious. 'You wouldn't leave me?'

'I don't think I said it was till death do us part, did I? I don't remember I was given the chance.'

'Is that what you want?'

'You'll have to ask me if you want an answer to that.'
'To marry you?'
'Isn't that what we're talking about?'
He stood up and went over to the window. 'That's right,'
she said. 'Think before you speak. Look before you leap. Don't
shoot till you see the whites of my eyes.'
'You like to put me in the wrong,' he said.
'Is that where you think you are?'
'I've got three small kids.'
'Well don't complain about it, Jess. Just one would make me
happy.'
He turned and faced her. 'I always have this feeling you have
your foot on the accelerator pedal because you know mine's
on the brake. If I took mine off the brake, you'd put it on
yourself.'
'But you don't dare in case your hunch is wrong.'
'Would you leave Rocky?'
'Do you want me to?'
He sighed, walked to his chair, and sat down. 'I don't know
what I want Arlene.'
'I know what you want. You want everything – me, her,
them, and the studio. Well you've got it. The lot. I admire
your control over your own life. I'd love to be in control.'
'It doesn't feel like control.'
'It's such control you don't even notice. You realize this isn't
Tuesday or Thursday. It took Marvin Major's death to get us
here on a different day.'
'I'm sorry Arlene. You're right. It's too mechanical. We
could . . .'
'No we couldn't,' she said. And then, 'God you make me
angry Jess.'
He poured some more wine. 'I'm bushed Arlene.' After a
silence he asked, 'Are you really thinking of going back to
Melbourne?'
'I'm thinking about it. I have to. It's a real act of courage on
Rocky's part. He'd have to go back and face the people who
gave him a big send-off. He'd have to say "I didn't make it so
I came home."'

'You'd have to give up your work.'

She nodded. 'And there's the big gamble. I might find myself living in Melbourne still married to a drunk.'

Jesse leaned forward, elbows on knees. 'I haven't got any rights. I know that. I shouldn't have said you put me in the wrong. I put myself there. But I love you Arlene. I can't think what to say except please don't go.'

She leaned forward and kissed his brow. 'D'you remember after your mother died – I hadn't known you were a Jew and you asked me did it matter? I said it didn't. That was true. It so much didn't matter it was embarrassing even to answer, because that might suggest I understood how it *could* matter – and I didn't. But after that conversation I thought about it for a long time. There was something I couldn't get hold of. A feeling. A hunch. And then all at once it came to me. It doesn't matter to me that you're Jewish, but it matters to you that I'm not.'

'No no no.' As he denied it he shot out of his chair and stood again at the window looking out. The denial was so vehement she knew she'd touched a nerve.

'Jess I'd like it better if you were honest with me. Your wife's Jewish. Your kids, your family, your friends. I don't know why it never occurred to me.'

'Yes but . . .' He shook his head. And then he said, 'Well, maybe . . .' – and at once she saw it differently. It was as if in that moment she'd offered him an excuse. Because probably there was something much more important than this Jewishness – something Arlene could hardly face. Jesse loved her. But that didn't mean he didn't love his wife.

So everything was on hold. Everything was under review. Rocky had to sort out his drinking problem. Jesse had to decide what he wanted. Sometimes it occurred to her that if Rocky became sober and Jesse offered to leave Judith and marry her, she would be faced with the need to divide herself down the middle like an amoeba and go off in two directions. But she didn't believe that both these things would happen. She didn't believe that even one of them would.

She worked on her script. Jesse encouraged her when she

looked for encouragement – otherwise he got on with his work and she with hers. Her money kept coming in. Rocky wasn't drinking, or not heavily. Bogart and Bacall came back from filming in the Congo and Rocky sometimes got a call to go sailing aboard *Santana*. Life was pretty good if you didn't think about the future, or the past, or what was happening in Washington and in the world. All the time the bombs were getting bigger, the tests blasting away in the upper atmosphere. The war in Korea raged on.

As a screenwriter Arlene was allowed a vote for the Academy Awards. That year there were five nominations in each category, but everyone was sure most of the big awards would go either to *A Streetcar Named Desire*, with Marlon Brando and Vivien Leigh, or *The African Queen*, with Bogart and Katharine Hepburn. Brando was the better actor, but Bogart was more popular.

The Awards ceremony was at the Pantages Theatre on Hollywood Boulevard. Arlene and Rocky went with a group from the Marvin Major Studio. They arrived in one of the studio limos. There were search–lights raking this way and that, crossing beams in the sky above the street. Crowds waiting to see the stars arrive were pressed back behind bleachers. Cameras flashed. As you went through the crowd you heard voices trying to identify faces. 'Isn't she . . .' 'No that's . . .' 'Wasn't he in . . .' 'He's not anyone . . .' 'Look there's . . .' The big stars got cheers and shouts of encouragement.

Rocky spoke and moved carefully. There had been a party at Paramount and he'd had some drinks – Arlene didn't know how many. Inside the theatre everyone seemed larger than life. They shouted greetings at one another, hugging and kissing as if each new encounter was astonishing and wonderful, and hooting as if every remark was brilliantly witty. Overhead, arches and fluted pillars shone in the light of the chandeliers. Arlene thought how healthy everyone looked, how unnaturally tanned and sleek. She felt removed from it all, and at the same time deeply interested, as if she'd dropped in from another planet.

They took their seats. The show before the awards were

announced seemed to go on a long time. It was slick and smooth and entertaining. It had to be. Everyone was eager for the announcements. Rocky came and went from his chair. Arlene was sure he was drinking and she didn't care. She felt a strange indifference to everything. All the show needed was Vic Mature to stand between the central pillars in a loin cloth and bring the whole theatre down in a final De Mille spectacular. Up nearer to the stage in the big auditorium she could see Jesse and Judith Fischer. They were with a group of friends. They seemed to be having a good time.

The awards began. One by one the winners were predictably modest, conscientious in thanking all those who had made their triumph possible. Bogart had said if he won he would say he had no one to thank but himself. By the time it got to the best actor award, *Streetcar* had collected best supporting actor, best supporting actress, and best actress. Now it had to be Brando or Bogart – the other nominees weren't in the race.

Greer Garson came out to make the announcement. Arlene remembered her from the war years in a picture called *Mrs Miniver*. She couldn't recall much of it – only a beautiful and stalwart Englishwoman finding a wounded German airman wolfing down food from her pantry.

Greer Garson opened the envelope. It was Bogart. There were loud cheers. Arlene looked for Brando and couldn't see him. Bogart went up, got his kiss and his Oscar, and made the speech everyone makes. He thanked John Huston, Katharine Hepburn, Betty Bacall, the crew.

That night there was a party at Romanoff's. Everyone was there. Arlene's recollection is that it was the new Romanoff's, and that there was a step down into the extended dining-room that hadn't been there before. Her friends argue with her and say the renovations and the new step went in later. Her answer to that is 'If they're right, Rocky fell down a step that wasn't there – and he was quite capable of that.'

He'd had a lot to drink and she didn't try to restrain him. It was up to him. She wasn't any longer going to be responsible. It was a good party and  :  was enjoying herself. Late in the evening Rocky decided  :e hadn't managed to get near his sailing friend who had won the big award. He set off across the room and fell conspicuously and loudly on his face.

Arlene got up and headed for the women's room. She arrived at the same moment as a beautiful blonde. That wasn't unusual – women's rooms in Hollywood usually had at least one beautiful blonde, and often several. The face was familiar, but not famous – or not yet. Arlene first thought it might be the actress she'd replaced in *Out on a Limb* – the one Dennis O'Donoghue had said possessed too much 'stellar quality' to be a one-scene secretary. But then she recognized her as Gary Cooper's wife in *High Noon* which had just been released.

So they went in together, and as Grace Kelly checked her make-up in the mirror she said idly, 'Who's that goon just hit the deck?'

Arlene put on her own stalwart Mrs Miniver face. 'That goon's my husband,' she said.

Grace Kelly, lipstick poised, looked at Arlene in the mirror. 'Well,' she said, 'he's got nice big shoulders' – and they both laughed.

# 21

I suppose everyone who visits Los Angeles brings away a different city. What they have in common is the sunshine, the smog, the freeways, and maybe the free ways. Professor Walt Ambrose lived in a lovely suburban street in Westwood, with wide tree-shaded sidewalks, Spanish bungalows, beautifully tended gardens, and neat signs spiked into front lawns saying ARMED RESPONSE. Over the low, red-tiled roofs of the suburb you could see the glass towers of Century City.

It seemed as if almost everyone jogged. Sometimes they carried dumb-bells so arms as well as legs got exercised. Some wore Walkmans as they ran, and stopped at intervals to check a pulse in the throat against a watch at the wrist. In the houses were weights and exercycles and rowing machines. Just about everyone ate health breakfasts and health lunches, and some fasted two days each week.

The university was close at hand. I could walk there when I wanted to use the library. I also had the use of Walt's second car, so it wasn't long before I set off to find Hollywood. Of course I knew – it had been explained to me – that there were two Hollywoods. There was the Industry, which was spread all through Los Angeles; and there was the suburb, or the city within the city, which had given the Industry its name. Still I think I expected something that would glitter – something bold, beautiful, glossy, brassy, ritzy. I strolled up and down the Walk of Fame. The big names were all there, under the padding feet and chewing gum. I looked at the hand- and foot-prints of the stars pressed in concrete in the forecourt of Grauman's Chinese Theatre. I looked at bookshops and glanced into Musso and Frank's where I knew William Faulkner and

Scott Fitzgerald had eaten pork chops. I sat in that place called Hollywood on Location listening to those old tracks and discovering that just as the walls of my soul were papered with scenes from old movies, so its corridors echoed with their tinny scores. This was the bad old diet that had preceded Keats and Wagner.

I remember in London in the 1950s getting to know an Indian graduate student from Delhi who was deeply disappointed at his first sight of Buckingham Palace. Wasn't it, he asked, the centre of the greatest Empire the world had ever known – the one on which the sun never set? Why then didn't the palace look the part? Why wasn't it grander, more imposing? I felt the same about Hollywood on that hot April afternoon. It wasn't just unimpressive. It was depressing. Everywhere there were drunks, drug-addicts, derelicts. I stood on the famous corner of Hollywood and Vine where it's said the young hopefuls of the 1930s and '40s came to see and be seen. Had Edie stood at this intersection? Had she walked along these dismal streets? Had they been as dismal then as they were now? Had she arrived too late and been a victim of the decline of Hollywood? We'd imagined her sharing in its affluence. What if, rather than that, she should be hidden away somewhere sharing in its poverty?

Driving back towards Westwood I pulled over to read my map. I spent a long time at it. When I looked up the street was closed off by police cars at either end. A cop with an RT was squatting across the street. Another, a marksman with rifle at the ready, crouched against a car parked back along the street from mine, looking up into a building above my head. I kept cool. I moved away very slowly, very smoothly. At the end of the street the road-block was opened enough to let my car pass. I was waved on, and I sped away. It was only later I began to wonder whether this had been real life or a bit of Hollywood in the making. In that building I couldn't see because it was directly above my car there might have been a crazed gunman, or there might have been a movie camera. Either was possible and there was no way of knowing.

I did my lectures for Walt. I tried, but largely failed, to work on the paper I was to deliver to a Keats conference in London. None of this was getting me any closer to Edie. I wasn't going to find her by cruising the streets.

Help came to me from the Department of Motion Picture Studies at Walt's university. A young man there, introduced to me as Richie, found copies of those two old movies, *Out on a Limb* and *Shooting*, in the Department's film repository. So I watched them again, or parts of them. There was my sister sure enough. The doubt that had crept in over the years vanished. It was Edie's voice, Edie's way of moving hands and body, Edie's eyes and smile. But the credits only listed the principal actors. In the 1940s, Richie told me, that wasn't uncommon. And the studio where those pictures had been made no longer existed.

I hadn't really explained to Walt Ambrose why I'd come to Los Angeles, but now, influenced I suppose by this new sense of certainty, I explained it to Richie. He said he wasn't experienced in what film historians did if they wanted to track down former actors and people who'd worked on old movies, but he would ask some of his colleagues who did that kind of work. Meanwhile he suggested I should go through the *Academy Players' Directory* for one of the years when the two films were made. If I couldn't find my sister listed as Edie Harper I should go right through looking for her, because every entry was accompanied by a photograph.

The directories were in the university library. I chose the year 1946 – that was volume 44 – and went to work. There was no Edith Harper. But she might have been married; or she might have taken an acting name. So I began to work my way through the women's photographs – from Eve Abbot on page 35 to Mary Young on page 230. With about seven to each page that made fourteen hundred faces. None of them looked like Edie. Or rather, they all looked like Edie, but none of them was my sister.

Then I discovered there were two more volumes – numbers 43 and 45 – for 1946. Most of the names and faces were the same as those I'd looked at in volume 44, but there were differences. Out of each page one or two actresses would have been dropped from one volume to the next, and one or two new ones added. So there was nothing for it but to go through the fourteen hundred beautiful faces a second time, and then a third.

As I walked back to Westwood that evening I felt slightly dizzy. I'm optimistic by temperament and every time I turned a new page I half believed this would be the one. Edie would be smiling out at me. But although I'd been disappointed I didn't feel defeated, I suppose because it was now clear to me that most things to do with the movie industry are documented. My quest had moved into the area of research, and research was what I was trained to do. If I could discover what Keats had for breakfast on the morning he met Fanny Brawne, I could surely discover what had become of a person who played minor roles in two movies of the 1940s.

That evening Richie phoned. I told him I'd had no success with the directories for 1946 and that I was planning to move on to 1947. But now he had a new suggestion. I should go to the library of the Academy of Motion Picture Arts and Sciences in Beverly Hills and ask for everything they had on the two movies. If the file didn't contain a complete cast-list, including bit-parts, I should make the same request at the library of the American Film Institute in East Hollywood. One or the other should have a list that would give me the name I was after.

And if I found the name, I asked – what should I do then?

'My colleague tells me he always starts with the LA telephone directories,' Richie said. 'LA's full of former movie actors. They tend to stick around.'

Each day brings on its common miracle. Even after so many years on the planet that seems to be true. Next morning I had my health breakfast, took a long slow spin on Walt's exercycle, read the *Los Angeles Times*, and set off on foot in the heat along Wilshire Boulevard.

It took some time; but that day I found what I was after. It was hard to believe Edie had gone by the name of Arlene Tamworth but there it was. I still have the xeroxed copy of the sheet I found in the library's file on the movie *Shooting*. It's headed MARVIN MAJOR STUDIO, and under that, CALL BUREAU CAST SERVICE. It lists the producer, director,

director of photography, scriptwriters, and so on. Then come the principals – the actors listed in the film credits, headed of course by Humphrey Bogart. Finally there's a heading 'Minor Parts and Bits'. Among the minor parts is that of the secretary, Joan Cromwell, played by Arlene Tamworth. What I hadn't expected was that Arlene Tamworth was also listed as one of three scriptwriters.

In the same folder there were stills from the picture. They were sharp glossy prints. The faces were clearer than they appear on the screen. There wasn't any doubt that the person playing the part of the secretary was my sister.

Back at Walt's place that evening I found Arlene Tamworth listed in one of the LA directories. Like a lot of Los Angeles listings it gave no address, but that didn't matter. It seemed I was only a phone call away from her. I walked around the garden a few times, went in, took a deep breath and dialled. No one answered. For the rest of the evening it was the same.

Next morning I began again and this time the call was answered by a man with a Spanish–American accent. He said, 'Sorry, sir, Meez Tamworth she's not 'ere.' And he hung up.

It took a few miles on the exercycle before I hit on a plan. I dialled the number again and the same Spanish speaker answered. I told him I was from Ace Delivery. We had something for Miss Arlene Tamworth but the wrapping was torn. We couldn't read the address.

He didn't seem to doubt this improbable story. He gave me the street and number. 'Oh sure,' I said, repeating it as if tracing it on the torn wrapping. 'And that's . . .'

'Pacific Palisades.'

Right. Pacific Palisades. So it was. I thanked him, hung up, and did two skips on the way to the bedroom. In my bag I had a copy of *Keats and Belladonna*, and a reprint of *The Keatsian Poetic*. I found some paper, wrapped them, addressed the parcel to Arlene Tamworth. Half an hour later I was cruising along Sunset Boulevard looking for the street which my map told me would run off to the left, towards the ocean.

Arlene Tamworth's house was white, sprawling, elegant. There was a paved courtyard at the front surrounded by a fence of black iron bars with spikes, and shaded by beautiful trees. The front door was open. I drove into the courtyard, went up the steps, and rang the doorbell. A young dark-haired woman answered. Down the corridor I could see a man vacuum-cleaning the carpet. Beyond him there were tall windows opening to a garden and swimming pool at the back.

I was told again that Miss Tamworth was away. I asked when she would be back. The girl turned to the man with the cleaner. 'Carlos,' she called, shouting above the noise of the machine, 'Meez Buchanan – when she be back?'

He switched off the machine and shrugged. 'She din say for sure. She say prolly – I dunno. Try tomorrow.'

It took a moment or two to sort this out. The girl explained that Arlene Tamworth was Mrs Buchanan. So what about Mr Buchanan, I asked. 'Oh.' The girl tossed her head, indicating a region somewhere above my head. 'Meesta Buchanan – he's dead.'

I handed her the parcel of books and asked her to see that Mrs Buchanan got them. 'They come from New Zealand,' I said.

'New Zillon.' She repeated it as if impressed, and looked again at the parcel.

I asked whether Mrs Buchanan came from New Zealand.

She called over her shoulder. 'Carlos. Meez Buchanan. She comes from New Zillon?'

'New Zillon?' Carlos looked judicious. 'Eez back east?'

'It's in the South Pacific,' I said.

'I think eez from back east Meez Buchanan. Maybe not. Maybe sheez from right 'ere.'

I began to walk away down the path. Then I turned back. After all, I didn't have long in Los Angeles. I asked where Mrs Buchanan was spending the day.

Carlos was consulted again. They discussed the question in rapid Spanish. Twice I heard them mention the Palomino Club. I thought perhaps they were trying to decide whether they should tell me anything or nothing.

'Sorry, sir,' the girl said. She gave me a beautiful smile. 'We don' know.'

'Sorry,' Carlos repeated, shrugging and raising his eyebrows. I found a place to have lunch and sat thinking what I should do next. I was reluctant to waste twenty-four hours. I asked the waitress what and where was the Palomino Club. She didn't know, but they were helpful in that place. They looked it up for me. It was in North Hollywood – open in the evenings. And they gave me the address.

That evening I found it. It was in a squat, dingy-looking building in a dingy street called Lankershim. I paid eight dollars fifty at the door and went in. The audience sat at long tables, served by waitresses. I ordered beer and tacos and a bowl of an avocado dip called guacamole. There was a stage, and banks of lights in the ceiling. A group called the Rhythm Pigs were setting up their gear. It took a long time and a lot of testing. There were three guitars, keyboard and drums. When they began playing my ears hurt so much I stuffed paper in them to deaden the racket. After a couple of numbers they were joined by a girl in a leather mini-skirt and felt hat of the kind my father wore in the 1940s. She went by the name of Gail Warning, and it suited her.

After the Rhythm Pigs and Gail Warning there was one of those breaks in which one lot of gear is dismantled and another set up and tested. The new group, three young guitarists and a drummer, all white, and an older black sax-player, belonged to the star of the evening, Screamin' Jay Hawkins, a black rhythm-and-blues man.

By now the place was filling up. There must have been at least three hundred people jammed in at the tables and around the back of the room. There was one table set aside for a group who were obviously Hollywood people. They were looked at and recognized, and you could see they were used to that. They looked only at one another, but they acted as if they were on a stage, in a play. Their gestures were larger than life. They were of mixed age and colour. In twos and threes they came and went from and to a door at the back of the club, but that table remained theirs. Nobody invaded their space.

When Screamin' Jay Hawkins came on he was greeted by cheers and whistles. He wore a blue satin suit patterned with dragon flies and strelitzia flowers, white shoes and white frills at wrist and throat, and a lot of jewellery. He must have been six foot three or four, wiry, athletic, hyperactive, loud, funny and overpowering. He sang, played the guitar, sometimes played a piano, mixed voodoo into his act, and screamed. From time to time he talked about people at that table. There was a TV producer, a movie star, a dress designer, someone who had promoted a great star of rock 'n' roll, the owner of a radio station, a producer. As Screamin' Jay mentioned them by name they waved or stood up while a beam of light swept down the table to show them to the crowd. It was Hollywood feeding off itself. Screamin' Jay's reputation was enhanced because they were there. Theirs was enhanced because he named them. Beautiful girls in the audience put themselves under lights in conspicuous places, hoping to be seen. The goddess Fame, whatever kind of battering she had taken over the years, was still being honoured in this place. And Screamin' Jay belted out his songs. He was a real pro – even a Keats scholar with paper in his ears could recognize that.

I didn't forget Edie. I looked for her. But how was I going to find her in this crowd? And why should she be here? I was pretty sure Carlos and the girl had talked about the Palomino Club, but I had no idea what they'd said about it.

Then in a break between numbers there was one of those shifts at the centre table. A group went out to the room at the back, and others changed places. A woman who'd had her back to me was now facing in my direction. It was Edie.

She was so much older she was a different person. And yet she was the same person. She was an American woman of mature years. But she was the beautiful sister of my childhood. I didn't have even a momentary doubt.

I stared. I was able to go on staring because, though she faced me now, she was some distance away and her eyes were turned towards the stage. When she looked away from the stage it was to address a remark, or an answer, to someone at her table. So Screamin' Jay danced and strummed and sang and screamed, while I stared.

After a while Edie yawned, stretched, and looked around

the room as if she'd had enough. Her eyes moved slowly until they came in contact with mine. There they stopped. Edie was looking at me. I was looking at Edie.

She showed almost no reaction – that was what seemed remarkable. Her mouth didn't fly open, her eyebrows didn't shoot up, her hands didn't go to her face. She simply took me in, thoughtfully, and there was no expression except just the faintest play of a smile around her mouth. She'd recognized me – I was certain of it – but she didn't show it. Was she going to deny she was my sister? It was a possibility that had never occurred to me until that moment of seeing her.

# 22

'No one you meet's a Los Angeleno.'

'There must be some. People get born here.'

Arlene was having lunch with Lee McConey and Baby Daniels at Musso and Frank's. She didn't like Musso and Frank's. Or rather, she liked the place, but it wasn't the kind of food she liked to eat for lunch. Grills. Kidneys. She loved kidneys, but middle of the day was bread time. Sandwich time. She was still a New Zealander in her eating habits.

'What does it mean anyway?'

'Los Angeles? The angels, doesn't it? City of the angels. I don't know any Spanish.'

'What about the English?'

'What about them?'

'Well, you know – Los Angeles. The English.'

Two blank faces. Silence. She explained, 'It's a pun.'

'Give me that bottle, Arlene. You've had too much to drink.'

'Los Angeles. The English.' She repeated it. 'Listen. I'll tell you a story I heard when I was at school.'

'Dirty?'

'Not dirty. Not funny. Listen. There were some English lads packed off to Rome as slaves . . .'

'When was this?'

'Oh God, I don't know. Centuries ago. When there were slaves. The Pope of the time he takes a look at them – they're in chains – and he says "Where did this lot come from?" And his chief slave-snaffler says "Your highness – your popeness . . ."'

'Your holiness . . .'

'That's it. "Your holiness," he says. "These are Angles."'

And the Pope takes another squiz at these blond blue-eyed
boys . . .'
'He was probably queer.'
'And he says, "They look more like *angels*."'
'Queer. I told you.'
'Why did the chief whatnot call them angles?'
'Angles. You know. As in Angles, Saxons and Jutes.'
They were staring at her again. Baby said, 'Arlene, you're
just doing this to us, aren't you?'
'Doing what? Listen. It's a big world. There's always some-
thing to learn.'
'Are you working on a movie about this poofter Pope?'
'I'm not working on any movie. Until Jesse gets on and
makes my comedy . . .'
'*The Runaway* . . .'
'*Tram*. That's the one. I'm on a go-slow. It's my protest.'
'What for God's sake are Angles, Saxons and Jutes?'
'They're the northern tribes, aren't they? The ones that drove
the Celts out of England. So the Welsh and Scots and Irish are
Celts and the rest are Anglo-Saxons. You know – Anglican,
East Anglia, Anglophone, Anglophobia, Anglicize, Anglo-
American . . .'
'Stop it, Arlene.' Baby put her hands over her ears.
'How come you know all this stuff,' Lee asked, 'and you
can't even name the capitals of the States?'
'It's what I learned at school.'
'In England?'
'I've never been near England. But we're part – I mean *they're*
part – did you know I'm an American? My citizenship came
through. New Zealand's part of the British Empire. Or
Commonwealth it is now. We sing "God Save the King".'
'Queen.'
'God yes. You're right. It sounds bizarre. "God save our
gracious Queen, Long live our noble Queen . . ." That'll take
some getting used to.'
Baby lifted her glass for a toast. 'You won't have to. We
salute you, fellow-Amurkin.'
'Thanks. I'm not sure I like it.'

'Who does? No one you'd want to be friends with likes being an American just now.'

'Well, I mustn't bite the hand that's feeding me.'

'It's better than being an Angle. Who'd want to be an Angle, for Chrissake?'

They laughed. They were all a little drunk.

'Did you see in the paper this morning? – some ex-Nazis have been allowed in as immigrants. They were investigated and it was found none of them had Communist connections.'

'I don't believe it.'

'It's true. It's in the paper.'

'And Eddie Robinson's grovelling to the Un-American Activities Committee again. Why doesn't he sell another painting and keep his trap shut.'

'How well is the hand feeding you, anyway?'

Arlene shrugged. 'No complaints. The money comes in. But New York leans on Jesse Fischer and he does what he's told.'

'So your tram's on the skids.'

'It's on hold. Or on the shelf. Or something. I don't get told anything. I just get fucked.'

They both stared at her.

'Not literally,' she said. And then, to the silence that continued, 'I shouldn't say things like that.' Suddenly there were tears.

'Arlene.' They both reached out to hold her hand, to pat her.

'Sheee . . . I am drunk.'

'You're not drunk, honey. You're just unhappy.'

'Who says I'm unhappy? My life's only an average mess. Rocky's getting cirrhosis of the liver and I've got cirrhosis of the lover.'

They laughed. The laughter died down and started up again. They didn't seem able to stop. 'It's not that funny,' Arlene said. But she went on laughing too.

'So there is a lover.'

She ignored that. She said, composing herself, 'Do you ever feel your life's out of control? People keep telling me I've hit the bullseye, or the jackpot. But it's never the one I was aiming for. I don't even know whether I was aiming at all. Everything happens too fast. It looks to other people as if I'm doing things. It even looks that way to me. But when I look back I can't see how it happened. I'm an American. I'm a screenwriter. But I'm not an American and I'm not a screenwriter. D'you know what I mean?'

She looked at one, then the other. She could see they didn't.

'You don't understand, do you. It's something to do with me. Something wrong. I'm the fruit of a blasted tree. Let's order ice-cream.'

'What blasted tree? Don't you like your family?'

'I hate them. My mother's a hysterical ghoul and my old man's a crypto-pugilist.' She was cheerful again.

'Is that true?'

'Probably not. Jesus! What's "true"? I don't know. I ran away from them and I still can't bear to think about them more than a few seconds at a time. Life's difficult enough without parents.'

They caught the waiter's eye and ordered ice-cream.

'I love my parents,' Baby said.

'Who's talking about love? You asked me if I liked them.'

'My God Arlene.' Baby shook her head. 'I can see why they buy your scripts.'

Arlene stood up. 'Where's the john? Hell's teeth!' She steadied herself. 'I'm not used to that stuff. I spend so much time keeping it out of Rocky's way, I get out of practice.'

She headed for the Women's Room. In there she spent long moments staring at herself in the mirror. She turned away and tried to catch a glimpse of herself by surprise. Lee came in.

'Are you OK Arlene?'

'I look OK – if that's me in there.'

'You look just great.'

'What about my waist-line?'

'Your waist-line . . .' Lee looked, and hesitated. 'It's just fine, isn't it?'

'Do you think my child will call me a hysterical ghoul?'

'What child?'

'If I have one. It's a hypothetical question.'

'Arlene – are you pregnant?'

Arlene laughed. 'Are you?'

She left Lee in the Women's Room and went back to their table. 'I'm pregnant,' she told Baby. 'Jesse Fischer's the father. He doesn't know. Neither does Rocky. You're the first to hear.'

Baby was overwhelmed. 'Why me?'

'Because everything you're told goes in one ear and out the other. No. That's not true. Because you're called Baby and I'm going to have one. That's not true either.'

Baby was upset. She didn't know how to respond. 'Are you going to have it?'

'I have it. It's in here. I guess in due course it will come out.'

'I meant . . .'

'You meant am I going to have an abortion.'

'Shush.' Baby looked around nervously.

'No abortion,' Arlene said.

Lee, returning to her seat, heard the word. 'So what's the news?'

'Can I tell her?'

'Please. Be my guest.'

Baby told Lee. Lee took Arlene's hand. Arlene let it be taken, but she still looked somehow distant, withdrawn from them. 'Are you pleased?' Lee asked. Arlene didn't reply. There might have been the threat of tears again.

There was a silence and then Lee said impulsively, 'Be pleased. You want to be – I can tell. Don't hold back. Who cares how it got there?'

Arlene smiled. She reached out and put an arm around each of them. 'Thanks for putting up with me. This is the nicest lunch I've had in ages.'

Arlene and Jesse were still meeting at the Beverly Hills. The room had been theirs so long now it was furnished like a little apartment. Her presents to him, his to her, were all kept there. Jesse was kind, generous, loving. They didn't talk much about work. He went there to forget it.

She knew there were difficulties now with everything. The brakes were on. Every projected picture had to be cleared with

New York, and questions had been asked about hers. But she blamed Jesse for not bullocking through with it.

Jesse was still her only real lover. He was comfortable, dependable, a refuge from Rocky's excesses. But he was no longer the man of power he'd once seemed. She found herself teasing him, sometimes good humouredly, sometimes with an edge of malice. He hardly ever responded. He just took each little cut, flinched, and carried on. She hated herself for it. She wished he would strike back, punish her.

Since Rocky's collapse at the previous year's Academy Awards it seemed as if she'd hardly ever seen him sober. She didn't remember when they'd last been lovers – it was long ago. So how did she tell him she was going to have a child? And what did she say to Jesse? Sometimes she thought of going to work on Rocky, somehow turning him into her lover again. Then she could tell him the child was his. That was one of many things she thought of. In the meantime she did nothing, and said nothing.

She felt vaguely ill most of the time. She slept a lot, and she didn't mind that there was no script to work on. Inactivity which would once have made her irritable was welcome. She could sit in a daze, letting her mind wander randomly, because the real work was going on without any need of her inter-ference. She felt a kind of immunity to most things. She might be at odds with the men in her life, but she felt at one with herself.

So she lay under those marvellous trees in the little park across the street from the Hotel – Sunset Park it was called in those days. She watched the sun fiery in an orange haze. Or on good days she watched cloud formations crossing high against a blue backdrop that might have been painted on the lot. Underneath everything, right down, there was contentment.

But if she felt herself in some way protected, she felt more than ever that others were not. She was given to rushes of powerful sympathy. The world seemed full of victims, and of victimizers. Those were the weeks when the news was full of appeals on behalf of Julius and Ethel Rosenberg, who had been convicted as Communist spies; and that couple, who seemed as the day of their execution drew near, so strangely innocent – innocent in themselves, whatever they may or may not have done – became increasingly Arlene's obsession.

There was a day when she was at lunch with Jesse at Oblath's. He'd had another long phone-call from New York and he was more depressed that she'd ever seen him. He told her Hollywood was finished. The great days were over. That was something she'd heard before, but never from him. What seemed to upset him now was not that it was over, but that the great days had been wasted. Money had poured in and poured out again. There had been thirty years of movie-making at full pitch – probably ten thousand movies – and how many would anyone want to look at in fifty or a hundred years' time? Maybe ten or twenty. Maybe a hundred. What did it matter? He was head of a studio and what did that mean? It was like being in charge of a big drain. Your job was to regulate the flow of waste.

She tried to listen and to feel sympathetic, but her mind was elsewhere. Just that morning she'd heard Harold C. Urey, a famous nuclear physicist, being interviewed about the Rosenbergs. He said he'd begun not knowing whether they were guilty or innocent, only knowing that they hadn't had a fair trial. Now he was convinced they were innocent. He was making a last appeal to the President, along with Einstein, the Pope, and the heads of state from many countries. It was essential for the health of America that the Rosenbergs shouldn't go to the electric chair.

As Arlene listened to Jesse the Rosenbergs were on her mind.

'Hollywood must have its highs and lows,' she said. 'Things will change.'

He shook his head. 'We had it all to ourselves. There was no competition. The whole world was at the pictures. Now there's television. It can never be like that again.'

'Well – at least we're alive.'

He looked at her as if that didn't make any sense. 'I was thinking about the Rosenbergs,' she explained.

'Oh the Rosenbergs.' He shrugged and looked around the room.

'Don't say "Oh the Rosenbergs" as if they don't matter.' She felt a rush of blood to the face.

'It's not that they don't matter. It's just I have other things on my mind, Arlene. I feel as if my world's collapsing. I've given my life to Hollywood . . .'

'Jesse don't. Please.'

'Don't what?' His face was blank, uncomprehending.

'I mean I don't want to hear how you've made yourself boss of a big drainpipe and now you don't enjoy it. Your world's collapsing. How do you think they feel?'

'The Rosenbergs?'

'The Rosenbergs. Who else? They're going to die. They've got two little boys.'

He shook his head. 'Don't attack me, sweetheart. I didn't send them to the chair.'

'But you don't care.'

'What's the good of caring? I mean of course I care. Jesus, Arlene . . .'

'OK. I'm sorry.' She sat grim faced. 'Let's get on with the serious talk. Isn't that how Hollywood turned itself into a waste-pipe? By talking about itself?'

'Oh God, this is stupid. If I could save the Rosenbergs I'd do it. Believe me. Since I can't, I find it a painful subject.'

'What have you done to help them?'

'Nothing. I've done nothing. What can I do? Have you done anything?'

'I've sent a telegram to the President. As a matter of fact I've sent three. And I've donated money. OK that's feeble. It's ridiculous. It's useless. But it's not nothing.'

'Good. So you've got a clear conscience. Congratulations.'

'I've got a conscience. It's not clear, but I've got one.'

He went back to his tuna salad. He looked past her, out into the little street towards the beautiful iron gates and pillars of the Paramount Studio entrance. His eyes were unfocused.

Why did she hurt him? He was going to be father of her child. She was afraid to tell him that. He might panic. He might fear she would use it to disrupt his life. She was afraid of Jesse's weakness more than she was of his strength.

206

And then her mind went back to the Rosenbergs – the victims. 'They're Jews, Jesse.'

Suddenly he was angry. 'So they're Jews. What's that got to do with anything? Do you rush to defend every goy on death row? Jews commit crimes, Jews get punished.'

'Being a Jew might be the crime.'

'I don't believe that.'

'You don't think maybe it helped? Did you hear over the radio that chant over the heads of the protesters in Washington? "Burn the rats. Fry the Jews."'

He looked around the room again like a man hunting for an escape. 'I'll send a telegram . . .'

'I don't want you to send a telegram.'

'. . . and a cheque.'

'I want you to care.'

'You want me to be someone I'm not.'

She looked at him. She felt herself unyielding. 'Yes, probably.'

'Well, get yourself another man.'

She smiled. 'That's the bravest thing you've said to me in five years.'

'I didn't mean it.'

'I think you did. You've had enough. You want out but you haven't the guts to say so.'

'This is ridiculous. We can't break up over the Rosenbergs.'

'We're not breaking up over the Rosenbergs. We're breaking up. And there's the Rosenbergs.'

'You don't mean that.'

'I do. And it's what you want.'

He shook his head. 'No.' There were tears in his eyes.

'There, you see. You can weep now. You can suffer – you will suffer. But it's what you want, and the way you want it. No blame. All my fault.'

He was still shaking his head. 'I don't understand you, Arlene. You're too quick for me.'

'Too quick to be your wife. Ideal for the back room. But it can't go on for ever, can it? The back room starts to invade the parlour.'

'Stop it.' He reached out to hold her hand. She was weeping now. She couldn't speak. There was a long silence in which they both composed themselves. They turned their attention to their plates and ate a little, picking at one thing, then another.

Out in the street he tried to persuade her to go with him to the Beverly Hills but she wouldn't. 'It's over,' she said.

She kept repeating that phrase and he went on insisting she didn't mean it. She did mean it. She knew he didn't believe she would stick to it. She didn't believe it herself, but she was going to try.

So began a time of withdrawal. She hadn't decided she must break with Jesse – not consciously anyway. But the decision had arrived, out of nowhere. Now she watched herself to see if it would be kept.

It was early summer. The weather was blustery, unsettled and unsettling. She had nothing to do at the studio but she was on the payroll and she went there every day. She read old scripts, tidied files, made notes for things that might be written in the future, spent longer than usual talking to friends in the commissary. In the early afternoons she dozed in her chair. Often she dreamed that she'd fallen asleep. In the dream she woke herself. To check that she was really awake she noted the positions of pencils, pens, scripts, paperclips, blotter on the desk in front of her. Then she woke really and found all these things in different places.

One day she phoned a man she'd met in the scripting department at Paramount. She told him she was looking for work. He knew one of the pictures she had a screen credit for, and he invited her to lunch. She took examples of her work, including *The Runaway Tram*. It wasn't a picture Paramount could make. The script belonged to Marvin Major Studios. But it would show them what she could do. A week later he phoned to say there was work for her at Paramount. They might prefer not to take her on salary. They would contract scripting jobs out to her and keep her on a retainer when there was nothing for her to do. The pay would be less regular, and less certain; but when there was work to do it would be good. Overall she might make more money that way. And she could work at home if she preferred. Nothing was concluded, but it looked promising.

There was no clemency for the Rosenbergs. On the day of their execution Arlene left the studio early. They were to die at sundown in New York. It was June. She thought that would be about 5 pm Los Angeles time. She drove down to the ocean, parked, and sat in the sun on a big flat yellow-orange rock, staring out at the Pacific, watching the surf roll in in long even lines. She tried to imagine the Rosenbergs taken from their cells, strapped into that awful chair, the electrodes attached, the bag over the face, the witnesses, the Rabbi's prayers, the switch thrown, the convulsions, the smell of burning, the limp bodies. She felt almost guilty to dwell on it so morbidly. But she couldn't do otherwise. She felt she owed it to them.

When the time came she didn't feel anger, or despair, or anguish. It was something worse – a kind of painful nothingness, as if her own identity had been wiped away. The sun was shining. The Pacific kept on rolling in and breaking on the rocks. The world hadn't changed. It wouldn't change. It would just go on.

Every morning as she drove up Woodville a conflict went on. Did she drive back along Mulholland to the place where Jesse might be waiting? Or did she go straight down to Sepulveda and on to the studio? It was as if she observed this conflict from the outside, never knowing which way it would go. And there was curiosity, as well as a hunger to see Jesse. If she weakened, would she find him waiting there? But she knew that if she went just once and he was there, then she would have lost the battle – not with him but with herself. She would be right back where she'd been before.

At the studio they hardly saw one another, and when they did, it was only in passing, with others present. Once she caught sight of him walking down towards the sound stages. She was looking down from her office window. The wind had ruffled his hair and turned up his collar. He looked vulnerable, and she wanted to rush down and hug him and smooth his hair.

One day he announced a meeting of producers, directors and other executive people, including scriptwriters. It was to be held in the evening because they were to be addressed by one of the company bosses from New York. New policies, and the studio's programme for the coming year, were to be announced. She wanted to go because she might learn something about what was to be done with her script. But more than that, she wanted to see Jesse – to be in a room with him, to watch and listen to him, knowing that she was protected from any personal contact.

She went home early that afternoon and cooked a meal. Rocky was sober – or as near to sober as he ever was these days. He was teaching himself to play the guitar, and he played her a couple of tunes to show her how he was improving. She sang the words. She got the words wrong, he played wrong notes, and they laughed. She thought afterwards it was a long time since they'd laughed together.

All through the meeting that evening she couldn't take her eyes off Jesse. She hardly took in what the man from New York told them. It was mainly to do with cuts, and increased efficiency, and faith in the studio, and optimism. If there was a message in it about the future of her script, she failed to decipher it.

Down in the carpark when it was over she couldn't start her car. The battery was turning the starter motor but the engine wouldn't fire. She had the door of the car open so the interior light was on. Someone loomed up out of the shadows. It was Jesse. He offered to help. She told him there was nothing he could do – he was no more a mechanic than she was. He said 'You'd better let me take you home.'

She felt panicky. 'I can get home.'

'If it won't start . . .'

'I'll call a cab.' But she knew there weren't any. 'I'll call Rocky.'

'Arlene . . .'

She got out and shut the car door. She was turning to go back towards her office. He put his hand on her arm. 'You were staring at me in the meeting.'

'You were at the front of the room. Everyone was staring at you.'

'I didn't notice the others.'

She knew she'd been staring at him. She thought of him as a palm-tree in a desert. 'You're a mirage,' she said.

'Let me drive you home.'

She broke away and ran to her office. When she phoned the house, Rocky answered almost immediately. He didn't sound too bad. She told him the car had broken down. He sounded pleased she'd called. He said he would be there in twenty minutes.

But when he got there he wasn't sober at all. He couldn't walk straight and his words were slurred. She said she should drive, and that made him angry. He said he'd got his car to the studio and he would get it back home again. He refused to move from the driver's side, so she got in beside him.

She was nervous. She kept jumping in her seat and telling him to take care. That made him worse. He drove faster. He missed the turn to Sepulveda, and when she pointed it out he said he knew that perfectly well – he was taking a different route home. Now they were careering down the long miles of Sunset Boulevard towards the ocean. Arlene had her hands to her face. She was terrified and she couldn't hide it, but the more it showed the angrier he became and the harder he pushed his car. She was yelling at him now, 'Please, Rocky, please . . .' At a curve in the road they seemed to rock over on two wheels, but they recovered. 'Rocky,' Arlene screamed. 'Don't kill me. I'm pregnant.'

His foot came off the accelerator. He hardly braked. There was a long gradual slowing down until they stopped. He hadn't even pulled over to the kerb. He had both hands on the wheel and his head hung forward. Without looking at her he said, 'Who's the father?'

She told him. He went to open the door. 'But it's over,' she said.

He nodded. There was a grim, tormented smile on his face as he pushed the door open and stepped, or staggered, into the road. He was lit up in what seemed like floodlights and then swept away in a horrible torrent of noise. She saw him carried away, together with the door that had been wrenched off in the impact, his arms and legs spread wide in the hard white light. When Arlene got to him the people from the car that had hit him were there already.

Bruce Burns, also known as Rocky Tamworth, was lying dead at the edge of Sunset Boulevard.

# 23

'Arnold. Candy. Then the fat lady. Her son was Victor . . .'

We are at the poolside again, side by side in deckchairs. We're trying to remember the names of the families who lived down the street from us.

'Holmes.'

'Holmes. That's it. Vic-*tor*! Vic-*tor*!' Edie imitates Mrs Holmes calling her son. 'Then – it was Cranch, wasn't it?'

'Cranch. Jesus – what a name. One of the twins was killed in the Tangiwai disaster.'

'Tangiwai?'

'It was a rail crash. A bridge collapsed. 1953, I think.'

'Oh yes. I remember. It was in the papers here.'

'The Queen was in New Zealand.'

'Which twin?'

'I think it was Jean.'

'Jean was the fair one. They weren't alike.'

'Then Surridge. Then the Brethren family . . .'

'Then the Macarthurs.'

There's a silence. We've touched on an old nerve? After a moment she laughs and pats my knee. 'Crikey, mate. D'you think survivors of concentration camps play this game?'

'Probably. Until someone's nerve breaks.'

The garden is enclosed by a tall stand of bamboo and a fence covered in bougainvillaea in purple leaf. Everywhere there are flowers and flowering vines. While we talk Edie is playing idly with Kapai. He brings her his stick, she takes hold of it, he holds his end growling and twisting his head this way and that. When he lets go she throws it. He likes having to dive into the pool for it. He has a way of getting up the wet slippery metal steps. That's the difficult part.

It's another warm morning. Indoors Carlos and Felice are cleaning the house. I've been with Edie three days. We've covered so much of the old ground, and of the ground in between, but there's no end to it. We have two lifetimes to exchange and soon I will be leaving.

'Let's take Kapai to the end of the street,' she says. 'He likes it down there.'

So we go through a side gate and into the street. Edie's house is only a couple of hundred yards from the cliffs. At the end of the street there's a small park with grass and shrubs and a seat where you can look down at the Pacific Highway and the ocean. The grass is brown and dry and there are mounds of red-brown soil between the clumps. Bushes and shrubs in the hollows look parched. On a near headland are houses, and one towering apartment block. We stand breathing the marvellous air that blows in off the ocean.

She says, 'This is what I missed when we moved from Santa Monica to Sherman Oaks. It was lovely there, but too hot on that side of the hills. And I always felt afraid of the summer fires. The chaparral just explodes in the heat. It's oily. It spreads its seeds that way, but everything else burns with it.'

She throws Kapai's stick and he plunges down after it into a hollow full of low shrubs.

'Rocky used to say Pacific Palisades was where we'd live when we were rich and famous.'

'He didn't make it and you did.'

'I think I made it because I wasn't trying. I walked into jobs backwards so it looked as if I was heading for the door. Rocky faced the way he was going and the door got slammed in his face.'

'The booze wouldn't have helped.'

She stares into the distance. 'It's a puzzle isn't it. Did he drink because he failed, or did he fail because he drank?'

I shake my head. 'Questions like that . . .'

'They don't help, I know. But there's a sort of fascination. Like, for example – my affair with Jesse. Did I get into that because my husband was an alcoholic? Or was he an alcoholic because I was unfaithful?'

'You're keen on causation aren't you Sis?'

She glances at me. 'I guess that's pretty unsophisticated.'

'Causation and guilt.'

'Oh well guilt – yes. Loads of it. Guilt about my family. Guilt about Rocky. Especially Rocky. People here remember him as a drunk. They never saw the best of him. And then there was that time when he was ready to go back to Australia. I ought to have jumped at it.'

'He shouldn't have left the decision to you.'

'You mean he should have bullied me?'

I laugh. 'No. I guess not.'

Kapai has found his stick. He brings it to me and I wrestle him for it. It's covered in slimy saliva. I throw it down the bank again. The sun is getting higher behind us. The sea looks very blue, very bland and beautiful.

Edie points out the big buildings on the near headland. 'A.B. made a lot of money out of those apartments. That's when we bought the house I'm in now.'

A.B. was her second husband – Allen Buchanan, a lawyer who dealt in real estate. He was some years older than Edie, with a son and a daughter when they married. So as well as her own daughter Edie has two step-children. All three are married now, with children of their own.

'Is it safe?' I'm looking at the apartment building. 'I thought you told me those cliffs aren't stable.'

'They're not. You see those houses over there. I wouldn't buy one of those. You might lose your garden. Or even the house. But houses are only built on the surface strata. To build an apartment block that size you have to go down to bedrock for the foundations. It's solid.'

Edie is wearing white trousers, a blue and white striped shirt, a blue jacket and dark glasses. Her hair is auburn – it must be dyed but you can't tell. 'You're still beautiful,' I tell her.

'Hey.' She laughs and kisses my cheek. 'You're not so bad yourself. Considering what we came from . . .'

'Maybe it wasn't so bad.'

'It was bad. But the genes must have been OK.'

Back at the house I look again at the photograph of her daughter, Ethel Rose, known as Rosie. 'Did Jesse Fischer know he was the father?'

'I never told him. I could see he wanted to ask but I think he was afraid of the answer. I left the Marvin Major studio when Rocky was killed. But I used to run into Jesse sometimes. He always stared at Rosie. But as far as the world knew it was Rocky's child. I owed that to Rocky. I had to preserve his honour in some way. She was Rosie Tamworth, daughter of Rocky Tamworth.'

'What about her? Does she know?'

'She knows now. She didn't when she was a child.'

'Does she mind?'

'I think she likes it. It gives her three fathers. There's her legal father who gave her the name Tamworth, although he was really Bruce Burns. Then there's her step-father, A.B. She loved him. He was the real father-figure. And there's her biological father. He was Jewish but he couldn't pass it on because technically Jewishness passes through the mother. But she says she's an honorary Jew because I named her after Ethel Rosenberg. Rosie visited Jesse a couple of times when he was old and ailing. I don't know whether she told him she was his daughter. Maybe it didn't need to be said. She thought he was a nice old guy.'

'So he's dead too.'

'Yes, the old sod. All my men are dead. I'm on the market.'

'Any takers?'

'Some. But I've made a rule. They have to be richer than I am so I know they're not marrying me for my money. I might make an exception in the case of a much younger man, but so far no luck.'

'And in the end you didn't like Jesse.'

'Of course I did. I loved him. I loved them all.'

'You said he was an old sod.'

'He was. He never made my picture. It's my one big grudge. That's how he punished me for leaving him. It belonged to the studio and he just left it on the shelf. Paramount wanted it but he wouldn't release it. And he wouldn't make it. It was the best bit of screen-writing I ever did.'

We're due for lunch at a house in Brentwood and Edie gets us there almost on time. The people are all old friends. They've known one another for years. Everyone hugs and kisses Edie, calling her Arlene. They're very demonstrative, and very welcoming to the man she introduces as her little brother. Among the people I meet are the two women Edie knew years ago as Lee McConey and Baby Daniels. I can't follow, or anyway can't keep in my head, the details of their respective divorces and widowhoods; but each is married now to a pink-cheeked white-haired man, two husbands so alike it's difficult to tell them apart.

The hosts are southerners and this is to be a Kentucky Derby party. We drink mint juleps in chilled silver cups. Lunch is cold ham and potato salad, beans cooked with pork, water melon and strawberries. There's a sweep on the horse race – everyone puts in two dollars. At two o'clock we gather around the television set. As the horses come out the whole crowd at the race track breaks into 'My Old Kentucky Home'. The words are flashed on the screen. It's a song Edie and I know from movies we saw as children, but when it gets to the line ''Tis Summer, the darkies are gay' the word 'darkies' has changed to 'people'. Edie leans over to me and whispers, 'Shouldn't something be done about "gay"?'

She has drawn a horse called Ayleesha. It runs well back but in the home stretch it makes a run and ranges up alongside a horse called Bet Twice that led around the turn. Bet Twice's jockey pulls his horse across Ayleesha's path. Edie hammers on my shoulder blades with her fists as her horse is checked and seems almost to go down on its knees. But now it's recovering, it's coming again, it wins by a nose.

It has become a noisy party. Edie is handed a wad of notes which she shakes under my nose saying it will be her shout at Gladstone's.

That night the two of us sit up late, drinking and talking. I tell her more of what happened in the family after she ran away. She says, 'I tried not to think of you all in those days. I

217

got bits of news from Veronica, but she was always inclined to melodrama and I didn't know what to believe. I think she liked to make me feel I was to blame.'

'You weren't to blame. You were just the occasion.'

'The occasion.' She looks at me over the rim of her drink. 'What does that mean?'

'Well – running away like that. It seemed to blow them apart. Our poor Mum became alternately hysterical and melancholic, and that seemed to drive the Hippo to violence.'

'But Bill darling – they were always like that.'

I don't think that's true but I don't say any more. I don't want to seem to be adding to her guilts.

We go to bed but I can't sleep. Too many mint juleps. I stand at my window looking down at the garden. A light breeze coming up from the ocean moves through the heads of the bamboos and feathers the surface of the pool. There's something in the back of my mind – some memory, not faint, quite distinct, but not available, like a word on the tip of the tongue which at a crucial moment you can't recall.

I get into bed and lie watching the movement of whatever faint light comes between the open curtains. Gradually I drift into something like sleep, but I don't think it's real sleep. The dream isn't a dream. It seems more like a memory. It's from a time when I was very young. Ellie and I are sharing a bedroom. I'm asleep and then I'm awake. We're frightened. There's noise. We're running. We open one door, then another. We have to reach up for the handles. We burst out of darkness into very bright light. Our mother is in the corner of the room, pressed against dark panels of wood. She's yelling something. I've never seen her yell like that. And our father is hitting her.

The night before I was to leave Edie took me to a fish restaurant called Gladstone's. It was down from Pacific Palisades where Sunset Boulevard joins the Pacific Highway, and it was advertised as the place where Sunset meets the sunset. The floors were of wood, scattered with sawdust. The seats and tables and partitions were all of sawn timber. There were big windows facing out over the ocean. It was very busy, and Edie pointed out to me famous people from the Industry. Floodlights shone down from the eaves and waves broke against the wooden piles under the windows. As it got darker gulls continued to scream and flash through the outside lights.

The fish was prepared in a mixture of Japanese and Hawaiian styles. It included red tuna, served raw, with a hot sauce that seemed to shoot up into your sinuses.

We stayed there a long time, and when we couldn't eat any more we went on drinking the Californian wine.

She told me she came to this place sometimes in the daytime and sat out on the deck eating oysters and drinking white wine. Especially at the time of year when the whales were migrating. You could watch schools of them going by out there.

Back at the house she put on a record – the kind of music that was popular when we were young. We danced – waltzes, fox-trots, the samba, the rumba. We hadn't forgotten how. Edie moved beautifully. Age didn't make any difference. She was still my big sister – the sexy one who'd run away to work in the movies.

The record ended and we went on dancing. We were in a haze of wine and food and mild exhaustion. In my head were those lines

> Darkling I listen; and for many a time
> I have been half in love with easeful Death,
> Call'd him soft names in many a musèd rhyme . . .

She turned the record and we went on dancing. Very slow; very dreamy. She was my Sister Hollywood. I was her Poetry Brother. New Zealand was a great way off. Sometimes when we talked she made me feel inexperienced; and there might have been times when I made her feel uneducated. But when we danced it was as if all the foreground vanished. We went right back to the beginning of the journey.

Next day, late in the afternoon, she drove me to the airport. I watched the lines of tall palms flicking by against an orange ball sun declining out there over the ocean at the end of another smoggy Los Angeles day. The remorseless traffic, four lanes each way and more at intersections and off-ramps, surged and slowed, merged and divided, like units in some mad spacies-parlour game, each unit contributing its smidgen to that brilliant Technicolor dislocation of light which is the Southern Californian sky.

At the Tom Bradley Terminal I checked in my luggage and we began to say our goodbyes in the big echoing concourse. I'd told Edie often she must come and visit us in New Zealand but she insisted she wouldn't. She couldn't. She didn't know why – she only knew that she would never set foot in New Zealand again. I was the traveller. I must come and visit her.

I said I would, but I didn't quite believe it. She'd brought me nearer than I ever wanted to be again to what we'd both left behind – and no doubt I'd had the same effect on her.

'No big farewells,' she said.

I kissed her again and stepped on to the escalator. She walked away from me, but before I'd reached the top she turned under the flags and waved one last time.